By Cristelle Comby

The Neve & Egan cases
RUSSIAN DOLLS
RUBY HEART

RUBY HEART

The Neve & Egan cases
Book Two

Cristelle Comby

Edition: 1

ISBN: 1492813435
ISBN-13: 978-1492813439

ACKNOWLEDGMENTS

Deepest thanks to my partners-in-crime Arthur V. and Kyle S. for their insight, Eric A. for his gorgeous 3D illustration of the Ruby Heart, and to everyone else who helped along the way.

Ruby Heart

PROLOGUE

Being a private investigator is nothing like as glamorous or exciting as books and films make it look. Some warning of those harsh facts before I opened my own Private Investigation agency is unlikely to have deterred me, but I wish we'd been a bit more perceptive about it all beforehand. "We" is myself and my former university lecturer, Professor Ashford Egan, now a good friend and colleague.

Although you could say I stumbled into the sleuthing world quite by accident, that accident was shocking and dramatic. I'd always led a very quiet, ordinary life, until the day my best friend was murdered.

That horror stopped short my meandering, easy life and so much changed. I had no idea this would result in my very first investigation, but it did. Egan and I put a stop to a Russian criminal syndicate — with its complicit upstanding British citizens — by delving into the murky worlds of human trafficking, arms dealing, murder and arson. Sounds horribly exciting and dangerous, doesn't it? It was... to the point where I was nearly killed, not just once but twice, and Egan was kidnapped.

However, I have since discovered that the everyday life of a PI isn't always so intense. Most of our cases involve suspicious spouses and lost items, or even worse... lost dogs. Life isn't always like it is in books and films, so why should the job of PI be so? We can't afford to refuse a client, even when the case is not as appealing as a mysterious unsolved murder or a missing painting on some tropical island. Our advert in the Yellow Pages claims, completely truthfully, that we provide "Comprehensive, all-round services. We diligently seek out the truth for our clients. Discretion assured."

Sitting in a small Italian bar, in the north of London, I cross my ankles — red Converse trainer brushing against red Converse trainer — and blow over the cup of my Macchiato as I wait for my esteemed colleague to arrive. I've learned there's an awful lot of waiting around involved in this profession. Just another part of this job that I'm not too fond of. I sigh, as I look back down — at least it gives me plenty of time to draw in the little sketchbook I always carry with me. I straighten my back, roll my shoulders, flip my long dark plait back over my shoulder, and close my grip on my pencil. I steal another covert glance at the barista, just to be sure that I have his bushy salt-and-pepper hair right and continue drawing.

I love quickly sketching snapshots of everyday life. Art is in my genes. My dad was a painter and, while I don't have anything like his level of talent, he did pass his passion on to me.

The page is nearly completed; it's a sketched portrait of the bar's owner, the bubbling and cheeky Luigi, balancing with practised ease a tray with four drinks in one hand and a huge coffee mug in the other.

I make some final touches to my sketch and flip the sketchbook shut.

'Anytime soon, would be appreciated, Ash,' I mutter to my half-empty coffee cup. Patience certainly isn't one of my virtues.

I let my gaze linger through the window. Still only mid-afternoon, but Camden High Street is already filling up. Must be the warm August weather, I guess. No one wants to be stuck inside on such a lovely day. If only this bar had a terrace, I'd be outside enjoying it too.

The doorbell rings, and I redirect my attention to the entrance, hoping to find a familiar round face topped with short, curly, ginger hair. I let a smile grace my lips when my eyes take in the tall man who's just entered, Ashford Egan, 40-something part-time private investigator, part-time history professor. He takes two steps inside, turns to his left, and takes precisely eight steps forward. He stops just a few inches before the table I'm sitting at.

'Alexandra?' He sounds a little hesitant, which is understandable. Although *Luigi's* is a sort of makeshift office for us, and we have a favourite table — the one furthest from the door, in a quiet secluded corner — there had been one or two occasions when it was occupied by someone else and we had to change location.

'Right here,' I say, and he sits down opposite me, behind the small wooden table.

'So —' I do not waste time, and voice the question I've been dying to ask for the entire afternoon '— how did it go?'

He settles himself, taking his time before replying. He carefully folds his white cane and places it on the corner of the table, then he brushes at invisible creases on the front of his off-white turtleneck pullover.

I don't need to look at his smug smile to know that he's drawing it out on purpose. He's recognised the eagerness in my voice, and he knows how impatient I am.

'Well,' he says, finally answering my question.

Gosh, talk about understatement. I fight the urge to roll my eyes, knowing any such gesture would be lost on my unseeing friend. I drum my fingers — as loudly and impatiently as I can — on the table instead.

The corner of his lip quirks upwards. 'I'm seeing her again, tonight,' he says. 'At the restaurant.'

'That well, then.' I'm impressed; I hadn't been sure our plan would work. 'So… the blind thing, it really does work.'

His eyebrows rise minutely above the rim of his dark glasses, and I understand he just rolled his eyes at me. 'Of course it does.'

I chuckle a little at the smug, superior tone; only Egan can elicit that feeling of light-heartedness that now rose up in me.

'I had to wait on her street for a solid twenty minutes, before her front door cracked open. I bumped into her — by accident, of course — on the pavement and then apologised profusely. I had no way of knowing she was there; couldn't have seen her for sure. She said it was alright and asked if I was hurt—' he smiles cheekily, and tilts his head to the side '—I thanked her for her concern and complimented her on the lovely timbre of her voice. It was dulcet, very pleasant to the ear.'

'Oh my God,' I chuckle. 'What I wouldn't have paid to see that — Ashford Egan, seducing a woman.' It's too bad I was holed up most of the morning going over official documents we had to fill in if we want to remain a legitimate business. Seriously, you wouldn't believe the amount of quadruplicate forms and official stamps involved in modern-day entrepreneurship.

A mildly indignant eyebrow rises up, above the rim of Egan's glasses. 'There's always the recording if you want.' He reaches into his coat pocket and retrieves the recording device with its little microphone that had been tucked into the inside of his coat collar.

He holds out the combination, and I take it from his hand — I'll download the conversation later.

'What time's your date?' I demand, growing serious again.

'Seven-thirty, at the Venetian.'

I whistle. 'It's an expensive place.' I doubt it was his choice, even if we can bill the meal as *mandatory expenses* to our client.

He shrugs. 'She's a rich lady.'

'No, *Mister* Cromworth is rich. Rich and currently away at a seminar, while his wife invites a complete stranger to some fancy restaurant.'

'What can I say?' He smiles with false modesty. 'It must be my irresistible charm.'

I laugh heartily at that. We both know how untrue that statement is. Egan has the decency to blush a little.

I know Egan can be charming, when he wants to be, but that's not very often. He's the type of man who likes to keep his cards close to his chest and doesn't let many emotions show through his carefully selected façade. He always maintains a carefully composed checked manner, at all times. It tends to make him come off as rather cold and uncaring. During the past few months, he's been melted a bit by my much-warmer-even-flaming-at-times maelstrom of a personality, but he's still rather coldly controlled in the presence of others. We often joke that we are as contrasted as fire and ice.

'Another marriage going down the—' Egan is interrupted mid-sentence, by a loud wail of pain coming from one of the men sitting at the bar.

I look up, my senses on the alert. There's some sort of commotion going on.

'Looks like some guy punched another in the face.' I look on, try to gauge if there's a risk of the situation getting out of hand. 'Who knows, maybe he found out his lady's cheating on him.'

Luigi comes to stand between the two men, effectively putting a stop to the burgeoning fight. With a few well-chosen curses, the wounded man leaves the establishment, a paper towel pressed firmly to his bleeding face.

'Show's over.'

Egan sighs, tiredly. 'Why are we meeting in this fine establishment again?'

I know the question is rhetorical, but I answer nonetheless. 'You know it's the best office we can afford. It's the *only* office we can afford.'

'Well, at least the coffee is good.' He waves a hand about. 'Silver lining and all that.'

I look back up, search for the barista, catch his gaze, and point to my friend as I mouth the word 'coffee.' Luigi nods happily.

He places a cup close to Egan's hand only moments later with a quick, 'There you go — sorry about that little hassle. Some men just aren't up to drinking too much alcohol.'

Egan reaches for his cup and Luigi trots back to the bar to greet new customers.

'Alright, back to business.' I reach for my own drink. 'You know what we need?'

'I know.' He takes a long sip. 'I'll do what it takes.'

I frown at the tone. There's something a bit off in it, a sort of resignation that I don't like. I scan Egan's face attentively, but his features remain guarded. I don't need to see the pain to know that it's there — drifting, just below the cold surface. It wasn't my idea to rely so heavily on his condition to get this job done. We argued about it a lot, actually. I caved in, at the end, but still think that using the non-seeing card is... well debatable, at best.

'Ash, you don't have to,' I say, in a gentle voice. 'We can always find another way.'

'No, it's alright. I don't like it—' he sighs '—but it's part of the job.'

I purse my lips, but hum in agreement.

Egan gives me a mirthless smile. 'You can be the one to announce the good news to the husband tomorrow, however.'

It's my turn to sigh. I hate being the bearer of bad news.

One thousand five hundred and fifty pounds: that is the fee for five days of surveillance on a cheating spouse. Of course, we provide a disk with recordings of incriminating conversations and several equally compromising high-quality pictures. Not included in the price: some mandatory expenses (with receipts), which are billed separately.

Mr Cromworth — an uptight middle-aged man who couldn't tell a joke to save his life — pays without a fuss and leaves *Luigi's* with a closed-off expression and a tight-clipped, 'Good-day.'

I can hardly blame him for his attitude. I have once been in a somewhat similar position myself, and still harbour ill feelings towards my ex-boyfriend. On a positive note, *that* did teach me a lot about self-preservation and sharpened my paranoia. I think this is, with my natural talent for observing things, what serves me the best in this job — even if hunting cheating wives is not the best way to hone those skills.

Still, a job's a job, and I take our well-earned money straight to the bank, that very afternoon. We have a joint account for the business — *Neve & Egan - Private Eyes Agency*, we're called (pun intended) — and although there's never much in it, it's satisfying to know we are our own bosses.

We launched, if you could call it that, the company at the end of May and have had exactly nine clients, in the two and a half months that followed: three wives, two husbands, one insurance company, two old ladies who lost their dogs and one who lost a nineteenth century jade pin.

Mr Cromworth was our eighth successful case (one of the dogs was never recovered). Business isn't booming, but between me sharing a flat with my mother and Egan working part-time as a lecturer for University College London, we make do. Luckily, this job comes with few expenses. We invested in a high-quality reflex camera, some security equipment, and a bunch of professional-looking business cards. We don't have an office, our advertising budget is close to nil and we get around town using public transportation.

As I walk back home, I wonder what the future holds for us. Who knows, a bigger case may be waiting just around the corner…

1

Upon my return home from the bank, I find a smartly dressed elderly woman in our living room, deep in conversation with my mother.

I frown for an instant, before remembering today's Saturday and that my mother finishes work at the shoe shop at noon on Saturdays. I've no idea who the guest woman might be, so I enter the room with a polite smile as I shrug off my vest. I try to fix my hair as I walk into the living room. I flip my plait over my right shoulder, pass a hand over the loose brown strands in the hope of taming them somewhat.

'Ah, here's my daughter.' My mother gestures to me, and the elderly woman stands up from the settee slowly and awkwardly, her joints cracking.

She seems hesitant; as she faces me, her gaze never fully rises to meet mine. *Ah! A client*, I understand.

The flat — which I share with my mother because the rents in London are… well, just like the rents in other big cities; they're astronomically high — also serves as a makeshift office for the PI agency. As we can't afford a proper office just yet, business is conducted in either the flat or the bar. Usually we prefer the latter, but when there's a need for privacy the living room is sometimes necessary. And then occasionally a client decides to show up unannounced to the address in our Yellow Pages advert.

'Alexandra Neve.' I motion for the woman to sit back down, before shooting my mum a meaningful glance that immediately has her standing up and leaving the room.

I sit down in the chair opposite the settee. 'What can we do for you, madam?'

'Mrs Doris Hargrave.' She offers me a her thin, wrinkled hand.

As I shake it, I feel small tremors run along her skin. I'm not certain if it's because of the stress of the situation or from some chronic disease. If I had to hazard a guess, I would go with the latter.

Mrs Hargrave appears to be past her eighties, with eyes slightly glazed over behind the thick, rectangular glasses perched on her wrinkled nose. Her thinning hair, although combed neatly and held together tightly in a bun, is as white as snow.

'What can we do for you, Mrs Hargrave?'

'I would like to employ you, to retrieve something that was stolen from me.'

I nod with interest, while fervently hoping that it wasn't her Chihuahua that had been taken from her.

She reaches down to her red leather handbag, unzips it, rummages inside and takes out a white envelope. She hands it to me with shaking fingers.

I take it, with curiosity, and find an old photograph tucked inside. The surface is cracked in the corners and parts of it have faded with time. It's a black and white picture of a couple standing in what looks to be a living room.

The simple clothes, the hairdos, and what I can see in the

background make me think of a scene from the thirties or the forties.

'My parents,' Doris Hargrave says. The touch of pain in her voice draw my gaze back to her. 'This was taken in nineteen thirty-seven. My father was a jeweller, in Germany, just like his father before him. The family ran a little shop in Magdeburg, an old city to the west of Berlin.

'People used to say that my father had hands of gold. He made rings and necklaces, all made of shiny, precious stones that glittered in the sun, just like stars sparkling in the night.'

I smile at the poetic description, which shows the memories of a little girl.

'He was very popular, people came from near and far to employ him,' she continues. 'He even made a wedding ring for a baroness once.

'Business got more difficult, after thirty-eight—' her shudder is visible, and her voice trembles with emotion '—they tossed bricks at my father's shop window that November night, and set it on fire.

It woke me up; it woke us all up. Thankfully my grandparents had already passed away and never had to see any of it.'

I let an almost inaudible sigh pass my lips; I haven't forgotten my History lessons. The broken Jewish shops, burned synagogues, all over Germany and the rest of the Reich. *Kristallnacht* — the night of crystal — a name way too beautiful for such a tragically dark time, and the foreshadowing of something much, much worse.

The old woman licks her thin lips nervously. 'Hargrave is my married name. My birth name, it's—' she stops speaking for an instant, hesitates, as if she cannot or maybe should not be telling me her real name '—it's Salzmann.'

I swallow, and nod to her to continue. I have an idea of where her story is going.

'My parents were Jews.' I can see her eyes tear up, and I smile in sympathy. 'They sent me away in late thirty-nine; they were deported in forty-two. The trains took them to Warsaw and later to Treblinka, and... well—' she waves a hand in the air '—you know.'

My gaze flickers back down to the photograph for an instant. The couple looked happy, holding on to each other and smiling brightly at the camera. They had no idea of what was awaiting them.

'I never saw them again, after I left. I've never seen anyone from my family, since.' She raises a shaking hand, to brush at her moist eyes, behind her glasses. 'I left on a train, in the middle of the night, with a small suitcase and a doll clutched in my tiny fingers. I was eight years old.'

Mrs Hargrave's gaze lowers to the photograph in my hand. 'This picture is the only one I have of my parents. This necklace—' she points at the image and I look back down, '—is the only heritage I had left of them, until it was taken from me.'

Looking down again at the black and white photograph, I notice around the woman's neck, a lovely heart-shaped pendant, hanging on a thin, silvery chain. Although the photo's lack of colour doesn't do the piece justice, I guess it to be sparklingly beautiful. Dozens of adjectives could qualify it, but the most apt to me would be *perfect*.

'It disappeared during the war, I lost all hope of ever seeing it again, until it was found in Italy recently.'

This perks up my interest greatly. 'But you don't have it anymore?'

'No.' She looks baffled. 'It was stolen from me. Stolen from my family, for the second time.

'This necklace was my grandfather's greatest achievement. A real labour of love. He spent years collecting exactly the right stones and then offered it to his wife on their wedding day. Later it was passed on to my mother, and she wore it the day she married my father.

'I was to wear it too, but alas…' She lets her sentence hang and brushes a hand over her eyes again. 'I never wore it, so couldn't pass it on to my daughter-in-law. My—'

Mrs Hargrave is interrupted by a long harsh bout of coughing. She takes several long sips of tea in an effort to stop it.

'My grand-parents had the happiest of marriages, you know, and so did my parents, until…' she trails off again. 'I wasn't so lucky. My husband left me, only shortly after my son's birth, for another woman. And my own son is now a divorced man.' She fixes me intently. 'Do you see?'

I see nothing more than coincidences, and tell her so, 'I'm afraid I don't, Mrs Hargrave.'

'You must see! It's the necklace! It makes marriages happy.' The sudden strength in her voice is at odds with her sickly frail appearance.

I'm completely bemused by this idea, and I allow myself a gentle smile. How on earth could a necklace have any effect whatsoever on a couple's relationship or save a sinking marriage?, I wonder.

Mrs Hargrave continues, unperturbed, 'My son's daughter is to get married this summer. When the necklace was retrieved, I really thought it was a divine sign.' She smiles brightly, as she momentarily looks up. 'Our necklace back, after all these years... a happy marriage for my beloved Lyssa. It could all end well.'

Her faces closes, as she licks her lips nervously. 'The police, they say they have no idea who did it. They're not looking anymore; they have other cases, more important cases than one stupid necklace.' Her tone takes on a bitter edge. 'But this jewel, you have to understand, Ms Neve, it matters so much to me. To my family.

'It's my only inheritance and it must be around Lyssa's neck, as she enters the church.

'Please,' she continues, pleadingly. 'My heritage, our history, it's all I have to give her. Her something old.'

The old woman faces me with wide, red-rimmed, pleading eyes and I feel my heart ache in sympathy. I do understand.

'I lost my father too,' I tell her, impulsively. I didn't mean to say it, and I don't know why I did, but I continue. 'I have very few mementoes of him, and most of what I had was destroyed in a fire recently.'

'Then you really do understand.' She looks at me with a hopeful expression. 'So, will you help me?'

I nod. 'We will do our best.'

She smiles brightly at my words, then another thought seems to strike her, and that bright smile falters. She lowers her head. 'I'm a very old woman, with rapidly deteriorating health. I know nothing about detective work, and I have no idea of your fees. I just saw that article about how you and your partner were honoured at that reception at Mansion House. So I thought you might be good…'

She trails off, and I grimace uncomfortably. Mansion House, the article — I remember both clearly. Egan and I were invited to meet with the Mayor of London at the end of our first successful case. Of course, journalists were there, and, of course, our mug shots ended up in the papers. It's just not my kind of thing. My mother forced me to get tardted up in a dress and high heels for the occasion — I still go cold just thinking about it all. For me that whole event had been one huge cosmic farce; the faked smarmy smiles, the abhorrent polite chatter just created an aching boredom in me. I just wanted to escape. Well, now it seemed I'd finally be repaid for all that agony. It had brought us a client.

'I don't have much money.' Mrs Hargrave brings me back to reality. 'My health can be said to be—' she pauses, as if in search for the right word '—*failing*, at best.' She smiles a little bitterly, 'This is actually one of my good days, if you can believe it.

'I really don't know who else to ask to do this vital job for me. It's the most important aspect of my life now. I know I have only a little time left and I must know that I'm leaving Lyssa secure in a long and happy marriage.'

I run some numbers in my head. We have just finished a case, and Cromworth's money is safely tucked away in the bank. It should cover half of this month's bills and — providing there are no nasty surprises — my share of this new client's payment, even if low, should be enough to settle the rest.

'It's probably going to take us time to track down your necklace.' I look up to Mrs Hargrave, with my most earnest expression, willing her to see that I'm speaking the truth. 'And there is no guarantee that we will find it.'

She nods. 'I understand that.'

'It will mostly be research and beating down the pavement — shouldn't cost us too much, except time.' I scratch at my chin while I do the sums. 'We can do it for five hundred pounds a week, plus expenses.' It's a fair bit less than our usual rate, but, if we can settle the case within a fortnight and take on a new client afterwards, we won't be in the red.

I force a smile onto my face, 'I'll have to ask you now for the first payment though.'

2

I meet up with Egan that same evening. As soon as Mrs Hargrave had gone, I left him a message saying informing him that I'd drop by his flat once he'd finished with his last class. Although the university is closed for the summer holidays, he still gives private tutoring classes to some students who are willing to pay for it.

We don't often meet at his place, but I know that he keeps several history books in his flat, and they might well come in handy with this particular case.

I rap my fingers on his door at precisely six in the evening. He has a perfectly functioning doorbell, but four quick knocks on the wooden panel is my way of letting him know it's me.

He opens up, moves to the side and lets me in with a courteous bow. From this angle, I can't see his face, but picture in my head the beginning of a smile part imperious, part peevish.

I chuckle, as I walk ahead of him and march down the corridor leading to his living room. Into his spotlessly clean living room, where everything is exactly where it should be and where everything is perfectly aligned. *Neatness freak!*

'So, how was your day?' I ask, coming to stand between his settee and the coffee table.

He huffs. 'Same as always. I spoke; no-one listened.'

'Nah. It's not true, they always listen.' I was one of his many students not so long ago, and I know for a fact that, while Egan isn't very popular as a person, his lectures are. He has a captivating way of recounting history in general, and battles in particular. 'They're just trying to be discreet about it.'

He comes to stand near the living room's entrance and offers me a stiff shrug of his shoulders. 'Well, they don't seem to remember much when the time comes for questions. Brains like tea strainers.'

'Again, that's just play acting. Students can't let their lecturers know they enjoy coming to university, can they?'

'Yes, that would be the end of the world, wouldn't it?' Egan replies, tonelessly.

I frown at him. He usually enjoys our little verbal jousts, but tonight he seems oddly distant. His face is closed, his posture too rigid. I remember how he moved to the side as I entered, more so than was necessary. I realised he'd been hiding his face from me. I take two steps forward and am presented with one last clue is in his eyes, a glinting wetness that I should have noticed right away, but that I overlooked. I can only blame it on the fact that I so rarely see him without his dark glasses.

I can see it now, a sort of contained sadness. It's very faint, repressed, but it's definitely there. Egan is fighting hard against himself to keep it from me. He blinks, once, twice, and I can see that he's loosing the battle. It has me rewinding our conversation and analysing his every word and inflection. It doesn't get me any closer to figuring out what is going on. Egan is the one who specialises in analysing people's tones of voice — he has the hearing of a fox and a natural talent for discerning lies. I'm only good at reading people's body language. It allows me to know when something is wrong, but doesn't help me figure out *what* that something is.

'Did something happen?' I ask, forced to fish for clues.

His face betrays nothing more, as he moves to the kitchen. 'Nothing worth mentioning.'

I don't buy it for a second. Egan isn't Mister Popularity at UCL, I know. The students, in general, don't like him and he doesn't have a single friend amongst the staff either. When I was there I think I heard others use most of the possible nasty nicknames. All this is because of his attitude. Egan is cold to all and sundry and he sometimes has a superior manner when talking to others. This can be somewhat unnerving. Now, I know it's just a façade — a way for him to protect himself — but when he was my lecturer and I was just his student, I admit to falling for the trick, same as everyone else. I wondered if today someone might have actually said something to his face, instead of just writing it on the toilet walls as sometimes happened.

When he comes back from the kitchen empty handed, I'm certain something happened, 'What's going on? What happened?'

'Nothing.' He leans against the low wall that separates his kitchen from the living room and crosses his arms over his chest. 'Drop it, Lexa.'

I take a step forward. If he really wanted me to back off, he would have called me Alexandra. It was only a half-hearted plea then — a sign although he doesn't want to talk about this, he knows he should.

He twitches and turns his torso almost imperceptibly in my direction. He's heard me move, I gather. 'Figgins asked me to his office.'

Any other day, I'd have turned this into a joke — something about him being called into the boss's office for a spanking — but today, I bite down on my tongue, hard. 'So, and what did the vice-chancellor want?'

Egan's mouth contorts bitterly and, for a long moment, it looks as though he isn't going to reply.

'He's learned of our—' another downward quirk of his lips '— business association.'

Huh? I'm surprised; this doesn't really make sense. What could the powers that be have to say about us? Sure, lecturers and students aren't really supposed to spend too much time together outside of the university, but I'm not a student anymore. I haven't been for months.

'So what? Unless he wants to hire us for something, I don't see what business he has poking his fat nose in our partnership.'

Egan frowns at me.

'He does have a rather fat nose,' I inform him. 'And my question still stands.'

'Lexa, don't.' Egan tries again.

I take a step forward, stop when I see it makes him uncomfortable. 'What did he want?'

Silence lingers and my friend's shoulders slump a few inches. 'He wants me to make a choice.'

'A choice?'

'Apparently, I cannot be a lecturer and a private investigator at the same time.' It seems to do him good to have said it out loud. He shrugs, as if the topic isn't interesting, as if he hasn't just confessed that he may be going to quit. To quit... *me*.

I swallow hard and force myself to keep my emotions in check. 'Why not?' I try to steel my tone, to not let him hear how uncomfortable I suddenly feel. 'Lots of members of the staff have jobs and they teach on the side. Why couldn't you do that too?'

'Because it doesn't sit well with them, Lexa. Because tricking some lady into cheating on her husband isn't the same as working part time in a law firm or a museum.' After running a nervous hand through his short ginger hair, he lets it hang dejectedly by his side again. 'Because Figgins doesn't like me, because he's been waiting for a reason to sack me for years and because he's finally found that reason.'

Bull! I bite my tongue yet again to stop impulsive words from rushing out; I take a moment just to breathe.

I look my friend up and down and he's the picture of misery. A well-contained misery, almost hidden and probably invisible to the unfamiliar eye, but very noticeable to me. I see it in his slightly slumped shoulders, his limp hands, his bobbing Adam's apple and, most of all, in the sad glistening wetness of his eyes. With a pang in my chest, I realise that he doesn't want to quit any more that I want him to.

'Ash.' I come to stand beside him. To anyone else, I would offer a reassuring smile to let my sympathy show, but instead I place a reassuring hand on his forearm.

I tighten my grasp comfortingly and he swallows thickly. 'Either way, he wins,' he says. 'There's no way out.'

Something clicks in my brain, at his resolute tone. 'It isn't the first time he's talked to you about this, is it? Why didn't you tell me?'

He shrugs again, heaves a deep breath, and angles his head away from me. 'Didn't seem relevant.'

'Not relevant! Ash, we're partners in this. Or did you fail to notice our two names on our business cards. I had them embossed for a reason, you know.'

The joke is rewarded by only a minimal upward quirk of his lips. 'Sorry,' he mutters, through clenched teeth. 'I didn't want to bother you with this. I thought I'd find a way out on my own. I looked into it, tried to contact people higher up in the food chain. I found nothing.'

I let my hand move up from his forearm to his shoulder. My second hand mirrors the first on the other side of his bowed head.

'You silly man,' I chide him gently, making appropriate tusking sounds. 'What part of the word "team" don't you understand?'

He lifts up his head a little to face me and inches forward. 'Sorry.'

'It's okay,' I murmur.

He lets out a long breath and slumps down even more. 'I haven't decided anything yet and… I need some time to think about it. Can we just drop the subject for now?'

'You completely sure there's no third option?'

'No. I'm afraid not. I'm in no mood for a long judicial battle.'

'Alright.' I swallow and force my voice to take on a lighter lilt, thankful that he can't see the tears pooling in my eyes. 'Whatever you decide, it won't change anything in our friendship.'

He smiles at that and nods in agreement. I tug at the back of his neck with one hand and he slumps forward until his chin settles on my shoulder. I close my arms around him gladly and he relaxes in the touch.

Our friendship, as a whole, is a very touch-filled one. When you lose one of your senses, it's a known fact that you rely more on those remaining. It figures this should also affect other aspects of your life, including how you treat your relationships with others. At least, that's how I understand it.

With Egan, reassuring smiles and well-meaning glances are not possible elements of our communication. The smiles have to be wrought into the tone of voice and the glances transformed into physical gestures: a pat on the shoulder, my hand sliding into his for a quick grasp, and the occasional, but always brief, hug. We've never really acknowledged or discussed the matter though. It's just something that slipped into our routine and that we've both come to accept.

This friendship, however unlikely, is something for which I'm ready to fight tooth and nail. I don't have many friends, but once I grant someone my complete trust, as I have with Egan, there's no going back. Although we are diametrically different — not just in age and cultural background, but also in spirit — we function very well as a team. Sure, there are little hiccups here and there — just like two elements not really meant to cohabit together. There is friction between us, sometimes, which creates sparks, which give birth to the occasional explosion. It's just like a cooking pan, sometimes you need to lift the lid to let out some of the vapour.

I take a step back when Egan moves away from me and retreats into the kitchen. While he busies himself with the kettle, I sink down onto his hugely comfortable grey leather settee that has become my official perch when I'm here. He comes back with a tray of teacups and biscuits, and I give him a recap of Mrs Hargrave's visit.

'So we are looking for a necklace,' he says, after I finish the first part of my rundown. 'Well it's certainly an improvement on lost dogs.'

Although his comment is funny, the circumstances stop me from laughing.

'Yes, we are,' I say. 'When the war broke out, Hargrave's parents were identified as Jews. When they were deported, the necklace was stolen by whoever came to arrest them. It was never seen again until Mrs Hargrave got it back briefly, this year.'

Egan scratches at his chin — an unconscious gesture he does when deep in thought — and leans backwards in his chair. He turns his head toward me and asks, 'How did she ever get it back?'

'Well, and this is where it gets interesting, the necklace was returned to her — exactly six weeks ago — by the Italian police.'

Egan's eyebrows rise up at that and he sits up a bit straighter on his chair, with his curiosity clearly piqued.

'Remember hearing about an earthquake that hit Northern Italy a while back?'

He nods.

'A little town, not far from Modena, was hit pretty violently and several houses crumbled. Mirandola, it's called.

'One of the rescue team found several invaluable items encased in a wall in the rubble of a house. It left the Italian police completely puzzled. They have no idea how it got there, but they imagine it stayed walled-in for several years, until everybody forgot about it, it would seem.'

I take a sip of my tea, before continuing. 'They found several paintings and a lot of jewellery. They've been trying to find the rightful owners of the lot ever since. They dated the paintings to the mid-thirties and that gave them something to go on.'

'Could they identify the painter?'

'No, but there were several landscapes; all of East-Germany scenes. Germany, mid-thirties, looted goods: the Italians did the Maths, and they inquired within the Jewish community. What with the Internet and all, it didn't take them too long to find the first owners.

'Thanks to the photograph Mrs Hargrave showed me this afternoon, she was able to prove that the necklace belongs to her family. Besides, she told me that her father's initials are carved on the back of the pendant, inside the metal frame.'

'Amazing.'

'Quite. Talk about a modern-day treasure story.'

'Can you describe it to me?' Egan says. 'The pendant, I mean.'

I take out of my shoulder bag a photograph Mrs Hargrave gave me. It's a close-up of the jewel that was taken by the Italian police when they made the inventory of the items discovered. It was thankfully taken in colour and high-resolution. There's a small fact-sheet stapled to the back, with relevant information.

'The heart in itself is about two by two inches and is composed of fifty rubies and fifty-eight diamonds. Basically, the middle is filled with carefully aligned and identically shaped rubies and they are surrounded by the diamonds.

'There's also a mini secondary pendant, above the first one, through which the chain passes — a tear-shaped silver frame with thirty tiny rubies.'

I gaze at it intently. It's absolutely beautiful to look at and I'm sure the actual piece must look even better. I can imagine it, reflecting sunlight on all sides, colours vibrating as if alive.

'I wish you could see this, Ash.' I let my thumb trace the curve of the heart-shaped pendant on the glossy photograph. 'It took true craftsmanship and dedication to make such a gorgeous piece. It's just… flawless.'

'Do you have any idea of its value?'

'The Italians had an expert do some research. It's impossible to say how much it would sell for at an auction or something like that, but each of the rubies are—' I flip the photograph over to peek at the description provided '—above one carat and the diamonds are even better. At current market value, it would sell for at least fifty thousand pounds. Of course, it was worth a lot less when Salzmann made it.'

Egan's eyes widen, the blue pupils darting upwards. 'Fifty thousand pounds for such a small necklace?' He coughs, as if the tea he just swallowed went down his windpipe.

I smile, unable to resist teasing him. 'Actually, that's just for the pendant; you'd have to buy the chain separately.'

My comment gets a derisive snort and an exaggerated eye roll.

I chuckle heartily. *Men* — they don't know the first thing about jewels.

'Anyway, the Italian authorities returning the necklace aroused huge publicity. There were several articles about it and there was even an interview on the BBC with Mrs Hargrave.'

Egan leans forward and rests his elbows on his thighs, lacing his long, lean fingers. Twin frowns lines mar his forehead.

'I know what you're thinking,' I say.

'— That this is how whoever stole it knew she had it.' He lets his chin rest on his folded hands, as he seems to consider his own words.

'My thoughts exactly.' I take a sip of tea.

'Whoever stole the necklace either found out from the papers or on the telly that Mrs Hargrave had it. The fact that it had already been stolen once could be a mere coincidence,' Egan offers. 'Maybe he or she just found it pretty.'

'Could be… but you know what I think of such coincidences.' I just can't buy them, especially when they're so big.

The corner of Egan's lips turn up. 'It's one hell of an assumption to make.'

'Chalk that down to intuition, if you want.' I place the photograph back in my bag. 'Whatever it is, I'm dead certain the two are connected. I just know it.'

He nods, flicks his hand in a 'Fine,' gesture.

'Whoever has the necklace knew about it. Knew where it came from and had been waiting for many years to get his or her hands back on it.'

'Or not,' Egan quips.

I shrug, not minding that he can't see me.

'Only one way to find out,' I muse.

Egan turns a derisive smile in my general direction. It unnerves me.

'So, we only need to find out who stole it in nineteen forty-two then. Piece of cake.'

3

'Alright,' I say. 'Bring me back up to speed on key elements of the World War Two era.'

Egan's eyes close to thinner slits and his brow crunches. If his gaze wasn't directed about ten inches to my left, he would be squinting at me.

'Why don't you tell me? I seem to remember you attended lectures of the highest quality on that time period, only last year. Tell me what you recall, and I'll fill in the blanks. Or are you a tea strainer too?'

'Seriously?' I'm bewildered. It shouldn't come as a surprise though, smug bastard. He wants to know if I paid attention to his lectures. 'Sure.'

I can do this. I can totally do this. Oh why isn't it pharaohs; that I can remember well. World War One and Two didn't hold as much interest for me. It was all too dark and depressing. I remember the main lines, but the finer details elude me.

'Nazi plunder.' The History professor nods at the apt technical designation. 'Art Theft committed during the Third Reich by Nazis, mostly of Jewish items. It started during the thirties—'

'Nineteen thirty-three.'

'Yeah, nineteen thirty-three and went on until the end of World War Two. Most stolen objects were traded to fund Nazi activities, but the best pieces went to high-ranking officials. We can assume the necklace suffered such a fate.'

Egan frowns at my words. 'Not too high-ranking, though. If the necklace had made it to Hitler, or say, Göring, who oversaw confiscated property, it would never have ended up in the basement of an Italian house.'

'You think it never made it that far?'

'Hmm, hmm.' He scratches at his chin. 'What you're thinking about is the Einsatzstab Reichsleiter Rosenberg (ERR) the Nazi party which appropriated cultural property during World War Two. They were mostly active outside of Germany; they raided most of Europe, looted about twenty percent of the entire European art, yes, but what they sought most were books and artefacts; things of particular historical importance.

'This necklace, although of great value, wouldn't have fallen into that category. What we should focus on is what happened in Germany.'

I look at him bemused, feel as if I have taken a trip in a time machine and I'm back to six months ago, when I was just a university student and Egan was only a professor giving me lectures.

I shake my head to clear my thoughts and focus on the matter at hand. Something Mrs Hargrave said comes back to mind. 'They passed laws, didn't they? To force Jews to register property?'

'Yes, the *Decree on the Registration of the Property of Jews*, nineteen thirty-eight. All Jews were required to value their assets and register them.'

'Nazis' little Christmas list,' I mutter darkly. They listed everything, and then they just had to pick up what interested them.

'They looted homes, when they came to ship the families to the camps, yes.' Egan confirms, in a quiet monotone. 'Following the aftermath of Kristallnacht, there were mass arrests made in Germany.'

'I suppose the necklace would have been listed, along with everything else that Salzmann owned.'

'Yes, a jeweller would have been kept under close watch by a lot of people.'

The appalling unfairness of all that hits me hard and I shuffle uncomfortably in my seat. I look at Egan with his calm, detached features, his straight back, his carefully held head. His attitude feels all wrong to me. I wonder if, after so many years of retelling history, he's forgotten how to care. These are real people he speaks of — he's describing mass murder, and it just doesn't seem to affect him. I stand up, feeling on fire as a sudden anger courses through me. I feel my hands close into fists.

'Lexa?' Egan frowns at my abrupt movements. 'Is something wrong?'

I stalk to the back of his living room, spat, 'How can you be so detached?' The words keep tumbling out of my mouth, 'Those are real people Ash, and they're just two amongst thousands. My God.'

He turns his head towards me, directed to where I stand, near one of the windows and exhales slowly. 'It's something one must learn to do, as an historian. We can't let ourselves be emotionally involved during our lectures. Think of it as journalism — we must remain neutral and simply recount facts as they've happened, without letting our personal judgments interfere.'

I scoff, dryly, 'That seems a very cold attitude to me.' Once again, I'm reminded that teaching history is the right job for Egan — a perfect fit to his personality. 'Suits you. Maybe Figgins' right and you should go back to being a lecturer full-time.'

The instant the words leave my mouth, I know it was a mistake to say them. *Porca vacca!* I inwardly curse, in my father's birth language, as I lower my eyes in shame and let a long breath out through my nose.

I push aside one of the long dark-grey curtains and peer at the quiet street below. There is nothing to hold my interest and I let the curtain fall closed again. I don't turn back, however, and continue to stare at the immaculate grey cotton. I'm too much of a coward to look at my friend right now. I cannot bear to see the hurt in his eyes, knowing I'm the one who's inflicted it.

Behind me, I hear him stand up. 'I demonstrate objectivity in my job, but that doesn't mean I don't have a personal opinions and feelings on the matter.' He pauses briefly, takes in a breath. 'I do not condone what was done any more than you do, Alexandra.'

The use of my Christian name in full doesn't escape me, and I grimace. I force myself to let go of the curtain and turn back to face him. He walked closer to me and his face shows no emotions, only cold detachment. Both of his eyelids are closed and he looks as though he was carved in ice.

I think back over my words, and know I couldn't have used better words to hurt him, if I wanted to. Once again, I let the flare of emotions get the better of me, and inadvertently hurt my friend in the process. I really need to learn to stop doing it; I need to learn to control this impulse and *think* before I talk. Old habits...

'I'm so sorry, Ash. That came out wrong.' My tongue feels thick in my mouth, as it forms the words. 'I just lost it — I don't know. I... I'm... you know how I am.'

'Lexa?' He reaches out a hand in my direction, blindly looking for me.

I grab his wrist, guide his arm, until his palm rests on my shoulder.

He squeezes it comfortingly. 'I know how emotional you can get at times, but you need to learn to distance yourself. You're going to get hurt otherwise.'

'Easy for you to say,' I say, *sotto voce*. He's not the one who sat in front of Mrs Hargrave, witnessed the hope moving forward her frail body, had to face her pleading, tear-filled brown eyes.

'God, I'm not really sure I'm cut out for this job.' The adrenaline rush is gone, and I feel drained and weak. I can't help but wonder if this isn't one huge mistake? Maybe I should have gone back to my studies after our first case, maybe this investigator's life isn't meant for me after all.

'Nonsense.' Egan tsks. 'You just need to learn not to take things too much to heart. This is not a personal crusade. You need to look at this case from an investigator's point-of-view. Look for suspects;

look for motives. What really matters is Mrs Hargrave and the job she's employing us to do.'

I sigh and close my eyes for a few seconds. He's right, of course. He's always right. Even with all the goodwill in the world and whatever I might do, I can't change what happened. I can't set right all of the wrongs that were committed, but, if the stars align, I can do this one thing. I can find this necklace and return it to Mrs Hargrave. Return to a survivor the only thing she has left of her parents.

'Alright.' I reopen my eyes. 'Suspects' list and motives — what have we got?'

Egan smiles and pats my shoulder one last time, before moving back to sit in his chair by the coffee table.

Forcing myself into a professional mindset, I return to my place on the settee. 'We need to investigate two thefts: the one that happened in nineteen forty-two and the one that happened last month.'

'Good thing there are two of us, then.' Egan offers me a small smile.

'Yes, we'd better split the work. It'll be faster that way. You could focus on the most recent case?'

He frowns at me.

'I know with your expertise, it would seem logical that you should take the forty-two case, but most documents pertaining to that a time will be just that... *documents*. You won't be able to find much on the Internet, hell, most of it must not even be typed yet.'

Egan gave me a tight-lipped smile and nods, reluctantly. I hate to think of him as anything less than what I am, but, sometimes, we are forced to face the fact that he's more limited than me, in certain areas.

'You can dig into what happened over in Italy. We need to know more about the other items that were discovered. Also, try to find out who owned the house — maybe it'll help us trace back what happened to that necklace.'

Faint traces of excitement begin to show in the lines of Egan's face. 'I can try to find out if someone else was interested in the jewel. Perhaps another person made a claim on it.'

'That would be a start. In the meantime, I'll try to find out what happened to the Salzmanns. If we can find out who came to take them, then we'll know who had the opportunity to steal the necklace.'

Egan nods his approval, reclining a little further in his chair and steepling his fingers under his chin. He's started to lose himself in thought, which I take as my cue to leave.

'I'll call you, if I need any specific information, or… a shoulder to cry on,' I say, in a softer voice.

He turns his head in my direction, showing me a sweet, honest and warm smile. 'Any time.'

I get up and see myself out.

On the ride home, I take my sketchbook out. Pencil in hand, I start to list what I need to research. The Salzmann family, the town they lived in, Magdeburg, Jews deported to Warsaw, and any particular historical event that took place in the area where the family lived.

My mother's already in bed when I come back and I move silently about the flat. I fix myself a sandwich and move to my bedroom, where I do all of my computer research.

There is a desk in a corner, and I've arranged it as a professional would. There is a computer and printer, several pencils within hand's reach, and just above the desk — screwed into the wall — a large white board.

I power up my laptop and get to work.

I manage to find listings of Mr and Mrs Salzmann in Yad Vashem's online Shoah Victims Names Database. They were listed on a nineteen forty-two Deportation List, along with hundreds of others.

I also discovered on their website something called *Pages of Testimony*. Documents filed by survivors of the Holocaust, listing deceased Jews during the Shoah. These have to be some of the most heartbreaking documents I've ever seen in my life. A single page of white paper, filled with basic information such as name and place of birth and a photograph — if the person filling in the form possesses one — and the only testimony left that those human beings actually existed. It's all they are in the end, a name and a picture on a list of thousands.

My throat tightens at the thought, and my eyes water. 'My God,' I say to myself. 'How could they let that happen?'

Egan's words come back to me, and I force myself to follow his advice and approach this case in a more detached way. It's hard to remember this is just a job and not a "personal crusade", as Egan put it.

I grab a black marker, sit up and write down a date at the bottom of the white board — April 14, nineteen forty-two. The date Mrs Hargrave's parents were deported to Poland; the date the necklace was stolen for the first time. With a red marker, I write "Suspects List" on top of the board.

I find a few online testimonies of survivors taken that same night. It's enough for me to get a relatively good idea of what happened to Mrs Hargrave's parents. There was a massive search, roundup and persecution in Magdeburg that day.

Two days later, a train arrived in Warsaw. There were a thousand Jews onboard.

In all likelihood, the local authorities knocked on Jews' doors and took them away. They brought them first to a local gathering place: a hotel or a community centre. They wrote down their names, stamped their ID cards with "deported" and confiscated all of their valuables. They left them with little more than the clothes they had on their backs. Afterwards, an SS detachment would have escorted them to the train station.

Two options present themselves here. The necklace could either have been carried by Mrs Salzmann or left in their home. My best bet is that she had it on her. From what Mrs Hargrave told me, her mother wore it all the time, often underneath her clothes. If the jewel was taken during this violent persecution, it should have been integrated into the lot of valuables seized that night. I don't need to find the inventory, to know that it wasn't. If there hadn't been something fishy going on, the necklace wouldn't have surfaced in Italy, seventy years later.

Someone took it for himself that night, and there were very few windows of opportunity to commit such a crime. The culprit either lay with the German police officers who brought the Salzmanns to the roundup, or within the SS unit who processed them.

I list both groups on my board. I have no idea which one to focus on, and, either way, finding out the names of the men who were there that night will be next to impossible. Talk about needles in haystacks.

4

Egan and I take a trip to east London on Monday to go and visit Mrs Hargrave. I want to have a look at the second theft's crime scene and it's only fair that my partner gets to meet with our client too, so we scheduled an appointment.

We take the Underground near his flat, and ride the Circle line to Greenford.

'So?' I ask, as our train departs. 'Have you made any progress?'

'Not much.' He shrugs, from his seat beside me. 'I've read about every article I could find online about the "mysterious treasure of Mirandola", but that's about it.'

The train takes a sharp turn and jolts me forward in my seat. I grasp at Egan — who is diligently holding onto one of the safety bars — for balance. 'Couldn't you get anything from more official sources?'

'The Italian police, the *Carabinieri*?' He chuckles. 'I can't find anyone who speaks a decent level of English amongst them.'

The level of contempt in his voice has me smiling. 'I'm sorry for you.'

'Maybe you could give me a hand with that, Signora Neve?' He turns his head around and arches an elegant eyebrow up. 'You are of Italian descent, after all?'

'*Non è possible.*' I snort. 'No can do. My father, although born here, was bilingual. I, on the other hand, should just about be able to order a pizza in a *ristorante.*' I let out a deep breath. 'What little Dad taught me, when I was a kid, is almost gone now.'

It's sad, when I think about it. It was a part of my heritage and I lost it to time and lack of practice. I'm sure, if my dad had known he was going to die of cancer before all of my adult teeth had grown, he would have gone about it differently, making sure that I paid attention and retained my lessons.

Egan's hand finds its way to my shoulder. 'Do you have contacts with your family in Italy?'

'No, there's got to be some distant second-cousins somewhere, but I've never known any of them. My dad's parents died a while back, and my two uncles feel more British than Italian.'

'I'm sorry for you.' He rubs my shoulder reassuringly. 'This case can't be helping.'

'It does stir up some bad memories, but you don't need to worry about me. I'll be fine. I'm following your advice scrupulously.'

He gives me a tight-lipped smile. 'If you need someone to talk to,' he offers, his tone cautious and hesitant.

Nah, I'm fine. *Really* fine. 'What about you?' I demand, in a vain attempt to redirect the conversation well away from me. 'You close to your parents?'

I expect a positive answer, but get the exact opposite. Egan's smile disappears and an icy mask of indifference comes up to cover his face. His hand disappears from my shoulder.

'Not really.' The coldness in his tone is enough to get me to bite on my tongue to stop any follow up questions I might have on the subject.

Okay, touchy subject — duly noted. I make an internal note to investigate the matter further at a later date though. I'm not nosy, but when you're a private investigator, curiosity is sort of part of the package.

'Hum, about our case.' I start, a little hesitant myself now. 'You wouldn't happen to know any historian colleagues specialising in World War Two?'

'Are you looking for something specific?' The change of subject is visibly a relief to him and his face regains some of its warmth.

'Documents from that time? If I could find a list of police officers and military personnel present in Magdeburg in the forties; that would be a big step forward.'

Egan frowns and his hand doesn't take long to come up to scratch at his chin — that little nervous tick of his makes me smile every time.

'I'm not sure I'll be able to help.'

'Oh, you don't go to the annual history professors' convention then? I hope you at least get the newsletter.'

The downward quirk of his mouth is priceless.

'I'll have you know—' he raises his hand, index finger imperiously held above the others '—that I'm a member of the respected Royal Historical Society.'

'Of course you are.' I have no idea what that is, but it does sound pompous enough for my friend to be a part of it. 'Do they have a newsletter?'

The intense drawing closer of his eyebrows, barely visible above his dark shades, is what I've come to know as his version of a murderous gaze.

He remains silent until I nudge his foot with the tip of one of my white Converse trainers.

'There are a few annual publications,' he mutters, and the index finger disappears, along with the others, into his coat pocket.

I chuckle. Egan can be so easy to get riled up sometimes.

'Fine, fine. I'm sure it's great.' I pat his shoulder good-naturedly. 'So, is there any way you can get in touch with these guys? Ask around if someone, by any chance, knows someone?'

He shrugs. 'I can try.'

We exit the Underground station, a little while later, and start walking west. Our client owns a flat on the ground floor of a little house built by the Grand Union Canal.

As we arrive at number 41, we find a one storey, traditional brickbuilt house, with a tiny, little worn-down garden in the front. We ring the doorbell, at just after four in the afternoon.

A middle-aged man with extensively tanned skin — clearly contrasted against his off-white cotton shirt — opens up the door. He looks at us and cocks a thick brown eyebrow upwards. He has dark rings of fatigue around his eyes, and the distraction of our arrival is clearly unwelcome.

I suddenly wonder if I got the house number wrong. 'Hi, we're uh… looking for Doris Hargrave?'

The eyebrow inches up. 'The PI's, right?'

I nod.

The man's tired face breaks into a polite smile, although he's clearly exhausted, as he moves to the side to let us in. 'I'm Robert, Doris's son.'

He leads us to a large room with a settee, two chairs and a coffee table. The living room is tiny and filled with too much furniture. You'd easily feel cramped up in this room, if it weren't for the large bay windows behind the settee allowing the bright summer afternoon's sunshine to stream in.

'Make yourselves comfortable,' Robert says, from the entrance door. 'I'll see if my mother is ready to speak to you.'

I help Egan navigate to the settee and we sit down together.

'Well?' He waves a hand about, encompassing the room.

'Exactly what I was expecting.' My gaze rakes over the shelves and other surfaces lining the walls of the room. 'Old furniture, covered with the sort of trinkets you amass with time, and a tapestry that belongs to the sixties.' My lips quirk up when I see several snow globes, on a small round table. My mum used to have some when I was a kid, but I managed to accidentally break them all.

'What surprised me the most, is the son,' Egan says. 'The strain in his voice was clearly audible, as if he was extremely tired.'

'Picked up on that, have you?' It amazes me, every time, how he manages to hear what my eyes can see. 'He did look tired. If I were to venture a guess, I'd say he's just come home from long holidays, somewhere sunny.'

'Heavily tanned, is he?' Egan asks, much to my amazement.

'How on earth…?'

He wiggles his nose slightly, purely for show, and replies, 'After-sun lotion. It hangs in the air… Aloe Vera, I think.'

With a frown, I close my eyes, focus on my nose and take a deep sniff. I have to inhale two more times to perceive the faint scent of something sweet and milky.

Noise reaches us from the hallway Robert has just disappeared into. He soon comes back in the room, with his mother at his arm.

Mrs Hargrave looks ten times worse than she did when she first visited me. Her features are taut, her skin sickly pale, with a clammy look. I immediately understand that the presence of her son at her arm is not for show — she wouldn't be able to stand without him. He helps her sit in a chair, finds a nearby Afghan and drapes it carefully around her.

'Thank you, Robert.' She slowly raises a weak hand to pat his arm.

'Can I get you anything to drink?' he asks.

She refuses with a weak shake of her head, stifles a cough.

Mrs Hargrave's glazy eyes lift up to meet mine and she offers me a feeble smile. 'Thank you for meeting with me here, Ms Neve. As you can see, I wouldn't have been able to make the trip to Camden today.'

'We can always reschedule,' I say. 'If you'd rather we come back some other time—'

'Nonsense.' She flaps a hand about. 'I'm used to my failing

health. Some days are better than others. Most of the time, I cannot leave the flat, except on some very rare occasions, when I feel like I'm twenty again. Like the last time we met.'

She fixes me with an intense, vibrant gaze. 'You are lucky to be so young, Ms Neve. Enjoy it, while it lasts.'

I smile a little awkwardly at the words and Egan shifts beside me. I suddenly remember that he's here with us. 'This is my colleague, Ashford Egan.'

He politely bows his head and Mrs Hargrave offers him a smile. 'It's a pleasure to meet you. Do forgive me if I do not stand up to shake your hand.'

Egan replies with a smile, a shade warmer than he usually bestows on strangers, 'It's quite alright.'

'Have you made any progress finding my mother's necklace?' Robert says, from the place he's assumed behind the old woman's chair.

'We're working on it,' I say. 'As I explained to your mother, it's going to take time. Documents from the World War Two era aren't the easiest to track down.'

The words seem to surprise the man. 'Shouldn't you be looking only into this year's events?' He narrows his eyes at me. 'Those old war stories are hardly relevant to our recent problems. Time is—'

'Let them do their job, Robert.' Mrs Hargrave snaps and her son shuts his mouth contritely.

'With all due respect, sir,' I say, with as much patience as I can, 'there is a possibility that the two thefts may be connected. So, to be absolutely thorough, we're investigating them both simultaneously.'

My answer seems to please Mrs Hargrave more than it does her son. Something tells me he doesn't approve of his mother's decision to hire private investigators. She quite possibly even came to seek our help while he was away on vacation, without him knowing about it.

'If you don't mind,' I say, trying to move the conversation back to safer ground. 'I'd like to have a look at the place where you kept the necklace.'

'Show her, Robert.' Mrs Hargrave flicks a hand to the side. 'You won't mind that I don't accompany you.'

'Certainly not, Mrs Hargrave.' I stand up and notice that Egan remains seated. 'My colleague will keep you company.'

Robert Hargrave takes me around the flat to a window, at the end of the corridor leading to the bedrooms.

'He came in this way.' He points at the window.

I can clearly see the alarm wire has been cut. 'The thief opened the window, just a fraction, and then cut the wire before opening it completely.' It requires a bit of know-how and some professional equipment to get this done without triggering the alarm first. 'This is not some amateur work.'

I crouch down, by the window, and inspect the floorboard: not a mark, not even a scratch.

'The police said they found no prints,' Robert says. He motions for me to follow him. He opens one of the bedroom doors and I follow him inside what I guess to be Mrs Hargrave's own room. The age of the furniture matches what I saw in the living room.

Robert takes a painting off the wall and it predictably reveals a safe.

'Someone opened it while my mother was sleeping not two feet away.' He makes a wide circle with his arm to encompass the bed, which lies just a little further ahead. 'Her hearing's not as good as it used to be, but it scares me to think what could have happened if she'd woken up.'

Probably nothing good. 'No prints found here either, I guess?'

'Nothing. What do you think?'

'That this is the work of a professional.' I inch closer to the safe. It doesn't look like it has been tampered with; there is no visible scratch mark. 'Who knew the code?'

'Only my mother.'

I raise a curious eyebrow up. 'Not even you?'

'No.' Robert's eyes meet mine steadily. 'My mother and I are not that close. I live in Islington. I just drop by every now and then to help, since her health has worsened. And before you ask, I was out of town, when the theft occurred.'

I nod.

'Alibi officially checked by the Metropolitan Police,' he adds, condescendingly.

Doesn't mean you didn't hire someone to do it for you, I think. Smiling, I say, 'I didn't mean to accuse you of anything, Mr Hargrave. I'm just gathering facts.'

With a pinched look, he adds, 'Not that I even would want that stupid necklace.'

I feel one of my eyebrow rise up at that.

Robert Hargrave notices. 'Has she told you about that myth?' He snorts loudly. 'That to wear that pendant is a sure way to "live happily ever after"?'

I nod with a comprehensive smile. 'I take it that you don't see it that way?'

'Of course I don't.' He scoffs. 'It's an old woman's delusion, but she's adamant my daughter should wear it on her wedding day, to avoid *the curse*,' he says the last word in a mockingly sinister way.

'And it gets better,' he continues, his voice heating up. 'My mother refuses to attend the wedding unless Lyssa wears the necklace — Lyssa refuses to have the wedding, unless her grandmother is present. My ex-wife blames it all on me, as usual. The groom is trying to pacify everyone, to no avail, and the rest of the in-laws are threatening to join in on it!' He throws his arms up. 'This damn jewel is making us all miserable. Trust me, if I had it, I would gladly give it back.'

I nod, at a loss for what to say. I turn back to look at the safe, taking a step closer to inspect it for a second time.

Several seconds pass without Robert saying anything, and I deem it safe to return our conversation to a more relevant topic. 'Do you think your mother could have given the code to someone else? A friend, maybe?'

'No. The police already asked her that.'

'Then whoever did this had the right equipment to get inside this safe, without leaving a mark.' Definitely the work of a professional.

'Was anything else taken?'

'No. There was a little bit of money, but the only thing missing was the necklace.'

'A professional working on a contract then,' I muse.

I take a few pictures with my mobile phone and Robert escorts me back.

The meeting with our client is cut short after my return to the living room, when the old woman stands up, apologises, and takes her leave to go, helped by her son, to lie down in her room. Robert seems pleased when I let him know that we'll see ourselves out.

'Did you learn anything useful from Mrs Hargrave?' I ask Egan, on the way back to the Underground station.

'I asked her the usual questions. Did anyone show a particular interest in the necklace; did anyone come to the house recently; and some other similar things.'

'And?'

'Nothing relevant at first, but then she suddenly remembered a visit which seemed a rather strange to her.' Egan falls silent.

Okay, now we're getting somewhere, and once more, it seems my peevish colleague has decided to test my patience. I decide to count to ten in my head, but give up at five. 'I have my expectant expression on,' I tell him and give him a little nudge in the ribs. 'Are you going to share what she told you this side of the twenty-first century, or not?'

He gives me a lopsided half-smile. 'A man paid her a visit, a few days before the necklace was stolen. He said he was from her insurance company and they had learned about the necklace from the news. He said he had to take a picture of it, so that it could be added to the list of things covered by the insurance. He also asked to see the safe, to make sure that it was secure.

'In her own words, he was "very polite, a real sweetie pie." She saw no reason to doubt him, or question his motives.'

'Hell, if this guy was the thief, it's no wonder he didn't leave a mark on the safe; she all but gave him the combination.' I pinch the bridge of my nose. 'And she didn't remember to tell the police any of this?'

'She had completely forgotten about that encounter until today. She wasn't overtly explicit, but I think she has serious health problems, and takes some heavy medications.'

'Yeah, she did look really bad today,' I confirm. 'Sickly pale complexion, clammy skin, glazed over eyes.'

'Now, is it just me, or does this impromptu visit from the insurance company seem a little dodgy to you?'

I snort. 'Not just a little, my friend. Could she describe the guy?'

'Average. About my age, she said. Brown hair, white skin. Nothing striking about him, and so very polite.'

'Very helpful.' I can' help being sarcastic. Couldn't someone one day come to us with something along the lines of extremely tall, with flashing blond hair, striking green eyes, and bearing an easily recognisable tattoo on his forehead that says, "I did it"?

We reach the entrance of the Tube station and I steer us to the right. 'Steps down,' I say, coming to a stop.

Egan slows down and reaches for the railing. I take the steps down at the same time he does.

We part ways in Central London and I head back to Camden alone. Once back at home, I continue my research. Later that evening, I get an email from Egan. As it turns out, one of the Royal Historical Society's Literary Directors in his youth, had studied for a few years abroad. He spent some time in Berlin and still has contacts there. The email provides me with his name, phone number and a very specific recommendation (in bold and capitals, no less) — **DO NOT DISRESPECT HIM WITH YOUR CHARMINGLY FLAMBOYANT MANNERS** — I grunt, as if I could ever do that. I hath manners, me lord.

I spend a little over twenty minutes on the phone with Mr Packard of the Royal Historical Society. He's a most charming man, who, at times, makes me think of my business partner, with his posh, superior speech pattern betraying an education of the higher standards. I start by presenting myself and explain to him what Egan and I have been hired to do and proceed to tell him what I'm looking for.

He rapidly quashes my hopes of finding military records. Such documents are very difficult to acquire, as most records were destroyed at the end of the war. When the rest of the world started to give German soldiers a dark look for what they had done during the Holocaust, they worked hard to cover their tracks. My politely-contained-and-perfectly-well-rounded manners do get me another direction to take my investigations in. Local newspapers. It's such a silly thing, but I must admit I have completely overlooked it.

I profusely thank Mr Packard and twice repeat the phone number he's just dictated to me.

Once I get back to the office corner of my bedroom, I glance at my watch to check the time — seven thirty — before dialling the number. Eight thirty in Germany, I guess it's not late enough for my call to be considered impolite.

A jolly voice greets me after several rings. 'Ja, Hermann Liebrecht.'

'Yes, hello. Mein Name ist Alexandra Neve.' I'm quite certain that my pronunciation is really horrific, but I try my best. 'Ich rufe von England.'

My interlocutor answers with something that I don't understand, and I curse myself for not having paid more attention to the single year of German I had while at school. Aside from listening to the occasional Rammstein song, I haven't practised German since then. Well, I guess Mr Liebrecht must be wondering what I want.

'Ich rufe von Herr Packard in London, und—' I quickly glance at the key words I pre-translated, before making the call, to find *need help* '—brauche Hilfe.'

I'm once more unable to fully understand the answer — the man's accent gives me a hard time. I catch one or two words though and I think he wants to know what I need. I try to explain to him that I'm a private investigator looking for copies of the *Magdeburg Zeitung* from nineteen forty-two until nineteen forty-four.

That gets me a lengthy reply. All I understand is a *what* at the beginning of his phrase and a *for* somewhere in the middle.

I quickly locate *necklace* and *stolen* on my list of words. And then scramble downwards for *during* and *war*.

Herr Liebrecht has the patience of a saint. He puts up with a good thirty minutes of my massacre of the German language. Twice, I have to keep him waiting on the line, while I resort to an online translator for some words I didn't think I would need. In the end, we manage to come to an understanding and we exchange our goodbyes.

Conversation in a foreign language is tiring and this attempt leaves me exhausted. I yawn loudly while stretching exaggeratedly; it feels good and seeing my bed out of the corner of my eye, the idea of sleep becomes irresistible. I flick off the desk lamp.

I guess I'll know how good my German is in a few days. If the parcel Herr Liebrecht promised to send me contains the microfilms I'm after, I'll brag about my natural linguistic talent to my esteemed colleague. If something else shows up, well… I'll blame it all on Google.

5

Why is it that every time I need to go to the Post Office, there's a meandering line of waiting customers worthy of the patient queues for a ride on the London Eye? Seriously, this is unbelievable. Every other time I just happen to be in the neighbourhood, the place seems to be deserted — and I come to this street often, as my Wushu classes are held in the building next door, but, today, the waiting area is jam packed. For heaven's sake, it's Friday — shouldn't people be at work or something?

I brace myself, take a preparatory deep breath and manage to squeeze into the tiny space in a corner which helpful established queuers indict as the tail-end of the line. Twenty-five minutes later, I can finally approach the counter and produce the official slip of paper that was left in our mailbox. It takes another four minutes for the woman serving me to find the right parcel and hand it to me. I'm practically bouncing from one foot to the other by that time.

I rush back home, toss my jacket and shoulder bag onto the settee and go directly to the kitchen to get a sharp knife to open the box.

'I haven't seen you this excited since last Christmas,' my mother says, lifting her nose from her crossword.

'It's for work.' I slickly cut the strong adhesive tape with the knife.

'The nice old lady that was here the other day? Mrs Hargrave?'

'Yes, I hope these are some old documents I've been sent straight from Germany. It may help us to find Mrs Hargrave's necklace.'

Finally, I get through all the sticky tape that practically covers the whole surface of the box. I plunge a hand through the polystyrene loose fill, like a kid rummaging through a Lucky Dip Barrel.

There are five 35mm microfilm rolls in the bottom. I take them out cautiously and find that there is a note tucked into one of them. It reads, "Liebe Alexandra, finden Sie hiermit die Magdeburg Zeitungsarchive. Mit freundlichen Grüssen, H. Liebrecht."

I turn back to look at my mother. 'Do we have a strong magnifying glass?'

She scrunches up her brow for a few seconds. 'Look in the sewing kit.' She shakes her head. 'My poor old eyes can never find the hole in those tiny needles.'

'Thanks, Mum.'

Shortly afterwards, but only after a quick trip to the shops, I'm sitting slumped over my desk, as I carefully look at every page through the magnifying glass in my hand. Mum's magnifying glass wasn't strong enough, and I'd had to go out to buy a more powerful replacement.

Mr Liebrecht told me that each roll contains about eight-hundred images of broadsheet newspaper pages, representing about a year of the weekly newspaper's content.

Moving on to the next page, I realise this case is turning out to be just as I have predicted: time consuming. In the extreme.

It's absolutely fascinating though, culture-wise, to be perusing seventy year old newspapers. It chronicles the life of people then. There are reports on how the war was progressing, depictions of events held in town, and more matters that are trifling. I don't attempt to read the articles, but I'm capable of making sense of some of the headlines, and I can learn a lot from the pictures.

I decide to start in April nineteen forty-two and move forward from there. As Mr Liebrecht had warned me on the phone, the newspaper's archive is not complete. I guess it should come as no surprise that certain dates have been edited out. I can find absolutely nothing on the day the Salzmanns were deported; it's as if that particular day had never existed.

As I near the end of July, my mother pops her head round the door of my room.

'I'm just going out to the shops,' she says, with a slightly embarrassed smile on her lipstick-reddened lips. She's wearing a pale red blouse of a matching shade, an item of clothing I don't remember ever seeing her wear before; must be a recent purchase. All of this has me raising a dubious eyebrow.

'All right, all right.' She flaps a hand about. 'I'm also going for tea with Bob. Do you want me to bring you something back?'

I snort. 'From your teatime with Bob? Hardly.' I correct myself, 'Sorry, no, thank you.'

'Don't be silly, Lexa.' She rests her hands on her hips. 'I mean from the shops.'

'I'm absolutely fine, Mum.' I turn back to my microfilm. 'Have a good time!' And don't do anything I wouldn't do, I think to myself, but manage to stop myself from adding out loud.

Bob is one of her clients from the shoe shop. From what she told me, he's interested in buying some moccasins, but he's having a really hard time making up his mind! Such a hard time, in fact, that he's had to come into the shop every week, for the past two months. It shouldn't take a professional investigator to figure out that he's more interested in the saleswoman than the shoes, but apparently my mother had remained oblivious. However Bob finally mustered the courage to ask her out for coffee last week. Today is going to be date number two.

I find myself smiling to myself at my thoughts. This has to be a good thing. My mother hasn't had a serious relationship since my father died, almost twenty years ago. I diagnose the problem stemming from the fact that she still loves him. Alas, a lost love isn't very good company on long boring weekends; nor is it a comforting, soothing, warm presence by your side on lonely nights. I should know; my dating track record, over the past couple of years isn't much better than my mother's.

I continue to peruse the German newspaper via the magnifying glass for the whole morning, and then escape to meet up with Egan for lunch. The day is lovely, sunny and warm and my strained eyes gradually relax as we get drinks and sandwiches from a local take-away and stroll towards Regent's Park to have lunch outdoors. This is a huge perk to living in Camden; one of London's largest parks is just a street away.

We find a bench that is partly in the shade and from which we have a good view of the ever intriguing straggle of London's inhabitants and visitors. We sit down, Egan looking stiffer and more straight backed than my flopped relaxed position. We start eating to the accompaniment of animal cries from the nearby zoo.

Funny old city. I smile affectionately to myself.

As usual, it seems Egan isn't going to start the conversation we've come here to have.

'So, have you made any progress?' I finally ask, before taking a second bite of my ham'n'cheese.

'I was going to ask you the same thing.' The corners of Egan's lips curl. 'I finally found someone in the Carabinieri who speaks decent English, so that's a step forward.

'A lovely girl, named Paola Plescia. I told her I was a PI hired by Mrs Hargrave and she sent me copies of some documents. Unfortunately, they're not at liberty to release everything, but it's a start.'

'So what did she send you?' I ask, through a mouth still full of bread. Egan frowns.

'I have the list of everything that was retrieved in Mirandola. They found a dozen necklaces, some earrings and some bracelets.' He carefully takes a bite of his sandwich only after he's finished speaking

'They found the other owners?'

Egan makes a point of chewing his mouthful and swallowing it before he answers me. 'Three, including Mrs Hargrave.' He takes another bite, chews and swallows. 'Actually, that's where it gets interesting. The other two owners were also from Germany.'

'Small world.'

He nods. 'Hold this, would you?' He gives me his half-eaten sandwich to hold. Once his hands are free, he takes some folded documents out of his pocket.

I recognise them immediately as his self-made notes. Egan once showed me how it works. He uses thick Braille paper, a slate and a stylus. The slate is made of two flat pieces of metal held together by a hinge at one end. The top part has rows of openings that are the same shape and size as a Braille cell (the small rectangular block of dots which represents a letter in Braille). The bottom part has rows of matching indentations. Using the stylus, a pointed bit of metal with a wooden handle, he can emboss the Braille dots onto the paper. With a bit of practice, it's as simple to use as pen and paper.

'The first item is a set of fine natural pearls necklace and earrings. It was returned to the Politz family. According to the declaration Mrs Politz made to the Carabinieri, the necklace and earrings were traded during the war to pay for the safe-passage out of Germany for their family.'

I hang on his every word with mounting interest, while not forgetting to finish my sandwich. It all makes sense — gold and jewels were worth more than paper money at the time. Precious metal and stones were always reliable — people knew they would never lose their value and could always be traded at a later date, when the economy improved.

'Then the second item,' Egan reads on, with his index finger, 'is a white gold and diamond necklace. It's a bit harder to understand what really happened to it, because the woman who owned it died quite a few years ago.

'Irena Harrowitz was born in Halberstadt, near Berlin. She died in Belgium, several years after the end of the war. Her daughter claims to have no idea how her mother escaped from her motherland, but… well, I think it's safe to assume it could not have been completely legal.'

Egan folds up his notes again and places them back in his pocket. I pass him back his sandwich and, with my own mouth now finally free of food, I start to tell him all about the microfilms.

He has to leave me, just before two o'clock. Finances dictate that he has to spend the whole afternoon doing his private tutoring. I enjoy the luxury of going the long way home, detouring through the park and making the most of the summer sun and the fresh air. It's delightful, after an entire morning spent hunched over old microfilms. The simple sights of children playing their games watched by chatting parents and friends sitting on benches in the park and scantily clad teenagers sunbathing really restores me, after all those hours spent pouring over grim World War Two reports.

When I get back home to the flat, my mother is still out on what she so stubbornly refuses to call her date. Feeling quiet and relaxed, I take a Coke from the fridge and retire to my room.

I kick off my grey Converse trainers and sit down at my desk.

'Nineteen forty-three, here I come.' Tucking a loose strand of brown air behind my ear, I switch on the desk lamp. Film in one hand, magnifying glass in the other, I bend forward once more to pore over one image after another in the old newspaper.

Finally, the next morning, my patience is rewarded; I stumble upon an article describing an event that happened in Magdeburg, in July nineteen forty-three. It isn't so much the text that catches my attention, but the accompanying pictures. They show a formal event, with all the guests wearing their Sunday best.

The first picture portrays a young military man, in an elegant dark uniform, with a row of medals pinned to his chest. He stands next to another, older man in a fine tailored suit. The caption reads: *Stabsgefreiter W. Strausser und K. Von Abschütz.* There seems to be quite a celebration going on in the background, with a crowd of people laughing and holding champagne glasses in their hands.

The second image has moved in to focus more on this crowd. It encompasses two men smoking cigars while engaged in an animated discussion and a group of smartly dressed young women, standing by the fireplace. The woman to the far right is the one who had caught my attention. She's tall, with light hair held up in an elegant bun. A few deliberately loose strands fall down the side of her neck, leaving the white skin of her thin collarbone exposed. A long, silky, dark dress hugs her slim figure and, just above the V-shaped cleavage, hangs the ruby heart.

6

I don't think my fingers have ever typed faster. The world could have ended around me and I wouldn't have noticed. I'm hooked on my laptop, eyes glued to the screen, fingers manically dancing on the keyboard.

Typing in *Magdeburg* and the date the picture was taken gives no answer. Typing the name of the man who held the party and the date gives no answer. Of course, why should it start to get easy now? I've never really been lucky — it would be unsettling if a streak of good fortune were to hit me, all of a sudden.

I guess we'll have to do this the long, hard way then. I revert to the microfilm, magnifying glass in one hand, keyboard below the other. I start to type out, word for word, the content of the article, then I switch to online translators and spend the better part of two hours creating an English version of the document.

It turns out, that the party was organised by one Kurt Von Abschütz, owner of the local sawmill and foundry, and according to the journalist, one of the city's richest men, at that time. It seems he was a pro-Third Reich kind of man. I suppose it all makes sense. Given his line of work, I'm sure Hitler's army was number one on his list of clients.

The journalist recounts that on July 18th, nineteen forty-three, there were about forty guests who attended the party held in honour of the German Army's recent progress. Several German soldiers were in attendance, including the man pictured, whose rank is the equivalent of a Staff Lance Corporal. At least five years of service are required to get promoted to Stabsgefreiter, but the kid in the picture barely looks older than twenty. My God, what a different world that was.

The article doesn't provide me with any names other than those two. The woman isn't mentioned within the smudgy lines, nor is the person in the foreground of her picture.

Straightening my back and rubbing my sore eyes, I let out a long frustrated sigh. How could I even think this would be simple? How could I think that it could be possible to solve a crime committed seventy years ago? *Lexa, you dolt.*

Closing the laptop — with a little more strength than I should — I stand up and go into the kitchen to find another Coke. God knows, I need the energy. Moving back to the bedroom, I mechanically let my eyes drift over the shelves on which we keep our phone, checking for the "you've got a new message" light. It's not on. Good thing, I wouldn't have listened to it anyway.

I walk back to my room and experience one of those light-bulb-blinking-above-your-head kind of moments. I rush back to my desk, sit back down, Coke immediately abandoned to one the side, and open up my laptop again. I start a search in the online Magdeburg phonebook and type in the name Von Abschütz. I'm sure the man in the picture must be long dead by now, but he could still have family in town.

I get four results, including the *Von Abschütz Metallurgie GmbH*. Huh, the family company lives on after all.

A quick parallel search shows me that Hans, Kurt's son, is now running the business — rather successfully, it would seem. His name is the third in the phonebook list and I dial it right away.

A woman answers, and I ask for Herr Von Abschütz in my warmest, kindest voice. A pause later, a man with a clear, authoritative voice greets me. I introduce myself, in German, and try my best to explain my profession to him.

He stops me after two sentences, 'Do you speak English?' he asks, and I smile in relief.

'Yes, Herr Von Abschütz. Alexandra Neve, from London. Private Investigator.' There, tons simpler, isn't it?

There's a hesitant pause on the line. 'What is this about?'

'I'm investigating a theft that occurred in Magdeburg in nineteen forty-three.'

'I wasn't even born then, how could I help? Are you sure you have the right number?' My interlocutor only has the slightest of German accents, and I understand he must be used to speaking in English.

'Your father, Kurt Von Abschütz held a party one night, in July nineteen forty-three. I have reasons to believe one of the guests was our thief. The only problem is, I don't know her name and I have no-way of finding it out.'

There's another pause and the words are clipped when Von Abschütz speaks up again. 'My father died a long time ago. I don't know how I could be of help to you.'

'Pictures were taken that night. Maybe you could have a look at them, see if you recognise anyone?' Once again, I force myself to sound as amiable as I can, hoping he will agree. 'I know this is unusual, but I don't have anyone else to turn to.'

I have to wait again for a reply. Finally, after a sharp sigh, he gives me his email address and promises to have a look at the images. He tells me, once again, that he has little hope of recognising anyone, before we exchange our goodbyes.

I go on to call the other two names listed in the phonebook. No one picks up at the first number and I get the answering machine at the second. I leave a message in German and my mobile number.

Moving back to the phonebook, I search for W. Strausser, with no luck. I do, however find one Margherita Strausser and an L. Strausser. I get an answering machine on the first number, and a young woman, who's just moved into town on the second.

Out of further ideas, I get up and drag myself over to the bed. I flop down on my back and massage my aching eyes. They feel hot and gritty from the effort of looking at those tiny microfilms. Before I have time for any more thoughts, I'm asleep.

Drifting back to consciousness a while later, with a groan and still gritty eyes, I sit up, massage my tensed neck, shuffle to the desk, and pop open the abandoned can of Coke. With the help of the online translator, I send an email to the Magdeburg newspaper agency, addressed to Jan Messer, a friend of Herr Liebrecht and the man I have to thank for providing me with the microfilms of the newspaper. I ask if by any chance he has more details of the event and the mysterious woman pictured.

I have half a mind to call Egan and let him know what I've learned, but upon seeing how late it is, decide against it. I guess I can drop by his place tomorrow and see if he's made some progress on his side of the investigation. Then, first thing on Monday morning, I'll go to a printing shop and get this microfilm scanned, so that I can transfer the images to Germany.

The next morning, I wake up with a start, to the chime of AC/DC's *Hell's Bells*. With a grunt, I scrunch my eyes closed and roll over. When Angus Young's first guitar notes reach my ears, I blink one eye open, and note by the lack of light that it isn't even six in the morning yet. Blindly reaching an arm forward, I grab my mobile phone and flip it open.

'Alexandra Neve,' I mumble into the receiver, wishing ten different kinds of hell onto whoever may be on the other end of the line.

'Ms Neve?' The feeble, almost rusty sounding voice has me opening both eyes wide.

'Mrs Hargrave?' I sit up and flick on the bedside table lamp.

'I'm sorry to bother you so early, Ms Neve. I just wanted to know if you have made any progress?' our client says. The words come out strained, as if it's painful for her to speak.

'As a matter of fact Mrs Hargrave, yes, we have got something. I found a sighting of the necklace in nineteen thirty-three. So, that will hopefully provide a clue as to what happened to it back then.'

'Do you know who had it then?' she asks me.

'Not yet, I'm sorry, but we're working on it. It's a good step forward though — it's just going to take us a bit of time to track it down.'

There's a long pause on the line, and I can hear some faint beeping sounds in the background — a familiar disjointed melody that I cannot place.

'I may not have much time left,' Mrs Hargrave finally tells me, in a still weak voice. 'My health is deteriorating quickly.'

Oh. I feel bad for her; suddenly the noise in the background makes sense to me — hospital sounds. 'I'm sorry to hear that, Mrs Hargrave. We really will work as fast as we can.'

She bids me goodbye shortly afterwards and I stand up, my stomach tied up in knots. I sigh — I hate hospitals.

I move to my desk, flick the lamp on and power up my laptop. One strong cup of coffee later, and I'm back to my research. All of my e-mails have gone unanswered and the only thing I can do right now is to enter strings of keywords into search engines, in the rather desperate hope that something relevant will turn up. 'Any time soon would be nice' I mutter, over the rim of my cup of coffee.

When the sun finally rises, I take the Northern Tube line down to Leicester Square. This early, on a Sunday morning, Shakespeare's statue stands lonely in the park and there's very little life in the square itself. With the cinemas and nightclubs now closed, I struggle to find a place to get a decent coffee.

Styrofoam cups in one hand, bag of croissants in the other, I move to the Underground again, and take the long escalator down to the Piccadilly line and ride the train to Russell Square.

The coffees are still warm when I arrive at Egan's with a long American for him and a double Macchiato for me. Between two bites of croissant, I tell him about the mysterious German woman that I still haven't managed to identify, and the various leads I'm pursuing to try to identify her.

Egan listens intently and then proceeds to recap the his own progress.

'I was on the phone with Paola yesterday evening,' he says with a minimal upward quirk of his lips. 'She's carried out a few more searches for me.'

I rack my brain, but can't place the name. 'Paola?'

'Paola Plescia, the woman from the Italian Police who's helping me?' He frowns at me. 'I told you about her on the train, didn't I?'

'Yes, you did. I didn't realise you two were on a first-name terms though.' A faint blush tints his cheeks at my words and I can't help myself, 'Should I expect a happy announcement by the end of the week?'

He all but splutters the gulp of coffee he's just downed. 'It's strictly professional,' he manages between two coughs. The red in his cheeks deepens.

'Of course it is.' I pat his hand in three times in rapid succession, my own version of a yeah-right smile. I bet it's the accent, or maybe she likes Italian operas like him. I decide to let him off the hook for now; either way: it's encouraging to see him interested in someone for once.

'So, what did Signorina Plescia have to say?' I ask.

Egan swallows a gulp of coffee down, before saying, 'There was no particular interest in the ruby necklace, other than Mrs Hargrave. She's the only one who filed a claim for it. Police officer Plescia—' he makes sure to emphasis the use of her formal title '—enquired after the other people who reclaimed heirlooms: nothing apart from the ruby heart has been stolen.'

'So this particular necklace really was the only thing our thief was after.'

'It would seem so.'

I scratch at my temple. 'And she's certain no-one asked questions about this necklace?'

'Absolutely.'

I swallow a long gulp of Macchiato. This can only mean one thing. 'Whoever hired the thief found out the necklace was here via the British press.'

'I came to the same conclusion.' Egan nods. 'The person we're looking for is in the UK.'

I hum in agreement. 'Have the Italians made any progress in understanding how those valuables entered their country in the first place?'

'The house that collapsed was abandoned. It had been so for many years already. It looks like the previous owner — someone named Marco Triba — mysteriously disappeared in the late nineties.

The house had been paid for in full so no one seized it. And because no one actually reported him missing, there was no investigation.

'Ms Plescia did, however, find some old criminal records for his name. He was involved with the local mafia. She told me that there is a small lake, near Modena. And that back in those days, more than one Mafioso was thrown in, complete with concrete shoes.'

I snort. 'Lovely.'

'Due to what they found in his house, they're investigating, but it's unlikely they'll find him. The Italian Police would welcome any additional information, and we have been respectfully asked to keep them informed of any relevant discovery we may make.'

'Naturally.'

I let out a puff of air. Damn, this whole case is getting more and more complex every day. A theft during the holocaust, a mysterious treasure found in the rubble of an Italian house and now Mafiosi throwing people into countryside lakes… 'What the hell have we got ourselves into this time?'

Egan's face lights up in a rare boyish smile. 'Exciting, isn't it?'

7

Well, "exciting" isn't exactly the word I'd use, but I do have to admit that this case is much more interesting than all the recent ones we've had. It's a pleasant change from lost dogs and suspicious spouses... and no one has tried to kill us yet.

'I also spoke with Stenson yesterday afternoon,' Egan says.

'You did?' I bluster, rather dumbly and it's my turn to blush slightly as I'm reminded of our friend within the Metropolitan Police's ranks.

Matthew Stenson is a Detective Sergeant at New Scotland Yard. We met some six months ago, when he interrogated me right after my best friend Irina's death. Finding out what happened to her had been, for Egan and me, our very first case. Stenson was of great help then; things could have gone horribly wrong in so many ways without him. And I don't mean the kind of wrong where you risk breaking a nail, but the kind where you could end up six feet under.

Another point worth mentioning about Stenson is that he likes me — he really likes me. And...if the truth be told, I kind of like him too. Not that I would ever admit that to anyone, least of all Egan, who entertains this crazy, ludicrous theory that there is *something* going on between the DS and me.

'I did,' Egan says. 'Matthew told me that Art Theft's not his division, but he pointed me towards someone who could help.' He

sends a crooked smile my way. 'Matthew says "Hello" by the way —
asked me to tell you that he hopes you're doing well.'

I can feel the red in my cheeks deepen. 'Uh, huh. Thanks,' I
mutter.

'Maybe you could give him a call,' he continues. 'Go for a coffee
or a meal.'

My eyebrows rise up as I goggle at Egan. The hell? I look him up
and down with surprise.

He's seated at one end of the kitchen table, shoulders relaxed
under the dark-brown turtleneck pullover that he's wearing today,
and he's still nuzzling his empty cup of coffee in one hand. His face
shows a relaxed expression and a faint smile, his gaze is absently
directed somewhere to my right. For one moment, I wonder if I
haven't dreamt the last part of our conversation.

'Did you just offer me dating advice?' I ask, bewildered. 'Who
are you and what have you done with my former history professor?'

His smile grows, but he remains silent.

I'm just about to tell him that I don't need his matchmaker
services when his phone rings. Saved by the bell, it would seem.

He stands up and moves to the low wall that separates his
kitchen from the living room. When he's at home, he always keeps
his mobile phone there. As soon as he comes in, he drops it there, in
the third purple bowl that decorates the top of the white wall.

I drop both empty coffee containers in the bin and wipe the
kitchen table; I'm just rinsing the washcloth when Egan comes back
to me.

'That was Stenson's contact in the Art Theft division. She's agreed to meet me—' he pauses '—Are you cleaning, Lexa?'

I turn my head to look at him over my shoulder and find that he's frowning at me. I turn off the water. 'Relax, I've only wiped over the table, not mopped your floorboards.'

I know he's a grown man, completely independent, and that he was living on his own just fine before we met, but I can't help but want to help him every opportunity I have.

He's still frowning when he moves back to the low wall to grab his wallet and glasses from purple bowls one and two.

'Well,' he says, putting his glasses on, 'are you coming along, or what?'

I place the cloth back on its hook and follow him outside.

'Who are we meeting with?' I ask, once we're in the street.

'DS Lingby, she works for the Arts and Antiques unit. She told me she has a meeting this morning, in the Strand, but she can meet with us at eleven, in a bar just around the corner.'

We take the Tube to Charing Cross and my phone chirps with a missed call the minute we come out. I have to wait until we're fully outside and Egan and I are standing in a quiet corner before peering at the screen. The call was from an unknown number with the +49 prefix. Germany. I dial back.

A young woman's voice greets me. 'Magdeburg Zeitung, Angela Hoss. Guten Morgen.'

'Guten Morgen, Alexandra Neve, aus London,' I say.

'Oh, good morning,' she says with a German accent. 'You

emailed us about a picture from our newspaper?'

Thank my lucky stars that the Magdeburg Zeitung has someone who speaks English. I quickly re-explain to the woman who I am and what I'm looking for. It's a good thing that I do, because my email was, according to her, somehow "puzzling." Egan sniggers by my side, when he overhears and I gently elbow him in the ribs.

Angela isn't really sure how to help us, because I'm the one with the microfilms. I describe as best as I can the mysterious woman: light hair, Angelina Jolie's eyes and nose, Anna Paquin's mouth with a front teeth gap and Reese Witherspoon's chin. Angela writes it all down, chuckles at some of my description and promises to try to ask around. From the sound of her voice, I estimate her to be younger than me, something between eighteen and twenty probably. The excitement in her tone tells me that this opportunity to play detective is appealing to her.

'Vielen Dank, Angela,' I say. 'Call me anytime, if you find something.'

I hang up and turn back to face Egan. He's still standing next to me, but his head isn't turned in my direction anymore. What faces me is his right ear.

'Overheard everything, haven't you?' I ask.

There's a soft smile on his lips, when he finally turns his head back to face me. 'I caught most of it.'

I snort: Ashford Egan, the epitome of modesty. If we were comic-book characters, his alias could be "The Fox", for he has the hearing of one.

The Fox: A history professor, once bitten by a radioactive fox, he now possesses super-human hearing. He roams the streets at night and brings criminals to justice, with the help of Super-Sidekick, portrait-sketcher extraordinaire whose pencils are sharp enough to kill.

I chuckle at how lame that pitch sounds, even in my own head.

'Something funny?' Egan draws me back to reality.

I drop the phone into my pocket and grab his forearm. 'Just imagining you in a cape and tights, my friend.' I start walking and he follows, with a dubious look.

The bar we're looking for is just a little ahead and we sit on the terrace a few minutes later. It's a lovely day and the August sun bathes the whole place in a warm glow. I'm only wearing light cargo pants and a slim-fit shirt, yet I feel warm and over-dressed. Even Egan has rolled up the sleeves of his pullover, exposing his pale, freckled forearms to the rays of sun.

A young man takes our drinks order and comes back a few minutes later with a large Coke and a lemonade, little ice cubes dancing at the top of both glasses.

I take a long sip. 'You know, you could try wearing some lighter shirts, and maybe one of those summer scarves,' I tell Egan.

When out in public, my friend only ever wears turtleneck pullovers and he's got a truly amazing collection of them. Thinner ones in cotton for warmer days, thicker ones in wool for winter; each sort in at least a dozen different colours.

Like everyone else, I had thought this to be just a personal fetish of his — another one of his eccentricities. But it isn't. I eventually discovered that he wears high collar pullovers to hide the long scar he has on the side of his neck. He's never told me how he got it and I've never asked.

'It's alright,' he says, taking a sip of his drink. 'I'm used to it, by now.'

I quirk an eyebrow up and mentally add "by now" to the list of information I've managed to glean on the mysterious life of the enigmatic Ashford Egan. *What?* I may have enough restrain to keep from rudely asking him point blank what happened but that doesn't mean I'm not curious about it.

'Well, if you ever change your mind… I'll be happy to assist. And because I'm such a good friend, I'll even go shopping with you, make sure that everything you buy matches your skin and hair colour, and, of course, follows the current fashion trends.'

He offers me a grimace of a smile in answer, before taking a sip of his lemonade.

'So, DS Lingby?' I ask, after a moment of silence.

'Yes, Matthew gave me her phone number. She's part of the unit in charge of Art Theft.'

'I wouldn't have put a necklace under the "art" category.'

'Maybe the historical value of the piece or—' the loud distressed scream of a nearby child interrupts Egan. I turn back in my chair to look for the source of the high-pitched wail. My gaze settles on a little kid — maybe five or six years old — with golden blond hair. He's looking up and waving a hand above his head. There's a bright red balloon — already some ten feet above him, and continuing to rise — its string trailing tantalisingly in the wind.

'Some kid let go of his helium balloon,' I explain to Egan, turning back to face him.

'Oh, that happened to me once too,' he says, with a lopsided smile.

When I try to picture him as a child, my mind goes blank.

I notice, behind his shoulder, a tall brunette in heels. She's sporting a dark blue pencil skirt and a white blouse and she's coming towards the bar. She looks over the people on the terrace, obviously searching for someone. When I see the way the thirty-something woman holds herself, with the silent assurance of someone who knows how to handle herself in just about any imaginable situation, I realise she's probably here for us. I quickly glance at my watch, 11:05.

'DS Lingby?' I ask, loud enough to be heard over the distance.

Brown spikes flutter in the wind, as the woman's head sharply turns in our direction. Her eyes narrow on me and she gives me a curt nod, pixie cut bobbing, before coming to our table.

'Martha Lingby,' she says.

'Alexandra Neve,' I extend a hand. 'And—'

'Ashford Egan,' she says, before I have the time to speak my friend's name. 'Yes, I've heard about you guys. The PIs who helped dismantle that human trafficking and weapon smuggling ring, earlier this year. You're a bit of a legend.'

'Really?' Egan raises a curious eyebrow.

'Well, Langford has quite a reputation, and it's not often than someone gets one over on him. Such news travels fast throughout the services.' She offers me a large smile, as she sits down.

DI Langford is Matthew Stenson's perpetually ill-tempered superior and he hates the sight of me. Well, guess what? It goes both ways!

DI Langford and I get along like cat and dog. So if I'm your regular kitty — rub it in the right way and it purrs — Langford is the short-tempered, barks at you for no reason kind of mutt; the kind with really bad breath and bared teeth always at the ready and aimed at your shins.

'So, Matthew's told me you're interested in the Hargrave necklace?' Lingby asks, growing serious again.

'Mrs Hargrave hired us to find the necklace,' Egan says.

'We were wondering if you could give us a run-down of your progress so far.' I add.

'It's one of my cases, but I've got nothing for you, I'm afraid. It was the work of a pro, and there was no evidence left behind. Quick and clean.'

'A pro working a contract?' Egan asks.

'Yes. There are two types of thieves, you see. Those who steal valuables of their choosing and then try to find buyers for their loot and those who are chosen by a buyer to steal a specific piece. Your guy's in the second category, that's for sure. And—' she frowns a little, her brown eyebrows knitting closer '—they're the hardest to catch.'

'Because they don't use receivers to get rid of their goods?' I say.

She nods at my words. 'And it's often one-time jobs. The thief and the contractor meet one last time to exchange the item for the money and then they go their separate ways forever. And if the thief is expert enough to leave nothing behind, it's damn near impossible for us to find a lead.

'Sometimes the method used allows us to pin the crime on a certain thief amongst the lot, but that doesn't get us any closer to identifying him or her.'

'Do you have any suspects in the Hargrave case?' I demand. 'Anyone with motives, or that you found suspicious?'

'Nothing of the sort. I looked into the son, and a few other acquaintances of Mrs Hargrave but found no one with the means or the motive to steal this necklace. Sure it's worth money, but hiring a professional would have made a big dent in any profit made from reselling the jewel.'

'So you've given up,' Egan says. I frown at him — not so much at his words, but rather at the tone he used. It wasn't a question. He stated a fact.

DS Lingby narrows her brown eyes and looks coldly at him. 'You have to understand, Mr Egan, that unlike you, I don't have just the one case to investigate. There's a pile, fifteen inches high, on my desk and only so many hours in a week. It's sad, but I have to prioritise.'

I understand what she means and nod understandingly. 'You'd rather focus on cases with higher chances of success.'

She frowns and the glare she levels me with turns even colder. 'It isn't by choice. We simply don't have the staff for extensive research into every single case and over-time is frowned upon. Besides, I'm not the one giving the orders. When the boss tells me to drop a case, I drop it.' She heaves out a deep breath, seeming to realise that frustration has seeped into her voice. When she speaks again, it's with collected professionalism. 'I'm sorry, but unless something relevant magically turns up, I'm afraid that this is yet one more item that will never be recovered.'

She reaches into one of her pockets for a small business card, before turning to face me completely. 'Trust me, I don't like to leave a job unfinished any more than you do, but I've reached the limits of my capabilities. I was thorough in my investigation, but nothing relevant turned up. I've added the necklace to the LSAD — the London Stolen Art Database — and that's all I can do. Items disappear everyday in London; I have to move on to other cases.'

She leaves her card on the table and stands up. 'I came here, because Matty's a good friend and he asked me to.' She pauses and looks down at the card. 'Call me if you find something tangible. I will look into any real lead you may find — it's the best I can do. I will email you a copy of what I legally can, but it won't be much.'

She leaves with pursed lips.

Egan and I finish our drinks in silence, and I pocket the business card before we leave.

'Back to square one,' my partner says, as we walk back to the Underground station.

'Yes.'

He blows out a long breath through his nose. 'I was sort of

hoping that she could at least point us in the right direction.'

'Yeah.'

Out of the corner of my eye, I see him tilt his head to the side. 'Something on your mind?'

'Hmm?' I feel him slow down, and I do the same.

'Monosyllabic answers aren't really your style.'

'I was just thinking about what DS Lingby said, that's all.' I'm not particularly happy with how this meeting went. I had hoped for more, and this leaves me feeling frustrated. Actually, this whole case is getting more and more frustrating by the minute.

'Do I detect a touch of jealousy to your words?' Egan questions, his tone slightly smug.

I stop dead in my tracks and turn to face him. 'What the hell are you on about?'

He arches an elegant eyebrow at my abrupt halt. If he thinks the gesture means he's right, he couldn't be more wrong. What reason could I possibly have to be jealous right now?

'"Good friend" could mean any number of things,' he drawls.

Yes, and the fact that she called him *Matty* is absolutely meaningless. 'Evidently,' I say, and anyway, I don't give a damn about it.

'Some friends are better than others — it's true. It's only normal to try to quantify the notion. Bad friends, average friends, good friends: it's just semantics.'

I roll my eyes at him, move back to my spot by his side and we start walking again. 'Whatever,' I half-say half-sigh, hoping the tone will convey all of my exasperation at his choice of topic.

'I'm sure you're a "good friend" to him too,' he continues and I look intently at the ground to avoid having to look at the condescending smile that I'm certain is plastered on his face. Damn, this partner of mine can be so annoying at times.

'Good can be a synonym for reliable or helpful. And—'

'Ash,' I interrupt him, having had enough. 'Thank you for your wonderful analysis of friendship. Now if you don't want me to change my inner filing system and move your name down a notch or ten — I advise you to drop the subject.'

'Of course, Lexa.' His voice tells me that the smile is still there. *Bastard.*

I hadn't expected the Metropolitan Police to solve this case for us, but a little more than "we've got nothing for you guys, sorry" would have been appreciated. Damn budget cuts! Where is this country going if the police can't even investigate cases anymore?

Sometime after lunch Egan and I part ways again, and I take the Tube back northwards. I spend the afternoon fruitlessly burning my eyes over the microfilms.

Angela Hoss calls me again in the evening and I pick up with a twinge of excitement.

'I have something for you,' the young woman says after greeting me. 'I think I found the woman you're searching for.'

'Really?' That would effectively turn a frustrating day into something much better.

'Do you have the microfilms?' she asks.

'Yes.'

'Go to Sunday 29th, August forty-three,' she instructs.

'Okay, hold on a minute.' I place the phone on the side of the table and grab the magnifying glass instead. I glimpse at the microfilm, every ten newspaper pages or so, and finally end up on the economic page of the twenty-ninth.

I press the call button again to activate the speakerphone. 'Got it, what am I looking for?'

She gives me a hesitant hum, 'Front page, I suppose.'

I move backwards on the microfilm and find a large black-and-white photograph of a burnt car and the words "Tödlicher Unfall" written in block letters on top of the front page.

There are two smaller pictures in the right column. The first is of a male in his mid-thirties, with short-cropped dark hair — the second is of a familiar young woman, with wavy long light hair.

'Tödlicher Unfall?' I ask, fearing I won't like the answer.

Angela's voice loses some of its cheerfulness, as she translates, 'Fatal accident.'

8

The words hit me like a sledgehammer. *Porca vacca!* Our mysterious woman — and our only lead — has been dead for sixty-nine years. Talk about a dead end.

'Danke, Angela,' I mutter eventually when I realise I've kept the young woman on the other end of the line waiting for far too long.

'Sorry I couldn't have better news,' she says. She honestly sounds sorry, though it isn't her fault.

I ask her for one more favour, 'Can you recap the article for me?'

'I don't have it here, because you have the microfilms, but I spoke with my grand-dad and he remembers the story — he worked for the police.'

'Really?'

'Runs in the family.' She laughs. 'My dad's in the police too… I almost joined myself.'

Well, that gives me a better idea why Angela is so keen on temping as a private investigator.

'It was my grand-dad's first case. He was fresh out of the police school, that's why he remembers it so well — first week on the job, actually. I have lunch with him every weekday and I mentioned our conversation.

'When I described the woman you were looking for, it reminded him of the female victim of that accident. It was my grand-dad's biggest case ever, the rest of his career it was rather quiet — sure it was war-time, but, you know, it's the countryside. Anyway, the accident and the party, it all happened roughly at the same time, so I thought maybe your mysterious woman and that victim were the same person.'

'Your instincts were right.'

She laughs heartily. 'Maybe I should consider a change of career — I could become a private detective too?'

I chuckle. 'It's not as fun as it sounds. Pay is dreadful and the hours are long.'

'Yeah, I thought so. Anyway, from what my granddad could find in the few papers he kept at home, Anna Levantiner — that's the woman's name — died in a car accident, along with her husband. She was twenty-five at the time. Her husband, Claus, thirty-seven years old, was Chief Engineer for Von Abschütz.'

Ah-ah, well, this explains her presence at the Von Abschütz party, a few months before, but that doesn't get me any closer to finding out how she acquired the necklace.

'Do you have more info on the accident?' I ask. The picture in the article only shows the mangled and burnt metallic carcass of a car, resting on its passenger side next to a large tree.

'Happened in the night, on some mountain road in the Harz forest, grand-dad said. The car went off the road at some point and tumbled down a cliff. It caught fire and both passengers died.'

'Any idea what they were doing there?'

'No. Granddad said they could never figure it out. They wondered if they were sightseeing or something.'

'I don't suppose your grand-father speaks English?' I ask, with no real hope of a positive answer.

'No, sorry. If you have specific questions, I can try to ask him for you.'

I think about it for a second. 'Not really, but I'll call you back if I do find I need something. I'd like to speak to my client, see if there's any connection between her family and the Levantiners. Thank you so much for all your help, Angela.'

'My pleasure, Alexandra. It was fun.'

We exchange goodbyes and I hang up. I take a deep breath, massage my tensed neck, grab a marker and write the name of Anna Levantiner on my white board. I add the symbol of a cross next to it and the date of her death.

'What was I thinking?' I grumble out loud. Was I really naïve enough to think that it would be that easy? That I would somehow identify this mysterious woman, and her identity would unlock the whole mystery. 'Stupid, Lexa,' I mutter to the board.

It's never easy; I should know by now — any real PI would know that. Hell, an experienced PI would probably never have even dreamt of being able to finish this case within a fortnight. I glance at the date on the calendar — and a true PI would never have agreed to work for such a low fee.

With a frustrated sigh, I get up and move to the kitchen to find a Coke.

'You shouldn't drink caffeine this late in the evening,' my mother says, as I pass by her, on my way back to my room.

'Not going to sleep anytime soon,' I mumble to her, retreating.

She turns to look at me. 'Lexa, dear. This really is no life for you.'

A frown is the only answer I have the energy to conjure up.

'You go to bed at odd hours — you eat at even odder hours. Then there's this trudging all around London that you do.' Now it's her turn to frown at me. Although she's a good head shorter than me, her looks have a threatening quality that only mothers can conjure up.

'And don't think, daughter of mine,' she goes on, 'that I don't know which shady neighbourhoods this job of yours takes you to.'

'What are you on about, Mum?' I raise surprised, innocent eyebrows. She can't know this accurately what we do. How could she know?

'I'm not stupid, Alexandra Neve,' she scolds. 'I see it when you come back with scrapes and torn up clothes. That doesn't happen when you take a walk in Regent's Park.'

I can't help but let a wry smile slip onto my I'm-innocent-don't-know-what-you're-taking-about face, for what she's referring to actually *did* happen in Regent's Park. Whoever said that recovering lost dogs is a straightforward job, was lying. Or maybe that person just hadn't met Mr Buggles, five-stones of Rottweiler with a peculiar fondness for the ducks in Regent's Park's pond.

'You're making up a story where there isn't one, Mum,' I tell her, in a placating voice.

'All I'm saying is that this job is too dangerous. It isn't for you, Lexa.' She sighs, and her eyes moist over. 'You worked so hard to get to university — you could have finished it, passed your exams. Then you could have done anything you wanted. Become a teacher or got a good job in some big company —'

'— And bring home pots of gold, buy a lovely house with a garden out the back, then get married and have one point five children,' I finish for her.

'Don't be like that, Lexa.' Her brown eyes blink furiously, and I understand that tears aren't far from falling.

I tone down the sarcasm. 'That perfect life isn't for me, Mum. It's your dream-life, not mine.

'I know the PI Agency thing isn't doing very well for the moment, but we've just started in the business and we're still learning the ropes. Okay?'

For an answer, she gives me a long, defeated exhale.

'I'm a big girl, Mum. You have to let me make my own choices, even if they don't seem to be the best ones.'

'Fine. But maybe you could consider taking a part-time job, like Ashford? That would be more sensible.'

My jaw tightens at the mention of Egan's work at UCL. My mother has unknowingly hit a sore spot and I try my best not to cringe at her words. 'I'll think about it. Night Mum,' I say before moving past her and shutting myself into my room.

"A part-time job, like Ash" — yeah right! Brilliant idea Mum, I think bitterly, because that's working so well for him.

I've been so focused on our case, lately, I haven't thought about Egan's current problem with the university's hierarchy. The two of us haven't talked about it since he brought it up and told me that he's might be going to quit our agency. I haven't even taken the time to think about this. But I really ought to know better than to play ostrich and hide my head in the sand. It's a huge decision, both for Egan and for me. The *Neve & Egan Agency* wouldn't amount to much without him. I would become the *Neve & No-one Agency* and that doesn't quite have the same ring to it.

I flop down at the foot of my bed and feel my eyes water. There wouldn't be much point in continuing without Egan. Sure, I guess the job would just about be feasible on my own, but I'm not sure I want to consider it. Together, we are a much stronger investigative team than either of us could ever hope to be alone.

Although Egan and I haven't talked about his decision, I very much doubt he will choose to quit UCL. Why would he turn his back on a comfortable life, with a secure monthly salary and no worries? Why would he choose to take on an uncertain and sometimes dangerous life?

Looking at the mess of papers and microfilm on my desk, I sigh. My mother may see her wish come true sooner than she thought. If Egan decides to leave, I fear this will be our last case.

'Well,' I stand up, blink back the tears, 'if this has to be our last case, I want it to be one we solve.' I move to the desk, seize my mobile phone and call Mrs Hargrave's hospital room.

It rings several times, before our client manages to pick up. She enunciates her name feebly, then coughs several times.

'Good evening, Mrs Hargrave, this is Alexandra Neve,' I tell her. 'Sorry to bother you so late, but we've found something.'

'It's alright,' she takes in a breath, 'I wasn't sleeping.'

I can tell from the sounds in the background that she hasn't left the hospital. 'I found the name of the woman who had the necklace in forty-three, Anna Levantiner, is this name familiar to you?'

I hear a few loud, deep breaths, then, 'No. I've never heard of her.'

'She lived in Magdeburg. Her husband Claus worked for the Von Abschütz Company. Do you have any idea how she could have come to be in possession of the necklace?'

'No, I'm sorry. Von Abschütz was some big company on the other side of town, but—' she halts to take in a breath '—the names are not familiar to me. What—' a severe bout of coughing interrupts her.

'I can call back later,' I offer, once she stops coughing.

'No… it's fine. Water in my lungs,' the old woman says, before taking a few breaths. 'I'm afraid it won't be any better later on.'

I don't know what to say to that, and remain silent.

'What happened to that woman?' Mrs Hargrave asks.

'She died in August nineteen forty-three. Car accident. I don't know yet what happened to the necklace after that.'

She hums. 'Thank you, Ms Neve—' she takes a few breaths '—for looking. I appreciate your hard work.'

'We're working as fast as we can,' I assure her.

'I know. I… I just want to hold it one last time.' She pauses. 'It's all I have left. It has to stay in the family.'

'I understand that.' I can't describe what I feel when I look at one of my father's paintings, but I wouldn't give that up for the world. It's a connection — intangible, but powerful — as if a part of him is still here with me. 'We are doing everything we can, Mrs Hargrave. I promise you.'

We exchange our goodbyes and I hang up, open the Coke and swallow a few gulps. I return to my microfilm and the article on the death of Mr and Mrs Levantiner, which I set myself to translate, in the hope it possesses some useful information: it doesn't.

When I really can't keep my eyes open anymore, I change to a loose T-Shirt and cotton shorts and go to bed. Settling down on the comfortable mattress and curling up under the duvet does wonders for my tense muscles. I sigh in relief. I close my eyes, wanting to drift quickly off to sleep, but various disturbing thoughts soon come to the forefront of my mind.

An impossible case, a deadline looming and a partner who's probably on the point of leaving our joint business… how is any sane person ever supposed to get to sleep with thoughts like that?

9

One headache and a few hospital-themed nightmares later, I wake up to a fully lit bedroom. Groaning against the bright light, I roll over onto my side and bury my head under the pillow. 'More,' I grumble, 'I need more sleep.

I have almost fallen asleep again, when a thought strikes me. *Light — what light?*

My bedroom window is facing south-west and rays of sun don't filter in until late in the morning. I sit up straight, in one quick movement, and snatch my wristwatch from the nightstand. Twenty past eleven, *porca vacca!* No wonder the room is as bright as Trafalgar Square on New Year's Eve.

I dash out of the room, cursing loudly, and shower in record time. I'm supposed to be meeting Egan for lunch, and I'm already way beyond late. *Porca vacca*, twice.

I leave the flat some twenty minutes later wearing yesterday's trousers and an old AC/DC T-shirt, chosen for the sole reason that it was on top of the pile. With my hair in untied strands and still dripping wetly, I run for the Underground entrance.

I find a seat on the train, sandwiched between some tourists who, to judge by their over-abundance of shopping bags, have evidently just visited Camden Town, We ride the Northern line southwards together as one compact mass of sweating human flesh.

On second thoughts, I wonder if it really was useful to shower *before* taking the Tube. My hair has dried, by the time we reach Leicester Square some twenty minutes later, but my skin is coated in a film of sweat.

I take the stairs upwards, two at a time, and make it to the park in record time. Amongst the crowd — a mix of Londoners enjoying lunch outside and tourists taking pictures of Shakespeare's statue — I find Egan sitting on a bench facing old William's fountain and sculpture.

My friend has once again rolled up the sleeves of his turtleneck pullover. His white cane is nowhere to be seen and, under this bright sun, his dark sunglasses don't look out of place. There's something about the image in front of me that I really like and I commit it to memory, to sketch down at a later date.

Egan's posture is relaxed and his head faces the fountain. If you didn't know him, you wouldn't know he's blind. I stop, a few feet away from the bench to look at him. His blindness is easy to forget, but that doesn't make it any less real and potentially dangerous for him. I've always refused to consider his condition as a disability, but — with my mother's words still fresh in my ears — I force myself to acknowledge the fact that this job is indeed dangerous. It's dangerous for me, and even more so for my friend. It's one thing for me to risk my life, but forcing him to do the same isn't fair. As much as I don't want him to quit, it would be the safer option.

Sitting down next to him, I realise the decision is his. Therefore, if he wants to go, I won't try to hold him back.

'Morning sir,' I say, to let him know it's me. 'Is this place free by any chance?'

'I'm afraid not, Miss.' He turns his head towards me, lips stretching into a condescending smile. 'I'm waiting for a friend, you see, but she's running late.'

'Sorry about that. I just woke up.'

A curious eyebrow rises above the dark shades.

'I didn't sleep very well and I didn't hear the alarm. Sorry to have kept you waiting, I know you don't have much time.'

Egan has some university staff meeting to attend this afternoon and it looks like our lunch break will have to be cut short if he wants to make it in time. Besides, we still have to find a place to eat, which — I look around at the bars and restaurant, all as packed as the Tube I've just left — is not going to be easy.

'I wouldn't say that.' He smiles bitterly. 'If I leave this very instant, I think I have just enough time to make it back to UCL for my meeting. A straight journey, of course, with no stops on the way.'

'Sorr—,' I start.

He cuts me off. 'Food is overrated. Who needs to eat, anyway, right?'

'I said, I'm sorry.' I try again, louder.

He turns his head away from me and I hear him exhale exasperatedly.

He told me, twice I think, to be on time. I have no excuse, I know, but I get so absorbed by what I'm working on sometimes. I know I need to learn how to be more responsible. It's what grown ups do, isn't it?

'Did something happen?' Egan asks eventually.

His voice brings me back to reality. 'Hmm?'

'Last night, I mean. You said you didn't sleep well.'

'Yeah, found something.' He turns back to face me, his interest for the case winning over his resentment. 'The girl from the German newspaper called me back. She discovered the identity of the mysterious woman — the one in the picture with the necklace.'

'Really?'

'Anna Levantiner, wife to some top engineer over at Von Abschütz.'

Egan expression turns hopeful. 'Is she still alive?'

'No, she died in a car crash, in nineteen forty-three.' My friend's hopeful face visibly sags. 'Her husband died too. It's another dead end. '

'I was up late last night, looking into this, but I have no idea who had the necklace after her, or how she even got it in the first place. I called Mrs Hargrave, but she sees no connection between her parents and the Levantiners.'

'She isn't doing any better, is she?' Egan asks, his voice full of concern.

'No.'

'This worries you, doesn't it? I have the impression it's more than just concern for our client. You—' he hesitates an instant over the word to use '—*relate* to her, somehow.'

Spot on! I'm surprised Egan caught this much — other people's emotions aren't really his forte. 'How?'

'It was in your voice when you mentioned her.' His lips turn into a sad smile. 'She really isn't doing well, is she?'

'No, she could barely speak. We didn't talk for long, but she let it slip that her condition is unlikely to improve.'

'Sorry to hear that.'

My stomach churns for a reason other than hunger. 'Yeah, me too.'

'All this, it makes you think of your father, doesn't it?' my partner asks, hesitantly.

'Can't help it—' I take in a deep breath and exhale through my nose '—I know what that feels like, losing a parent too early and only having objects to remember them by.'

'I'm sorry.' Egan says. 'I wish I knew what to say…' He sighs, looks remorseful. 'I'm not very good friend material.'

'You're just perfect, Ash. I assure you.' I smile at him and hope he can hear it in my words when I add, 'and I'm glad we're friends.'

I reach for his hand and curl my fingers around it for an instant. I'm tempted to ask him to stay, to go to his meeting at UCL and announce to the staff that he's quitting. My heart wants to beg him not to leave me, but my brain makes a smart decision, for once, and keeps my mouth shut.

'Have you—' I stop, when I realise how pained my voice sounds. I swallow, try to get a grip on my emotions and try again '— have you made any progress at your end?'

He shakes his head slowly. 'I read through the documents that

DS Lingby sent us, but there's nothing useful. She's done her job correctly: interviewed the people I would have thought to interview; got in touch with some well-known jewellery receivers. Nothing came up.'

'Nothing new on our mysterious insurance guy?' I ask.

'I called Mrs Hargrave's insurance company and they confirmed that they'd never sent anyone. This either was our thief or an accomplice.'

'So we have no ID and only a vague description.'

With deft fingers, Egan pushes open the protective glass of his wristwatch and presses his index finger over the dial. He frowns.

'Time for you to go?' I suggest.

He nods and stands up.

I follow suit, 'Ash, I'm really sorry for being late. I'll make it up to you, okay?'

'Just find me one of those vending machine on the way.'

I hum positively, offer him my arm and direct us towards the Underground entrance. 'Dinner tonight?' I ask. 'My treat?'

'Dare I enquire as to what you have in mind?' he asks, with forced mock-up cheer. 'A date at the Venetian? Should I dress up, dear?'

I chuckle. 'With my budget, it will be take away at your kitchen table, *darling.*'

'Oh, Lexa. You're such a romantic. No wonder Sergeant Stenson is so interested.'

I don't bother replying, and punch him lightly in the arm.

He tuts at the gesture. 'After dinner, we could go over Lingby's report again. You may see something I missed.'

I sincerely doubt it, but it's worth a try. 'Sure. In the meantime, I'll take the microfilm to a printing company to get a digitalised version.' I'd already found one offering this service in Ealing. As I process the thought, something clicks into place in my head. 'Oh *porca vacca!* In my haste to get here on time, I completely forgot to take the microfilms with me.

'What was that?' Egan asks, with raised eyebrows.

It takes me a second or two to get the true meaning of his question. 'Oh that… Italian. It's the equivalent of "damn it".'

'Oh,' he says, with a smile. 'And may I enquire as to what has you so upset that you feel the need to swear in a foreign language?'

'I left the microfilm at home.' Damn it, damn it, damn it.

'Can't you go get it?' he asks, with a puzzled expression.

'And waste another twenty minutes in a packed Tube just to go home. Get the microfilm and then spend another twenty minutes sweating to get back to the starting point, then take the Central line for another forty-five minutes.' I sigh. 'I'd rather die!'

Egan chuckles.

On a regular basis, I like taking the Underground. It's a fast, convenient means of transport and it beats spending hours stuck in traffic jams, true. However, I like it a lot less on stuffy warm summer afternoons, when the outside temperature reaches thirty degrees and it's even more underground. 'I'll go first thing tomorrow morning, when the supposedly fresh-air is still *fresh*.'

'Can't blame you for that.'

Maybe I can go to the library while Egan is at work. UCL's library may have some specialised books on World War Two and Eastern Germany. It won't hurt to have a look. I wonder if I can find testimonies of people who escaped Germany at that time. 'How long do you think you'll be?'

He frowns in concentration. 'We can never be sure, but I'll probably be done by four. You want to stick around?'

'Yeah, I'll hit the library.'

Egan slows down and when I turn to look at him, I can see on his face that something is bothering him. 'What is it?'

'Maybe you could go shopping. Or go watch a movie,' he offers, hesitantly. 'Do an activity that's not work-related, for a short while — take some time-off.'

Yeah, right, like I have the time to laze around! 'I can't really picture myself phoning our client to tell her we haven't made any progress because yours truly took the day off in a spa.' How can Egan even suggest something like that?

His tone is colder as he eventually says, 'Forget it. I was just trying to— Ah, forget I said anything.'

I realise my last comment was maybe a bit too cutting. I try to soften my tone as I say, 'There's no time to waste, you know it. We have to find a lead.'

The way he nods in reply is too stiff to be anything other than a controlled gesture.

I turn to face him. 'What is it? What's on your mind?'

'Forget it,' he says. 'We'd better get going.'

He takes a step forward, but I place a hand on his forearm to halt him.

Egan's lips part, as he takes in several breaths. Several seconds pass without him saying anything. 'I'm just trying to…' He falls silent again. 'I just don't want you to get hurt, is all.' He turns his head away from me, after the last word.

Oh! he's trying to look out for me, I realise. It must be a bit of an alien concept for him. Or, at the very least, something he hasn't done in a while.

I shake my head with fondness, take a step forward to be at his level and briefly squeeze his hand. 'Thanks for your concern, but I'm okay.'

He appears uncomfortable, as he nods.

We resume walking in silence.

I go through with my plan, and spend the afternoon in the university library. There were several ways to leave Nazi occupied territories, at that time. Some involved having fake passports or visas to travel to neutral countries, others required the use of a smuggler to discreetly cross the border. All of that cost money, and it wasn't uncommon for people to pay with valuables such as jewellery, silverware and other rarities.

Egan joins me once his meeting ends and we walk the short way back to his flat, stopping at a little Chinese shop for some cheap takeaway. As promised, we eat at his kitchen table, and, once we're done, I let myself slump into the comfortable confines of his leather settee.

'Thanks,' I say, as he hands me the dossier DS Lingby left us.

He stands awkwardly near his chair and I raise my gaze to look at him expectantly. It predictably has little effect on him, but I so rarely see him hesitate, that I wait a little longer before saying, 'Is something the matter?'

'UCL's History Department scheduled a meeting next week to discuss next year's program. I'd just like to write down some notes, while today's talk is still fresh in my head, to help prepare for the meeting.' He swallows nervously. 'Will you be okay on your own?'

What a dumb question is that? 'Course I will,' I smile at him. 'I promise to call you if I get so much as a paper cut.'

He shakes his head and retreats down the corridor that leads to his bedroom. I've never entered it, but I suppose he must have a desk in there with a computer, for I've never seen one in any other room.

With a sigh, I open the manila dossier and start reading the police report on the theft of the necklace. As I peruse the interview summaries, I can't get Egan's stupid question out of my head. In all the time I've known him, I've very rarely seen him hesitate. I glance around me, at his spotlessly clean flat. He's as much of a control freak with his emotions as he is with anything else: a master of self-control. The few times I have seen him doubt were when we broached some personal matter or when he was trying to be compassionate. Why in the hell was he hesitant about leaving me on my own to go and write down notes?

I flip a page, start to read the interview of the nurse who

sometimes visits the Hargrave's flat. I find nothing particularly interesting. This entire report is exactly as you would expect a police report to be: emotionless and factual. It's a huge pile of data, with nothing groundbreaking in it.

Egan's attitude still doesn't make sense when I reach the end of the last page.

I drop the dossier back on the coffee table, stand up and straighten my back. About two hours have passed, I notice. I look around the place aimlessly, until my eyes settle on the only decoration in this room. There's a framed portrait on top of the expensive radio unit that stands on a shelf against the wall to the right. The portrait is one of mine and is a sketch of us both. I hate to draw myself, but, on rare occasions, I can be persuaded to make the effort.

The drawing is of the simplest type, all lines and no shades. My strengths as a portraitist normally lie in subtle shading, but, with Egan, I've been forced to draw as a comic book artist might when creating a character. I used special paper for this sketch, a sheet much thicker than I normally prefer, and a stronger pencil. The portrait was drawn using as much strength as I could to scar the paper without actually tearing it.

I guess you could call the final result an embossed drawing or something. I smile at the name. The label isn't important — what matters is that this is a drawing my friend can actually "see". I removed the glass from the frame and it allows him to run the tip of his fingers along the lines whenever he wants to. By mapping the image this way, he manages to, somehow, *see* it in his mind.

It's a rare gift, Egan told me. He doubts this would work with someone who was born blind, but because he only lost his sight as a young teen, he still remembers shapes and forms enough to be able to conjure up a mental image close enough to reality.

With one last look at the portrait, I walk to Egan's room and find he's left the door ajar. I push it open, and rap my fingers on it, out of politeness.

As I'd guessed, there's a large desk facing one of the walls of the room, and just next to it, a large bookshelf filled to the brim with Braille books. The rest of the room is as neatly arranged as the rest of the flat, and it follows the colour theme of grey and whites, with notes of purple here and there.

'Have you found new ways to torment those poor students yet?' I ask.

Egan smiles, from behind his computer. He's typing with one hand, and reading from Braille notes resting on the desk with the other. 'Worse than that.' He offers me a fake evil grin. 'Looking into this year's exams.'

'Ouch, exams: that terrifying creature that tries to claw its talons into the flesh of terrorised students once a year.' If there's one thing I'm glad to be done with it has to be that.

'Did you find something?' my friend asks. I see him push the rest of the notes to one side, before he closes the document he was typing.

'Nope.' I sit at the foot of his bed. 'Didn't get a paper cut either.'

He spins on his chair to face me. 'It's not what I meant, you know.'

'What did you mean?' I ask, with curiosity.

'I—' he pauses, and there's that damn hesitation again.

I look at him, at his desk, and my mind finally connects the dots. He'd been trying to look out for me again. 'It was your way of saying "Sorry to leave you to go work on my other job" wasn't it?'

He swallows, Adam's apple bobbing tellingly.

'I still haven't decided,' he admits. 'I'm sorry, Lexa. I—'

'Don't,' I cut him off. 'As long as you do your bit on this case, it's fine with me. Take your time.'

'I will, of course — do my bit, I mean.'

'Then, it's—' I don't get to finish my sentence, as my phone suddenly starts to ring. I fish it out of my pocket, frown upon reading the caller ID: Matthew Stenson.

I haven't spoken to him since our last encounter, months ago. What could the DS want with me, now? I hit the answer button eagerly. 'What can I do for you, Sergeant?'

'Alexandra, I'm glad you picked up,' the young man says, in his familiar baritone. He sounds stressed, I note.

'What's going on, Matthew?'

'Something's happened to your mother.'

10

The words take the breath out of me. My voice is almost a whisper, as I ask, 'What's happened to her?'

I can feel Egan tensing on his chair.

'I'm at the hospital with her, can you come? She's okay, but she wants to see you.'

I don't hear anything beyond the word "hospital". I manage to stammer barely coherent words, 'Why? Wha—what happened? Is she alright?'

'She's going to be fine.' Stenson's voice is calm and patient, on the other end of the line. It's a professional tone, that of someone used to dealing with emotionally conflicted people. 'It's just a broken arm.'

The tone, more than the words, finally gets through to me. 'Thank God.' I let out a sigh. 'Where are you at?'

'The Royal Free Hospital, on Pond Street.'

'I'm on my way.' I stand up. 'What the hell happened?'

'Some sort of break-in at home… I don't have all the details yet.' I can hear someone calling him in the background. He mumbles an apology, before telling me on which floor to find him, and hangs up.

I pocket the phone in a daze. Someone broke into our flat… *what the hell is going on?* Something nudges at my shoulder and forces me to move forward. I'm too dumbstruck to protest. It takes a little time for my brain to understand that Egan is guiding me back to the bed and forcing me to sit down on it. I hadn't even realised that he had got up.

'Are you alright?' His voice is hesitant, as he sits down next to me.

'Yeah, think so.' I swallow hard. 'You heard?'

'Hmm, hmm.' He rubs at my arm in a soothing motion.

It's hard for me to gather my thoughts. Mum, assaulted by some criminal, in our own home… dear God. A multitude of different scenarios, all quite dreadful, flash before my eyes.

'Come on, Lexa.' Egan shakes my shoulder a little. 'We should get going.'

After what feels like the longest train ride of my life, but that is in reality only thirty minutes, we finally reach the hospital to find Stenson seated on a plastic chair in one of the waiting areas. He's wearing black trousers and a light-blue shirt so wrinkled it makes me doubt that this guy ever irons anything. Either that, or he's been working shift after shift without even breaking for a change of clothes.

He stands up when we arrive. 'Alexandra, Ashford, good to see you guys.'

Egan barely has the time to edge in a short 'Hi' before I ask, 'Where is she? Is she alright?'

'She's with the doctor.' Stenson jerks a thumb to the left to indicate a nearby door. 'They're putting her arm in a cast. It shouldn't take them much longer.'

I breathe out a world of relief.

'What happened?' I have to force myself to ask the question that's been haunting me since I hung up the phone. 'Why are you here? You don't do home break-ins… If you show up, it usually means that there's a body.'

Stenson seems surprised by my question. It's an odd reaction and I raise a hand to my mouth, as my stomach summersaults. 'Oh, my God,' I mutter through my fingers. 'Is there a body?'

'Relax, Alexandra. Nobody's dead.' He raises a soothing hand and offers me a large smile, complete with stubble-covered dimples. 'One of your neighbours called the police — when they showed up, your mother gave them my name.'

'Why would she do that?' I ask in surprise.

'I don't know.' He shrugs. 'She probably wanted to see a familiar face — you can ask her, when she comes out.'

'Why didn't she call me?' Stenson frowns and I quickly add, 'Not that I'm not happy to see you, but—' I wave an awkward hand about '—you know what I mean.'

The young man smiles at my words. 'She said she didn't have her phone with her, and, in the confusion, couldn't remember your number. I offered to call you while the doctor was seeing to her arm.'

I blow out a breath, as relief washes over me.

Stenson pushes both hands into his trouser pockets. 'So… it's been awhile,' he says, hesitantly, 'how have you been?'

I'm not sure what to say. 'Good, thanks… You?'

He smiles nervously and shrugs. 'Good.'

With all that panic finally receding, this leaves room for awkwardness and embarrassment to fill up my head. 'Hope this—' I wave a hand around, to encompass the room '—didn't interrupt you at some bad time.'

'Nah.' He shrugs again. 'My shift was nearly over anyway.'

I look back at the door he's indicated, impatience creeping in. It's crazy how hard one can wish for some doors to open, but they remain unnervingly closed.

'Good.' I mumble, for lack of anything else to say. I look up at the door again, to avoid having to look at either of the two men next to me. I'm sure Egan must be smiling at the awkwardness of the situation. Hell, if it didn't involve me, I'd find it funny too.

Out of the corner of my eye, I see Stenson run a nervous hand through his dark curls.

'So… how's business?' He asks turning to include Egan.

'Enamoured,' my partner replies, before I have the time to say something. I instantly feel my cheeks turn scarlet and I move to face the door fully on.

'We're totally enamoured with it,' Egan continues, in a tone I can only describe as syrupy.

I'd give him a dark glare if I could. As it turns out, he's lucky to be out of my reach, or he would get a good kick in the shins.

'You're still looking for that necklace?' Stenson asks. From his tone, I know that Egan's not-so subtle message has eluded him. Thank God for small mercies.

I'm saved from any more innuendos, when the door I've been

staring at finally opens. A man with salt-and-pepper hair and a white shirt comes out, and pauses next to us.

'Family of Laura Neve?' he asks.

I take a step forward. 'I'm her daughter. How is she?'

'Fine.' The doctor gives me a polite smile. 'The shock is passing and the arm is in a cast. Her ulna is broken—' he raises his forearm and taps a finger on it to indicate the location of the bone '—it's a common result of a direct blow to the outside of your arm when you have it raised in self defence.

'There was little swelling, which is always good, and it only broke in one place.'

'No need for surgery?' I ask concerned.

The doctor offers me a polite smile. 'No. The bone is not out of place, a cast will suffice. The healing of the fracture needs to be closely monitored though. Your mother will need to set up appointments for several x-rays to make sure there are no shifts in position.'

I nod, attentively committing the instruction to memory.

'If all goes well, the cast can come off in a month or so.'

I give the doctor a relieved smile and shake his hand. 'Thanks. Thank you very much.'

He returns my smile, before leaving us, and I enter the room.

I find my mother sitting on the side of a bed, with her left arm covered in pristine white plaster. I give her a quick once over, but don't find any visible wounds, aside from the obvious. She engulfs me in a one-armed hug, the second I'm close enough for it.

'Oh Lexa, it's so good to see you.'

'Are you alright, Mum?' I ask, pulling myself out of her crushing embrace.

'Yes.' She lets go of me, and gives me a smile that is on the right side of dopey. 'They gave me some good pills.'

I nod in understanding. 'They obviously did.' I reach for her handbag that sits on the nearby table and her coat, before walking back to her. Egan lingers, somewhat hesitantly, near the foot of the bed and the detective stays by the entrance door.

'Do you two have a place to stay?' Stenson asks, and I turn to look at him questioningly. 'Your flat's been burgled, forensics are still there — might be best to stay somewhere else tonight.'

I hadn't thought of that. 'Can you stay with Bob?' I ask my mother. 'Or with your friend Marie?' She blushes at the mention of Bob, but nods nonetheless.

'The forensics should be done in a matter of hours. They'll make sure to disturb the place as little as possible.' Stenson says. 'I have to ask, Mrs Neve: did you get a good look at the man who hurt you?'

She shakes her head. 'No, I was just going up the stairs to our flat when this man came down running. I was in his path. He didn't give me time to move out of the way, just knocked me off balance and I fell. I didn't even know he'd been in the our flat.'

'Did you see his face?' he asks.

'No. He had one of these sweatshirt hoodies on — I only saw that he was white, but nothing else. I'm sorry.'

'It's okay,' Stenson says.

I turn back to look at him. 'Can we drop by the flat? To pick up a few things?'

'I'll arrange that.' He takes his phone out of his jacket pocket. 'I'll call ahead and let them know we're coming.'

The detective leaves the room to make the call and I can't help but smile as I watch him leave. I'm glad my mother called him. Even though I won't admit it out loud, it's nice to see him again. Kind, amiable, reliable Detective Sergeant Stenson, with his perpetual three-day beard, and tuft of dark hair.

'Forensics,' my mother says, as if she's only caught up with the word now. 'Why would there be forensics in our flat?'

'To look for prints, Mum. To find out who did it.' I shrug. 'It's the standard procedure.'

'Oh, right,' she says, frowning. 'You would know that of course.' The dopey look is starting to fade, and her gaze takes on a harder edge. 'Has this got something to do with your job?'

What? 'No! Of course not, Mum.'

The look she gives me is proof she's not convinced.

I stand straighter, take in a deep breath. 'Home burglaries happen all the time. There's no telling if it had anything to do with my job.'

'Oh yes.' She snorts derisively. 'Just like it wasn't your job's fault our last flat exploded.'

I cringe; she's got a point — that bomb definitely *was* job-related.

My mother stands up fast. The change in demeanour is startling. Just a minute ago, she seemed doped to the eyeballs and now she's moving with the swiftness of angry flames. Adrenaline, I suppose.

She fixes me with a pointed look, holding her plastered arm protectively close, with the other hand. 'I warned you, Alexandra. I told you that you should get out of this kind of work.'

I try for a placating voice, but it's not easy to counter her heated tone. 'I'm sure this has absolutely nothing to do with it, Mum.'

She stares me down hard, with smouldering brown eyes. Then her gaze moves to the left and she points her index finger at Egan.

'What about you?' she asks. 'Can't you get her to see reason, Ashford?'

A twin set of ginger eyebrows rise up, behind the dark shades, and for a minute, my friend looks like he's just swallowed a fly.

'You're supposed to be the grown up one in this partnership.' She takes a few steps forward and jabs her index finger into his ribs. Well, if he hadn't known about the accusing finger so far, he certainly does now.

She pokes at him a few more times and my friend looks about ready to flee the hospital room at rocket speed.

I chuckle. Egan can stand his ground in front of juvenile students, deprecating colleagues and dangerous suspects, but my petite five-foot-three mother has him ready to back off into a corner. I guess that's the *Neve effect*.

'Alright, that's enough, Mum.' I say, holding out her handbag. 'None of this is Ash's fault, and you know it.'

One handedly she grabs her stuff, and with one last 'humph', leaves the room. I follow her outside, with her coat folded over one arm and Egan holding the other. Damn, she can be infuriating at times.

The car ride to our flat doesn't take long, but it's spent in a tense quietness. My mother and I sit in a muted silence on the backseat of Stenson's Volvo, while Egan rides shotgun.

As we reach our destination, the detective parks on the curb, next to an official police car.

'Stay in the car and try to relax a bit,' I tell my mother. 'I'll pack you a bag.'

She doesn't offer any answer, and fumbles with her phone. I exit and move to stand next to Egan. A young constable reaches us and politely greets the sergeant. They exchange a few words, before she allows us to enter.

As we near the building's entrance, she warns me, with a pointed look towards Egan, that the place is a mess.

I quickly find out the constable didn't exaggerate. Everything that had been on our living room table is now strewn across the floor. There's a small cabinet next to the wall, to the left of the telly; all of its drawers are pulled out, the contents tossed all over the floor.

I guide Egan over to the settee and let him stand there, with his hand on the dark leather. 'You should have stayed downstairs,' I say.

He huffs a breath. 'With your mother?'

Yeah, right. I can see why he would rather risk breaking his neck up here. 'Stay here,' I tell him, with a pat on his arm. 'The place is a mess.'

'Get your stuff,' Stenson advises. 'And try not to touch anything unnecessary.'

I nod, move forward, distractedly notice the kitchen has been spared, and enter my room. *Oh, God!* Well, if the rest of the place looks upside down, I don't know how to qualify what's in front of me. It looks like a tornado ripped between my desk and my bed.

Everything that wasn't firmly screwed to the wall has been tossed in a heap on the carpet. Our case files, personal documents, old university manuals — everything is scattered about.

I squat down and push at a few papers. I easily locate the photograph of the ruby heart; I catch sight of a few printouts I've made of nineteen forties documents. What I find — or rather, what I don't find — leaves no room for doubt.

My mother was right. This was not a random home burglary. Whoever did this knew exactly what they came for, and they left with it.

'Well,' I say, coming back to the living room with two sports bag, filled with clothes and basic toiletries. 'Just about everything's still here, as far as I could see. I don't think they took anything of value.'

Egan turns his head my way. There are two deep lines marring his forehead and I gather he caught my lie. I'm glad he decides not to challenge me on it, though.

Thankfully, Stenson doesn't seem to be quite as talented when it comes to playing lie detector — the downside of having five senses to rely on.

'I'm not surprised, I don't believe this was a random theft,' the sergeant says. 'There's one more thing you need to see.'

I stop next to Egan and am about to question Stenson, when he closes the front door. With dismay, I discover words have been spray-painted over the white pane of wood. Whoever the messenger is, he wanted to make sure we'd get the message — to be absolutely certain we wouldn't miss it, he took the precaution of writing it in thick, capital letters, with blood-red paint.

GIBST AUF ODER STIRBST

'Give up or die,' I translate, in a thick voice.

11

'So,' Stenson says in an even voice. 'What have you two got yourselves into this time?'

'Exactly what I told you over the phone.' Egan answers. 'We're looking for a stolen necklace.'

The detective narrows his eyes at me. 'Nothing more?'

'Nothing more,' I promise. 'I don't understand. We haven't got that far yet. We don't even have a lead.'

Stenson's lips press to a thin line. 'Really?'

'Nothing relevant,' Egan confirms. 'Why would someone threaten us?'

'One way or another, you must be close to finding out whoever did it.' The detective points to the door again. 'The thief wouldn't have risked getting caught otherwise.'

'Does my mother know about this?' I nod at the message, mentally crossing my fingers, in the hope of a negative answer.

'No. She hasn't been back up here yet.'

'Good. Please keep it that way. She's shaken up enough as it is; I don't want her to worry for no reason.'

Stenson nods his agreement. 'Are you sure you have absolutely no idea who's behind this? Not even a hunch?'

I shake my head. 'Not a thing.'

He thrusts his hands into his trouser pockets with a weary

expression. 'Normally this would be the time where I advise you to drop the case and stay out of this for your own safety, but—' he shrugs '—I guess that would be a complete waste of breath.'

Damn right it would. There's no way I could be coerced into giving up now, not when this case has just reached a whole new level of *personal*. I chance a look at Egan — his straight back and squared jaw tell me that he feels the same way. 'Hell will freeze over first.'

Stenson lets out a long, exasperated breath, looks at the door and then back at us, with a defeated expression. 'Can I at least advise you to be careful?'

I look him straight in the eyes.

And Stenson returns my stare with just as much determination as he says, 'Whoever is behind this knows your home address. He could come back, and leave something a bit more permanent than spray paint next time.'

He's right, I know, but I'm not ready to back down. My mind is quick to come up with an alternative. 'We'll clear the flat, for the time being, and go somewhere else until this case is over.'

Stenson blinks, averts his eyes, and I know I've just won the argument. When he looks up again, it's with a pleading look. 'You need to be cautious,' he says, as he points his index finger at me, then at Egan, 'the both of you.'

'We will be,' Egan says.

'I mean it, Ashford.' Stenson's voice takes on a harder edge, the words coming out sharp and clipped. 'I don't need to remind you what happened last time, do I? You almost died.'

I swallow hard as those not too distant memories resurface. The sergeant is right — there's no need for a reminder. I haven't forgotten my best friend lying on the cold concrete floor of a warehouse by the docks, bound and gagged, surrounded by armed Russian thugs. The moment when I was looking into the barrel of a gun had been hard, but seeing that same weapon directed towards someone I care about made my insides physically ache. I close my eyes for a second and force the memories away, knowing that, reminder or no reminder, I'll never forget that day.

When I reopen my eyes and look in Egan's direction, I see a shudder run through him. His face has turned a shade paler, and every one of his features seems to be carved out of ice. He clearly hasn't forgotten the ordeal either; I mentally curse at Stenson for bringing it up.

I take a step closer to my partner, snake my fingers around his for comfort. Egan lets out a faint, relieved breath, as he curls his fingers around mine.

'Thank you for your concern, Sergeant,' my voice takes on a harder tone — not entirely unlike my mother's, I realise — but I don't bother to soften it at all. 'Now if you don't need us for anything else, we'll see ourselves out.'

Stenson raises pacifying hands, as new emotions play on his face. 'Don't get angry, Alexandra. I just want you to promise me that you'll be careful.

'And I'll keep an eye on the investigation and let you guys know if Forensics find anything here. In the mean-time, you two must be on your guard.'

I nod in agreement, my anger receding and giving room to what feels like the start of one massive headache.

'Call me, if you need help,' Stenson adds, before stepping aside. 'Please.'

'Will do,' I say. The set of dark eyebrows above the detective's almond-shaped eyes rise up in question. 'I promise.'

We all take the steps down and find my mother waiting by the car. As I give her one of the bags, I notice she's calmed down some.

'I called Bob,' she tells me. 'I'll be staying with him for a few days.'

'A good way to test the waters,' Egan suggests, with a smile. It's too bad that he misses the dual set of disbelieving eyes that turn to him at his words.

My mother gives me Bob's address and phone number, just in case, and Stenson offers to drop her off, seeing as it's on his way. I watch the dark Volvo disappear in the dusk with a clenched heart. I hate to have to lie to my mother, I hate to have to keep her in the dark about my work and its consequences, but I know the truth would only cause her to go mad with worry.

Egan gallantly offers me his couch for the night, and it must be a testament to how my headache is progressing that I don't find anything snider to say than a polite, 'Thanks.'

Egan and I leave the Forensics and the constables fretting near the building's entrance, and make our way to the Tube station on foot.

The ride to my partner's flat is spent in a companionable silence and we reach our destination within the hour.

'Oh, dear Lord.' Egan sighs, as he sits down on his settee. 'And I thought you had problems managing your emotions — your mother's even worse than you are.'

I snort, dropping my bag under a shelf in the living room entrance. 'Had to learn from someone.' I sit next to him and slump back tiredly, my eyes closing of their own accord. 'Gosh, I thought she'd never get off my back. Thank God she's alright though.'

'Stubbornness: another inherited trait, it would seem.'

I open one eye just long enough to gently smack my partner on the side of his arm.

'"Heaven has no rage like love to hatred turned. Nor hell a fury like a *mother* scorned"' he says, his elegant baritone taking on a pompous edge.

I chuckle, fair enough. 'Tell that to her face, if you dare.'

My friend, predictably, remains silent.

I've almost fallen asleep when Egan's voice rouses me. With a serious tone, he asks, 'So, what did the thief take?'

I sit back up, reopen my eyes and answer with the same seriousness, 'What he came for: the microfilm.'

'Our only evidence.'

'And the only copy.'

Egan sighs, as his hand comes up to scratch at his chin. 'I don't see the point of it. So we found out Anna Levantiner's identity, but what does that matter. She died, a long time ago, so even if she had something to do with this — she couldn't be of help to us.'

'She has to fit into the puzzle somehow.' I massage my aching forehead. 'Matthew was right; they wouldn't have gone to the trouble of leaving us this message, if we weren't onto something.'

'Well, whatever clue was on the microfilm is now lost.'

An idea strikes me, and that too hurts. 'I'm not so sure.' I stand up, rummage through my shoulder bag until I find my sketchbook. It takes me a bit longer to find a pencil.

'Lexa?' Egan asks in a perplexed way as I turn back to him. He's leaning his head to one side with a puzzled expression.

I smile, what I'm doing should become clear to him soon enough. I sit down on the coffee table, open the sketchbook to a blank page, and start to draw. It isn't too complicated — by now I've looked at that mysterious woman often enough. I committed her visage to memory, to make sure I would recognise her, if I were to see her face again on another photograph. I start with her eyes and nose, then work on outwards.

'Can you remember her face well enough?' Egan asks, having picked up on the familiar sound of graphite scratching paper.

'It won't be as perfect as if I had the picture at hand, but it'll be close enough.'

The lines come easily and, within half an hour, I have an almost perfect portrait of our mysterious woman. She stands in her evening dress, as she did in the photograph, with the necklace elegantly hanging around her neck. I shade the background lightly, and her light hair stands out, the bun looking chic and elegant.

'There,' I say, finally satisfied with the portrait. 'I'll email it to Germany tomorrow to see if Von Abschütz's son recognises her. I could send it on to Angela too.' I drop the sketch and the pencil on the table and move to sit back on the settee — well I *slump* back on it to be more accurate — with a contented moan. Damn, that thing is comfortable.

'Thanks for letting me stay here, by the way,' I mutter, yawning. I was a little surprised when Egan offered me his settee for a few days. He was very uneasy, the first time I came to visit him in his flat. Although he has got over it now, I'm still surprised he feels comfortable enough around me to allow a longer stay.

'No problem.' He smiles, with only the barest trace of nervousness. 'Just don't move things about too much and—'

'Yeah, yeah I know.' I wave a tired hand about. 'One place for everything and everything in its place.'

'I was going to say you can have my bed, if you'd rather,' he pouts his lips, deliberately so, 'I'm not so inclined to offer it anymore.'

'S'alright,' I slur, getting comfortable. 'Don't want it. I'm fine here. But—' I poke him in the ribs '—your outdated chivalry is duly acknowledged, my dear Sir.'

He chuckles an instant, before growing serious again. 'Do you think Matthew was right?' he asks. 'Are we in danger?'

'Given our usual luck, we probably are.'

The headache is building behind my eyes. I shut them, raise a hand to massage my temples, but it does little to relieve the tension.

My aches make me think of Mrs Hargrave. She's counting on us to find the necklace, and she's fast running out of time. I want her to have it back, and to finally see her granddaughter walk down the aisle wearing it.'

'We can't give up, Ash.'

'I know. I never said we should.'

I feel Egan move next to me and I reopen an eye.

He seems uncomfortable where he sits, his back straight, his hands nervously flexing. 'I just...'

The words die on his lips. I reach for one of his hand and wrap my fingers around his. 'I know. I'm not going to let anything happen to you, I promise.'

He smiles briefly and relaxes a fraction. He doesn't let go of my hand.

'Matt's an idiot for bringing up the warehouse,' I say.

Egan lets out a nervous breath at the mention of the incident. He covers it up with a forced smile, as he says, 'That young man's just worried for you. He likes you, you know.'

'Yeah, I kind of got it the first time you said it — thank you, Captain Obvious.' I still don't know how I feel about Stenson, though. I think I like him, but it's too complicated to envision... something. There are other things to be focusing on right now.

'Enamoured', I snort. 'Did you really have to say that to his face?'

A short chuckle escapes Egan's lips, as he shakes his head with mirth. 'Alas, I'm not sure he got the message.'

Luckily for me. 'Ash, I adore you, but please stay out of my love-life, okay?'

The chuckle returns in full. 'I can't make any promises.'

'Let me rephrase that, my friend.' I let my voice drop a little and hope it will sound more serious. 'Stay out of my love-life or I will seriously start poking my nose into yours.'

The fleeting look of terror that crosses Egan's face is priceless. 'I'll try,' he mutters.

'You'd better… if you don't want to learn the true meaning of the expression *blind-date*.'

We lapse into a comfortable silence after that. Night has long since fallen and the feeble glow coming from the pendant lamp on the ceiling is the only source of light in the room. A car drives by, in the street below, and bright light momentarily filters through the windows. I watch, as shadows dance on the floorboards, before disappearing, engulfed by the darkness again.

'What now?' Egan asks, eventually.

I find sleep to be the most appealing answer to his question, 'Tonight, we rest,' but sleep won't solve this case, I know, 'and tomorrow we find everything we can on Anna Levantiner.'

Egan nods in agreement. 'I'll get in touch with DS Lingby, tell her what we've found and see if I can get her to take this investigation out of the cold cases pile.'

I let a soft 'Hmm' of approval escape my lips. The headache is waning, or maybe it's me who's falling asleep. Egan's hand is warm in mine, and a reassuring weight.

Once more, I realise I don't want him to go. He's my friend, my best friend, and I need him. I swallow hard, at this thought, because he's also the man who almost died, a few months ago, due to my reckless actions.

'Do you still have nightmares… about the warehouse?' I hate to ask this, but I need to know.

'No.' His hold on my hand tightens. 'Not unless I think about it.'

I let my thumb stroke the back of his hand, the only comfort I can give him. 'I'm so sorry, I—'

'Don't,' he cuts me off. 'You had no way of knowing what would happened, and then you found me — that means a lot to me.'

I open both eyes to look at him when he says this. There's a faraway look on his face and his gaze seems more distant than ever. I have a feeling there is more to his words than I hear, but I don't know how to ask. I'm not even sure that I have the right to ask, but I can't help it. 'Ash?'

There's no answer, but the grip on my fingers tightens.

I push the fatigue away and sit up straighter as I observe him. He's leaning against the side of the settee, and, to a casual observer he would look relaxed. I've learned how to look beyond his carefully constructed exterior and find tenseness running just below the surface, and pain. The pain is so intense and raw, I can almost physically feel it.

I understand that the surge of emotions not only has to do with the warehouse and this case — it has to do with his life. It's connected to what happened before we met, echoes of the past. I know so very little of that part of him he keeps locked out of sight, and that he so stubbornly refuses to share with me.

'What happened to you?' I ask, in a gentle voice, knowing I won't get a real answer.

He takes in a deep breath, but his voice is breathless, as he says, 'A lot.'

I wait, patiently, for him to elaborate, he doesn't.

After a long moment of silence, he gives me a humourless smile. 'I just forgot what it's like to have someone you can count on and who cares.'

The sheer honesty of his words cuts deep. I wish I had something better to offer than another, 'I'm sorry.'

'Don't be. Just promise me you'll stick around.' There is a rare open honesty to his tone.

'I will.' I lean down and kiss him delicately on the forehead, deciding for once against a hug, for fear that he will find the gesture condescending.

He offers me a sad smile and a nod. 'It's late; I should go to bed — let you get some sleep.'

I lean back against the cushions and slump comfortably. 'Yeah, you should.'

He doesn't make a move to get up, I don't move either and continue to watch the occasional play of shadows on the furniture.

Eventually, I feel Egan tilting over to one side. He lets out a contented sigh, as he falls asleep, his hand still in mine.

I'm about to succumb to sleep too, when an old Italian proverb comes to mind. *"Chi trova un amico, trova un tesoro."* I have no idea where it comes from — probably something I heard as a child and that floated around in the dark recesses of my mind until today. It translates as, "He who finds a friend, finds a treasure".

I smile, as I drift to sleep. It couldn't be more true.

·

12

I wake up to the sound of the distant clinking of china and cutlery. At least, I think it was the clinking that woke me up. Either that or whatever is poking at me, just below my ribcage.

With a groan, I twist an arm beneath me and pull on that whatever. Opening one eye, I find a folded white cane. The second eye opens, as my mind slowly starts to process the thought. *What the hell?*

Sitting up, I realise that I'm not in my bed, but on my friend's settee and things slowly fall into place as I remember yesterday's events. Our flat: raided — my life: threatened — me: homeless… and it's only Tuesday.

More chinking noises, this time more like pots and pans draws my attention to the kitchen and I stand up and stretch myself. I untie my hair to let it breathe, and join Egan, who's busy preparing breakfast.

He looks perfectly presented and ready for his day: short ginger hair neatly combed, dark-blue turtleneck pullover and black denims creaseless. I let out an involuntary yawn, as I pass a weary hand through my tangled hair. With the other hand, I straighten my rumpled shirt, as I manage a tired, 'Mornin'.'

Egan inclines his head my way and replies with a smile, 'Good morning to you too, Lexa. I hope you slept well.'

'Would have,' I say, holding out his cane, 'if that thing of yours wasn't so rudely poking at me.'

A flustered look crosses over his face and he fumbles a chaotic sort of bewildered apology between two coughs. Going back over my words in my head, I can see where the confusion could have arisen. I'm tempted to let the innuendo linger just a while longer, but whatever he's cooking smells good and I'm starving.

'I meant your cane, of course.' I tap his shoulder with it, and he reaches out a hand to take it, muttering another string of confused words, 'I... huh...well... thanks.'

'What on earth did you think I meant?' I ask, the amused lilt in my voice the vocal equivalent of wiggling eyebrows.

The red in his cheeks reaches his ears, as he focuses intently on the pan in front of him, stirring deftly what looks to be an omelette. With a parting laugh, I retreat to the bathroom.

When I come back to the kitchen, Egan's waiting for me, leaning against the kitchen worktop with his arms folded over his chest and a pensive look on his face.

'I had an idea,' he says.

'I'm listening.'

He motions to the table he's set up for two — mushroom omelette already served and steaming. 'Sit down and eat. We're on a tight schedule.'

I gladly obey. 'Are we?'

'Yes, we are,' he says, as he pours himself a cup of coffee, 'I thought back on that portrait you did of Mrs Levantiner.'

I offer a distracted 'hmm' over a mouthful of omelette. It could do with a bit more salt, but other than that, it's quite good.

Egan pushes the coffee pot my way and I grasp the handle, pouring myself a cup.

'Thought you could maybe do the same with Mrs Hargrave,' he says.

I offer a second, slightly more inquisitive 'Hmm' this time.

'I mean for you to draw the mysterious man who came to visit her. From her description from memory.'

That really is a very good idea. I like that a lot. I swallow down some coffee and then query, 'Haven't the police done that already?'

'I took the liberty of calling DS Lingby to check,' Egan says, sounding only slightly smug. 'They haven't.'

'How come?'

'Well, between Mrs Hargrave having initially forgotten all about the encounter and her recent hospitalisation, they never got around to doing it…'

'And with the case having officially hit a standstill, I guess they never bothered to round off the edges,' I finish, reading between the lines.

He gives me a nod, as he takes a bite of his omelette. Damn budget cuts.

As soon as we're finished with breakfast, we leave the flat and head for the hospital. As we enter it, a slight tremor of apprehension passes through me. I know it's completely pointless. After all, a hospital is only a place; it can't hurt me or have any influence on me, but I have so many bad memories associated with just such places that the very name has become a synonym for discomfort to me.

When my father became ill with cancer, I was only a child and I spent long hours within those white corridors, surrounded by the antiseptic smells that became all too familiar. Although I was very young, I could understand, at least on some level, I was surrounded by the sick and the dying. And then, after one admission, Daddy never came home.

I hate hospitals. Fact. And I don't believe that will ever change.

Egan must have sensed something was wrong with me, because he moves an inch or so closer; or maybe he just doesn't like hospitals either. I suppose he must have seen his fair share too, through losing his sight.

We ask after Mrs Hargrave at Reception and are directed up to the fourth floor. She's in room 428 lying under a thin light-blue cover on a complicated looking electric-powered hospital bed. Tubes are going in and out of her arms and bedside machines blinking and beeping at intervals.

As we enter, she fumbles for the remote control of her bed, and offers us a feeble smile, as we draw closer.

'Thank you for receiving us, Mrs Hargrave,' I say, coming to stand at her bedhead. Egan lingers near its end.

'It's no problem. I hardly have anything else to do all day.' She tries to make a joke out of it, but the harsh rasp of her voice stifles her intent. She sounds as if there isn't enough air in the room. There's also a sort of wet sickly quality to her breathing; the kind of breathing you might imagine from someone who's just been saved from drowning and has swallowed gallons of water.

'Have you made any progress?' she asks.

'Some.' I don't really wish to go into details and I would rather spare her the most recent events, not wanting to alarm her needlessly. I reach into my shoulder bag instead and produce my sketchbook and a pencil.

'Alexandra is quite the talented portraitist,' Egan says, with a smile. 'We thought maybe you could describe to her the man who came to enquire about the necklace.'

'Oh, I'm not sure I can remember him very well,' Mrs Hargrave says, frowning deeply.

'Well, it won't hurt to try.' I motion towards the foot of the bed, silently asking permission to sit down. She raises a shaking hand and waves her agreement.

'What can you tell me about him?' I ask. 'Is any detail particularly prominent in your memory? His eyes, or maybe the shape of his nose or—'

'His chin!' she interrupts me. 'It was angular; really very angular "as if it'd been cut with an axe" I remember thinking.'

Alright: chin! I grab my pencil and start drawing chin lines with straight angles. Once I'm done, I rise the sketchbook up for her to see, and get a nod of approval. 'What of the rest of him? Were his cheekbones sharply cut too?'

She frowns for an instant. 'Yes, yes I think they were.'

Right, so it's yes to Angular Chin and Prominent Cheekbones. This is an odd kind of way to draw, I think to myself. Personally, I prefer starting with the eyes, the window to the soul, as they say, and then move onto the nose. I then expand outwards, finishing the rest of the face and keeping the hair until last. Today, it feels as if I'm working backwards.

I have to be flexible with my artistic preferences here, because this portrait is so vital to our case. This man — this mysterious stranger slowly taking shape under my hand — may hold the key to this entire mystery.

The process of describing one person to another is a very long task. It takes time to precisely describe features. There are hundreds of different types of noses, for instance. Long, fat, curved, slightly askew, bearing the marks of one too many punches received in younger days… Mrs Hargrave's memory is fuzzy over some details. At some point, I resort to gathering magazines. I turn the pages for her, she points at some actor's brow, some politician's ears, and so on.

Sketching the portrait of our mystery man takes me half the morning. We have to stop several times to allow Mrs Hargrave to rest. Her health has declined tremendously. Aside from the very evident breathing problems, she also suffers from some acute chest pain. One long bout of coughing has me almost reaching for the alarm bell to call some medical staff over. She dissuades me with a weak wave of her hand. After a few more coughs, her breathing calms again.

Egan disappears from the room at some point, professing the need to stretch his legs. Once the portrait is finished, and Mrs

Hargrave and I have exchanged goodbyes, I leave her room to look for him. I eventually find him sitting on a plastic chair on a nearby terrace.

I turn my back on the glaring noonday sun and sit down on the adjacent uncomfortable chair, with an audible 'eh.'

I clasp my sketchbook firmly in my hand. I'd completed the portrait and had finally received Mrs Hargrave's seal of approval for its representation of her "insurance man" visitor.

'How did it go?' Egan asks.

'She seems satisfied that we've done the best we can. I suppose the next step is to drop it off to DS Lingby on our way home.'

He nods his agreement. 'I talked with one of the doctors, while you were busy.'

His face looks grim and I gather the prognosis must be poor. 'How bad is it?' I ask.

'Mrs Hargrave may only have a few days left, they reckon — a few weeks at the very best. Her entire immune system is starting to fail. If they can get rid of the pneumonia it will buy her a few extra days, but she's unlikely to see the end of the summer.'

I swallow hard. 'I'm so sorry for her. It's crazy, she looked good, the first time I met her. A little tired maybe... like she had flu or a cold, but I would never have guessed it was so bad,' but then again, I had seen my father two days before he died and he hadn't looked "so bad" either.

A chill runs through me at the thought. 'Shall we go?' I ask.

Egan sits up with a nod, holding out a hand to me. I take it, and keep it in my hand for a few seconds more than necessary.

Later that night, I get a phone call from DS Lingby to thank me for the portrait we had dropped off at the Arts and Antiques Unit office that afternoon. She hadn't been in at the time, and we'd left it with one of her colleagues. Apparently, she's also had a chat with *Matty* (I can't help but cringe at a shortform that sounds over-familiar to me) who had told her about my flat being raided. She informs me that, given the latest development, her unit is officially reopening the case — new cost-efficiency policy be damned.

She promises to keep me in the loop with the case's progress, and I hang up with a sigh. 'A dying man's last hope,' I mutter, as I place the phone back on the table… or rather a dying woman's, in this instance.

Another saying comes to mind, "Don't put all your eggs in one basket," and I decide to take to the advice. I can't, after all, rely solely on the police finding our mysterious man. I reach for my phone again, and place a call to Germany.

Angela Hoss picks up on the fourth ring. 'Guten Abend, Alexandra,' she says, her voice as joyful as it was the last time we spoke.

'Evening, Angela. How did you know that was me?'

'I don't get that many calls from England, you know.' She chuckles.

'Of course… Look, I've got a favour to ask you.'

'Go on.'

'I'd like to ask your grand-father a few questions, about the Levantiners' case. Do you think you could play translator for me?'

She takes a little while to answer and I rearrange the documents on the corner of Egan's coffee table in a neat pile. 'Sure,' she says. 'Call my mobile tomorrow at noon — I'll be with him then. It'll be easier that way.'

'That's great. Thanks Angela.'

We exchange goodbyes and hang up.

Leaving the phone on the table, I get up and, while heading for the shower to get ready for bed, I start mentally preparing questions to ask the retired police officer.

13

On Wednesday morning, Egan leaves early to go to UCL. He actually leaves so early, that I wake up to an empty flat. I might not know anything about History Department meetings, but it seems unlikely that they start at six thirty in the morning.

My jaw's set tight, as I get up from the settee. I'm sure Egan got up early to avoid having to run into me. Cunning bastard. He wanted to avoid having to fess up to the fact he was going to that meeting. Because his attendance means that he hasn't made up his mind yet — he's still considering pursuing his teaching career. My throat constricts at the thought.

I open a window, and tiredly rub at the back of my neck. Yeah, a really neat move to have left early. Skirting around issues isn't a dance I do very well; I'm not smooth, I'm not subtle and I hate having to be diplomatic or keep my mouth shut about something. '*Porca vacca!*' I sigh. 'One of us is going to have to own up at some point and acknowledge the big elephant in the room.'

Turning my back on the already bright sun, I move towards the fridge, but stop when I see the kitchen table is set with toast, marmalade and butter all ready to be wolfed down by one hungry private investigator.

I call my mother after breakfast to inquire about her health, but she doesn't pick up. With a grimace, I leave an awkward message on her voicemail.

'Hey Mum, it's me, Alexandra. I was just calling to see how you're doing. Call me back when you have a minute, okay? Love you, bye.' Yeah, I know, I'm pathetic at leaving messages on answering machines.

My weekly Wushu class is next and I take the Underground north to Camden. Soon after I moved into this neighbourhood, I walked past the front of the club by accident after taking a couple of wrong turns, and entered on a whim. I've been going to classes once or twice a week ever since.

Wǔshù, I've learned, literally means 'martial art', in Chinese. It's a sport, with a complicated set of rules and points given to certain manoeuvres. I do not care about that side of the art, and told my instructor so on the very first day. I'm only interested in learning the routines, so I can hold my own in a fight.

In my line of work, a little bit of self-defence knowledge is pretty essential, if you intend to stay alive. Trust me, I know what I'm talking about. On our first case, I'd been taken off the streets and thrown into a moving van in which two guys held me down. They had every intention of inflicting real damage for sticking my nose in where it wasn't wanted. I still shudder at the memory — I barely made it out alive

Today, we practise extended kicks and striking techniques. Our instructor demonstrates a wide range of impressive acrobatic kicks that have me, and the other students, gaping in awe. He whirls, runs and leaps, with such ease that it's quite unnerving.

In the span of an hour, we learn two moves: a long uppercutting punch and a whirling roundhouse kick that has me falling on my bum several times.

I lack grace and balance, or so the instructor tells me. 'You need to be bamboo, Alexandra, be flexible, bend with the wind, adapt to the circumstances'.

I like to think I'm a strong English Oak tree, like the ones which grow in Camden Park, firmly rooted and stubborn.

After the class is over, I stick around a little longer to punch at a sandbag, on my own, and God, does that feel good!

Right straight punch, crouch, jab, stand, left hook. Repeat.

I love the repetitiveness simplicity of the action sequence; there's nothing better to let out some of my frustration and the raw force it allows me to expend does wonders for the psyche. And guess what? It's also good for the figure. Okay, it probably won't make you look like one of those women from the adverts — the ones who look like they've been baked with abs and biceps of steel in some special pre-formed mould — but it will help if you have, like me, a special fondness for Spaghetti Carbonara with a double serving of cream.

I punch the bag with renewed strength, thinking that I'm stronger, faster, firmer... and all that's missing now is the chorus of *Eye of the Tiger* blasting in the background.

Besides a newfound ability to look good in tight denim trousers, I know that if I should ever be jumped by some bad guys again, I would now have a fighting chance of making it to round number two before being knocked out.

When my knuckles start to ache, I call it a day and head for the showers.

Once back out on the street, I stop at a nearby bakery for a sandwich which I hungrily chomp on my way back to Egan's flat.

Just after one o'clock, I call Angela, sketchbook in hand, pencil and questions at the ready.

I start with some general questions about the accident. 'Where did it happen, what were the Levantiners doing there?'

I can hear Angela's grandfather's voice in the distance and the young woman's cheerful voice starts to translate, as best as she can, 'Third day on the job, we were called to the scene late at night. I remember that it was raining a little. We went to the woods, on the east side of the Harz Mountain. The car was on fire when we arrived, the rain wasn't enough to put out the flames. I still remember it vividly. This carcass of metal engulfed in red and orange flames, standing out in the dark night — and the water pouring down on us.

'They left me and another young policeman to guard the scene all night. We had to wait until the morning, for the fire to die down. When the officers came back, we discovered the bodies of two victims in the wreckage — a man and a woman; he was the driver and she was in the passenger seat.'

'Can you ask him if the woman was wearing any jewellery?' I ask Angela.

'Wedding ring — they both had one. Nothing else. I was sad to find out they were married — I had just got engaged myself, a few weeks before.'

'How did you identify them?'

'Car licence plate — it was the only way. We didn't have DNA analysis back then. First thing we did was go to the Levantiners' home but there was no one there — they were never seen again so we declared them dead. Car accident. Simple case.'

'But you never understood what they were doing on that road?'

'No, there was nothing on the mountain but bunkers and military outposts. Civilians didn't really go there, at the time. And it was a dangerous road, especially at night, with rain.

'We thought maybe they went to visit some of the military. Herr Levantiner worked for Von Abschütz and the company did a lot of business with the Army back then.'

'Do you remember anything about Mrs Levantiner? What she was like, if she had any hobbies?'

'Of course we would have asked around about them, but it was all a long time ago and my memory isn't what it used to be. I think she was well liked. Everyone was sad to learn about her death.'

'And her husband?'

'I remember going to the Von Abschütz factory to enquire about his whereabouts — a huge building with dozens of local people working the metal, and as hot as hell. My boss talked with Von Abschütz himself. He was a very reputable man; his company benefited the entire town. We didn't really mind that he was working with the Reich as long as people had jobs and earned enough money to feed their families.

'He said he and Levantiner were friends and shared the same

views on a lot of things. There was one thing he said about Mrs Levantiner that I've rarely ever heard being said of a dead woman, and that puzzled me. "She still had to learn her place." It could have meant any number of things, so we didn't dwell on it, but I still remember it. The rest wasn't as striking and is rather blurry.

'We closed the investigation shortly afterwards. As I said, it was a simple car accident. The only reason I remember it so well, is that it was my first case. I would have forgotten all about it otherwise, there really was nothing remarkable about it.'

'Thanks again for your time, sir,' I say and I can hear Angela translating my words.

We say our goodbyes and hang up.

I look down at my notes feeling rather baffled. "She still had to learn her place." What on earth could that possibly mean?

You don't make such comment about someone who has just died. Von Abschütz knew the Levantiners well. He spent a lot of time with the husband — probably saw him every day or so.

I lean back in my chair and concentrate on thinking it all through. If Claus Levantiner was anything like the rest of the male population, I'm sure he must have complained about everything and anything that was going wrong in his marriage to his mate. Moreover, for Von Abschütz to come up with such a strong statement at such an inappropriate time, our Herr Levantiner must have complained a lot.

'Trouble in paradise,' I mutter, as I write the quote down on my sketchbook before circling it twice.

The rain maybe was not the only thing responsible for the Levantiners' deaths. They could have been arguing in the car, or maybe even fighting. But that still doesn't explain what they were doing on that road, late at night.

I roll my shoulders and heave in a deep breath. I don't know much about the forties — hell, my own mother wasn't even born then — but I know couples. It's the same shenanigans no matter which century: when one is unhappy, one goes somewhere else, searching for that elusive bit of greener grass.

This universal truth does bring forth another question: would a man who spends his entire day arming the Third Reich really give his wife a necklace created by a Jewish craftsman? And if not, then who would?

14

When I wake up the next day, Egan's flat is as empty, as it had been the previous night. Stretching slowly and lazily, I reach for my phone and flip it open to see if I missed any calls. I find two from my mother, I frown, look at my watch and get up quickly, swearing. Mum had called to meet me for breakfast in town ten minutes ago. Damn it, again.

I'm thirty minutes late, when I actually make it. I find my mother morosely stirring an half-empty cup of tea. She's a strange sight. She's wearing a loose T-Shirt with the left sleeve hanging at odd angles, the cotton fibres caught on some parts of the plaster of her arm cast. Her hair's not done as well as usual either; the greying curls are messier than I'm used to seeing. But she smiles at me as I sit down, so I take it she isn't getting on so badly after all.

'Sorry, I'm late.' I begin. 'Forgot to set my alarm clock… again.'

She shakes her head, smiling at me in a rather forced way. 'It is good to see you, Lexa.'

I smile back, 'Good to see you too.'

I motion at a passing waitress for some scones. 'So…' I say to my mother, 'how are things over at Bob's?'

She seems a bit flustered. 'He's a charming man.'

'And?'

'And he cooks me breakfast.'

I smile. 'Funny, Ash does that too.'

Her eyes open up, comically wide. 'Does he?'

I shrug. 'Well, it's his flat after all. And he doesn't really like me going through his stuff — something about me being too messy or something.'

That seems to calm my mother some. 'Ah, yes of course,' she says.

I get an odd feeling of déjà-vu and go back over my words to see where the innuendo could have been this time. I find nothing. Why the hell would my mother have assumed there's something going on then? Unless, she—

'What exactly did you meant by "he cooks me breakfast", Mum?' I ask and she blushes.

'He makes the breakfast, and then we eat it,' she mutters, eventually.

'And where exactly do you guys eat that breakfast?'

Her silence is answer enough.

'Anyway,' she starts, after a gulp of tea. 'Have you talked with that kind detective? Does he know when we can go back to the flat?'

'Called him on the way here: Matthew says we can go back anytime we want. He also said he would give me a list of security devices we could install. You know: better locks, chain, alarm and stuff.'

Although the answer should please her, she frowns.

'Nothing's stopping you from telling Bob it's better to stay at his place a while longer, of course.' I wiggle my eyebrows suggestively.

Her face takes on a sadder expression. 'Are you okay with this, Alexandra dear? I mean, I haven't really had anyone since your father died and—'

I raise a hand to stop her. 'If you're happy, then it's fine with me.'

'Are you sure? This whole thing happened faster than I anticipated.'

'It's alright Mum. Dad's been gone for a long time now and you're allowed to be happy with someone else.'

She gives me a smile. 'I just thought you would find someone first. What about that detective? Do you know if he's seeing anyone?'

I let out a long-suffering sigh. Why does everyone seem to want Stenson and me to be an item?

'What about Bob?' I ask instead. 'Is he good in bed?'

That effectively shuts my mother up. She looks down at her tea and mutters something incomprehensible. It's just as well, because I don't think I could bear to listen to a proper answer anyway. I'm tired of people trying to push their way into my personal life and I don't want to learn the details of theirs either.

Once she's recovered, she redirects the conversation to some more conventional topics. The deep blush in her cheeks remains.

'What about your job?' she asks, eventually. 'Have you found that necklace yet?'

'No, we're still looking.' I swallow a large mouthful of tea. 'But we've made some progress.'

'And you're getting paid, yes?'

'She made a deposit when we took the case, we'll get the rest when the job's over.'

'And this case…' She seems hesitant. 'It is safe, isn't it? It's just a stolen necklace, not a murder investigation or anything. You're not going to get hurt, or…'

She lets her sentence go unfinished and I force a smile as I say, 'It's just a stolen necklace. It's as safe as can be.'

Technically, it's not a lie. However, if something bad were to happen to me, "technically" would be of little comfort to my mother. I hate lying to her, but if she knew of the message left in our flat, she would forbid me to continue with the investigation. And I wouldn't put it past her to lock me away in a cell somewhere until I was grey and past it all.

'Mr Hammond called…' she begins.

There's no need for her to finish her sentence. Mr Hammond is our landlord, and he only ever calls about rent.

'I gave you my half, didn't I?' she asks, worried lines etching her forehead. 'I thought you'd already made the transfer?'

I swallow, I would have if I could. I shrug. 'Things have been a little hectic lately.'

'Lexa! I thought we discussed this already.'

'I know, Mum.' I look down, try not to let my embarrassment show. 'I'll figure something out, ok?' I suppose the company's account can be in the red, again, for a few days.

'This is no way to live your life, Lexa.' She slams her cup onto its saucer and the china clinks audibly. 'This whim of yours is dangerous.

It's been months and you're still struggling to get by.'

'"Whim"?' I repeat, aghast.

'Yes, daughter. A childlish, foolish, irresponsible whim. That's what it is.'

The words cut deep.

'Look at you,' she continues, waving her non-plastered arm about to show what she means. 'Obviously dressed in a hurry, your hair's a mess and you look like you haven't slept decently in a week.'

'You're exaggerating everything, Mum.'

'No I'm not. I'm worried for you, Lexa.' She huffs. 'How can you expect to run your own company, when you can't even remember to set your alarm to meet with your mother? And you hold meetings with your clients in a bar. In a bar, for Heaven's sake, Alexandra.'

'There's nothing wrong with that,' I butt in rather lamely. 'It's—'

'And what about that potential client you told me about last month who called the meeting off, after you gave her the address? Why do you think that was? You really have absolutely no idea what you're doing, my girl. This all needs to stop now!' She taps hard on the table for emphasis.

My mother's words almost set me alight, and I have to make enormous efforts to keep my possible biting retorts in check. I know throwing a tantrum would only prove her right.

I resort to doing things adult style. I push back my chair, stand up, and place the serviette back on the table delicately. 'I'm sorry that you see things this way, Mum.' I push the chair back against the table with controlled movements, pick up my shoulder bag, reach for my wallet and place my last tenner on the table. 'My apologies again for being late. Now, if you'll excuse me, I have a job to get back to.'

That said, I turn on my heel and leave the bar.

I put off going back to Egan's flat and go round to our own with a pot of white paint and a large brush. I spend time straightening out the living room, tidying all our stuff into its rightful place and it becomes home again. Finally I start painting the door. My mother's words are still ringing in my ears. Am I really being a child? Is this private investigator's business really such a bad idea?

Defeated, I plonk myself down on the corner of the coffee table, wet brush still in hand. Tears spring to my eyes as I look up at the half-painted door.

'What am I doing here?' I ask the door. 'Is this really what I want — a life of death threats, take-away food and short nights?'

The door offers no answer other than the mocking scarlet red "give up" painted on the wood.

No-one said it would be easy. Nothing is ever easy. I learned that lesson a long time ago. 'Life is hard like that, kiddo,' my father told me once, 'but without the bad, you wouldn't be able to appreciate the good'.

Papa. What would he say today? What would he think of me? The letters on the door blur, as the tears begin to fall.

A distant voice drifts back to me, from the furthest recess of my mind. 'Always follow your heart, child.' I close my eyes as my throat tightens. 'You will never be wrong that way.'

My father's blue eyes and kind smile fade away as I reopen my eyes, and the door returns. I stand up, dip the drying brush into fresh paint and cover the remaining letters with resolute strokes. Time to grow up, Lexa.

After I'm done with the front door, I move to my bedroom to straighten that out too. It really took the brunt of the tornado. As I'd already noticed, all of the microfilms are gone along with most of my notes. Whoever has been here even erased my white board.

I sit at my desk and scribble the most important points onto the white board again, thinking that such an interest in the necklace is baffling. Sure, it's a gorgeous piece that is worth quite a bit on the market, but it's not the crown jewels. Why would someone risk a prison sentence for it? And exactly how far would that person go to get it?

My thoughts are halted by the chirping of my phone. I fish it out of my pocket and it flashes with Stenson's caller ID.

'Hi,' I say, in a cheerful voice that has me blushing when I realise just how cheerful I sound.

'Hey, Alexandra,' he says, in a tone that matches mine. 'I've got some good news for you.'

'Great, what is it?'

'We've found the guy who redecorated your flat.'

Yippee. 'Good, where is he? I'd like to give him a piece of my mind.'

He chuckles. 'Calm down, Alex. I didn't say we have him yet, we've only just identified him. CCTV caught him when he left your place — it just took us a little bit of time to match a name to the picture.'

I don't really consider two whole days to be "a little bit of time", but I make a successful effort to keep my mouth shut.

I hear the sound of rustling papers down the line and Stenson says, 'Steven Stuart, aka Stony Stu. Small-time thug. Been busted for some minor and some not so minor things: drunk-driving, drug possession, assault, the list goes on...'

'Know where to find him?'

'No known address, but we have an idea where to start looking. I'll text you his picture, so you can be on the look-out — just in case.'

'Thanks.'

'I'll let you know when we find him,' the sergeant says.

We exchange our goodbyes and he hangs up. My phone chirps again with a text message, seconds later.

'Well hello, Stony Stu,' I mutter to the phone.

The picture Stenson has sent me is of a young man, thirty-ish, with dark brown hair that fall in long bangs over his face. He has the tattoo of a star on his neck and brown eyes that have a dull look to them that can only mean one thing — he was under the influence of something when the mug-shot was taken.

I try to commit his features to memory, to make sure that I would recognise him, should we ever cross paths. I'm about to flick my phone shut, when a thought strikes me. The tattoo. I zoom in and look at it more closely before letting out a small 'Ah' of victory.

This is more than a tattoo, it's an emblem branded on skin,

much like a cattle brand. This unique symbol — a five-pointed star made of barbwire — is always inked on the forearm or the side of the neck of a *Fiver* to expose his membership to everyone else.

The *fivers* — one of the many gangs that operates in Hackney, in the E5 postal district — is mostly comprised of young men carrying knives and committing small-scale robberies. They are also known to do some drug dealing, but they're not major players. Their business stays very local and no one has died at their hands… yet. They're not particularly violent — mostly, they just acquire stuff to sell so that they can keep buying their daily doses.

If you believe the newspapers, Hackney has the highest number of separate gangs of any London borough. I agree with that statement. Before moving to Camden earlier this year, I lived in Hackney for over a decade. I've never been part of any gang, but I've known men who were. One especially. As the saying goes… the nice girls always fall for the bad guys.

15

I'll concede that entering the local hangout of a street gang on your own, when you're a twenty-four year old girl armed with a bottle of pepper-spray and a lot of good will may not be the most intelligent plan ever. True.

I could have taken Egan with me; probably should have taken Stenson with me and at some point today I'll most likely regret not having just stayed at home in bed. Nevertheless, I walk in, with my head held high, and my black Converse trainers stomping on the concrete floor in my best attempt at steady and decided steps. My hair is tied in the usual way, and the plait bounces over a red leather jacket that is too hot for the season but that I believe gives my look a cool edge. I also decided to forgo blue jeans and chose to wear black denim trousers instead for this mission.

I walk to the bar of the little joint — *Eddy's counter*, the neon sign outside used to spell, but someone smashed the 'o' and the last two letters a few years back — and sit on a stool.

'What can I get ya?' the barman — a middle-aged, lean and balding, Texas-born guy — asks, with his back to me.

'G&T if you would be so kind, Eddy,' I order, steadily.

The man turns around rapidly. He eyes me, up-and-down, for a full minute, before offering me a bright smile. 'Alexandra Neve, I never thought I'd see you round here again.'

I smile back, my jaw relaxing fractionally.

'How long's it been?' he wonders, in his southern States drawl.

'About four years,' I reply, my smile faltering at the thoughts the words stir up.

Eddy's smile stays strong. 'One Gin and Tonic comin' right up, kiddo.' He moves to the left and prepares my drink.

'So how you been?' He asks, dropping ice cubes in my glass, and holding it out to me.

I take a long gulp before answering. 'Good.'

'Walking the narrow path, eh?' he asks, with a wink.

I nod. 'You know me.' I give the place a good, long look. 'Can't say the same about you.'

There are two groups of men seated in the room. One group of four, two tables from the entrance door. One group of three, seated on the opposite side of the bar, by the window. All the patrons are men and they're all dressed in dark colours. There's a generally heavy and menacing vibe to the whole place…

Eddy shrugs. 'You know how it is. Business is business. They pay, I serve.'

Although he welcomes gang members into his joint, Eddy doesn't have any tattoo on his own neck or forearm. He is (for the most part) an honest man trying to make a living. It hadn't been his choice for his bar to become the number one hangout of the *Fivers*, but when they started gathering here to discuss business for endless hours while drinking a lot, he didn't throw them out. He and the gang leader came to some kind of an agreement. As long as the boys behave and pay for their drinks, they'll always be welcome at Eddy's.

I give him a wry smile. 'Do you still have the same clientele?'

'Mostly.' His expression grows serious again. 'What'cha doin' here, Alexandra? You were a good girl, and I always liked ya. I don't mean to be rude, it's nice to see ya again, and I'm happy to note that—' he waves a hand encompassing me '—you seem to be doing fine, but this ain't no place for good girls.'

'I'm looking for someone.'

He leans in closer. 'Not that scum you were with, I hope?'

I huff. 'God, no!' I'm well and truly done with that guy. Ben was the worst mistake of my life actually.

I take one of my business cards and hand it out to Eddy.

'Private investigator,' he whistles. 'Didn't see that one comin'. Weren't ya gonna go to university or somethin'?'

I shrug. 'Didn't turn out as I'd planned.' I take my phone out, and show him the picture. 'I'm looking for this guy. He's one of the *Fivers*, right?'

Eddy glances down at the portrait and nods. 'Yeah. I've seen him a few times. Stu… something, I think'

'Stony Stu.' I drop the phone back in my jacket pocket.

'Yeah, that the man.' He exhales loudly. 'What d' ya want with that knucklehead?'

I remain silent as I debate what to answer. I actually worked some shifts in this bar a few years back, when I was saving money to put myself through university. I know Eddy's a good man and I may have some lingering fondness for him — from the day he drove me back home and helped me up the steps, because I was too hammered to make it home on my own — but not enough to tell him everything. 'Need to ask him a few questions. Do you know where lives?'

'Some flat on Leaside Road, next to the storage building.'

I finish the drink and stand up. 'Thanks Eddy,' I say, reaching for my wallet, with every intention of tipping him kindly.

He stops me with a wave of his hand. 'It's on the house.'

I smile at him. 'Thanks.'

'No need to thank me, kiddo. It was nice to see ya again.'

I nod and walk out of the room, doing my best to ignore the many dubious looks I can feel burning into my back.

'Stay out of trouble.' I can hear Eddy mutter, just before I walk out the door.

'Sure thing,' I mutter back, as I step out. That's exactly what I intend to do.

On the pavement, I find that cotton white clouds still cover the sky, and I'm thankful for the shade they provide. The day is hot enough even without direct sun and my shirt clings stickily to my skin under the leather jacket.

As I set out for Leaside Road, I thank my lucky stars for that "successful" sortie into my dodgy past and gradually release the vice-like grip I have on the bottle of pepper-spray in my jacket pocket. The visit to the bar could have gone a lot worse, if some of my old acquaintances had been in attendance. I didn't hang out with the *Fivers* much, but the guy I was dating at the time was one of them.

God, was I stupid when I was younger.

The *Fiver* I was with — Ben Cobart, but everyone called him Ben *Crow*bar — was a long-time member of the gang, and a terrific skater. He's the one who taught me all about skating, and I got really good at it. I have the scars to prove it, and my knee joint still locks sometimes when I exercise too hard. Our story was a lot like that Avril Lavigne song, *Skater Boy*, except it didn't end so well for either of us. It cost me more than I like to admit, and I hate the possibility of bumping into him or any of his crew ever again.

Finding Stony Stu's building isn't difficult, but finding his flat number is. Of course, his name doesn't appear anywhere on the row of postboxes.

A young girl with freckled cheeks and pigtails — ten years old at most and playing with dolls in the entrance — recognises him on the picture I show her. She refuses to tell me which floor he lives on, unless I give her a tenner. I take one of the crisp notes I got from the ATM this morning and hold it out to her. She then asks for another ten-pound note to tell me which of the three flats on the fourth floor is the right one. I try to bargain, but eventually give up. Damn kids really grow up fast these days.

I've almost reached the second floor when I come face-to-face with a man about my height walking down the steps. He's wearing a dark sweatshirt with a hood thrown over his head, and long brown bangs hide most of his eyes. I freeze mid-step in surprise.

I didn't have much of a plan to begin with — I was actually going to use the time it took me to climb all four floors to come up with one. I haven't reached the second floor yet so I'm still a long way from anything concrete.

I can see in Stu's eyes the moment he recognises me. He drops the joint he was smoking and pushes me back to one side with both hands. A second later he's running down the steps. I manage to hang onto the railing with one hand, only just keeping myself from tumbling down the staircase behind him. As soon as I'm upright again, I start going after him.

'Wait,' I scream between two breaths, 'I only want to ask you a few questions.'

Although I'm sure he's heard me, Stu doesn't stop.

I keep running down after him. I do have longer legs, but that doesn't help in rushing down a staircase, but I hope it'll work to my advantage once we reach the ground floor.

I'm still coming down the last flight of stairs, when Stu pushes the front door open and is outside. I run out of the door mere seconds after him, and then stop briefly searching left and right, fill my lungs and start running again. I follow him down the road, my plait horizontal behind me in the wind, my shoulder bag bumping with each step. My strides are longer, and I'm closing in on him as he reaches the end of the block.

I extend a hand forward and my fingers just stroke the hood of his sweatshirt, when he abruptly turns left into a narrow passageway between two houses. I stop sharp, take a step back, and enter the passageway at a full run again. The surprise manoeuvre made me lose ground, and I'm now ten steps behind again.

The man is not a good runner, but he knows the terrain. He makes several sharp turns between worn-down brick houses, and keeps throwing everything he can get his hands on in my path. I have to jump over three dustbins, and a rusty shopping trolley almost has me on the ground.

My knee starts to hurt, and I curse loudly when I realise the distance between us is increasing. This chase needs to end soon, or I'm going to lose my quarry.

I thrill to see Stu make the mistake of trying to cross a large patch of desolate wasteland. *Wrong move*, I think and push harder. I run as fast as my ragged breath allows and thank the stars I've been exercising more recently. Still, I don't run very often, and now there's a searing pain in my leg muscles and my bad knee is starting to ache violently. I promise it an icepack tonight, and charge on. I push forward, long strides bringing me even closer to the young man. When I feel I'm close enough, I throw myself at Stu, rugby-style, and we smash to the ground together in a flurry of limbs and groans.

When the world eventually stops spinning, I find myself on my side, with my back to the man I was after. I push myself up onto my knees and palms, and turn to look at Stu, who's trying to do the same. His face is a mess of dirt and stray hair, and he looks confused. His cheeks are red and large beads of sweat cover his forehead. Our gazes meet for an instant, and I can see the faint haze of drugs in his pupils.

I don't give him time to figure things out. I shift all of my weight onto my left knee and hand, and kick him in the guts with my right heel. The blow sends him toppling backwards, and he lands on his back with a "humph" as all the air leaves his body. I see him gaping like a fish taken out of water.

I stand, on shaky legs, bend over a second to get in a few more deep breaths, and move forward, pepper-spray bottle in hand.

I haul Stu up, pin him close to me, his back to my chest, and twist one of his arms behind him. I pull on his hand, as hard as I can, and he screams. The move is something I practised in class and I'm pleased to find it comes naturally to me in real life.

With my free hand, I raise the spray bottle up, hold it inches away from his face.

'Know what this is, Stu?' I ask, my breath coming out in short bursts. 'I heard it hurts… a lot.'

The junkie nods in a quick gesture, his breathing accelerating.

'Also,' I continue, and pull the hand in his back a little higher up, 'I could break your arm.'

He yelps in pain again. 'What d'ya want?'

'You know who I am?'

He nods again.

'I want to know where the necklace is.'

'What necklace? I know nothing about no necklace,' he pants out.

I twist his arm a little. 'The ruby heart! The one that was on the microfilms you stole.'

'Aaah,' he screams. 'Stop, please. I stole the microfilm, yes.' I ease a little on his arm, and he takes a few deeper breaths.

'Keep talking,' I advise, waving the spray bottle under his nose.

'"Steal the microfilm and get rid of all notes pertaining to it", that's what I had to do. I know nothing of no necklace.' He pants. 'Didn't even know what microfilm was.'

'Who hired you?'

'Don't know.' He tries to squeeze out of my grasp and I twist his hand again.

'Who hired you?' I ask, louder.

'Some old bloke,' he screams. 'Looked a hundred at least. Came up to me in some fancy car, said I was recommended to him...' he starts gasping.

'Keep talking,' I order.

'Gave me an address and... and told me what to get. S'all I know.'

I twist his hand again. 'And the message on the door?'

'Yes, yes. The message, yes. It was on a piece of paper... he said I had to copy it in... in red paint.' He pants. 'Please stop hurting me. I don't know nothing about no necklace.'

'And the man. The one who hired you — you saw him again. Where?'

'Empty warehouse lot... east of the E5 area... later that night. I gave him the microfilm and he gave me five grand. Cash.'

'What's his name?' I ask, twisting the hand a little more.

'Aah — Don't know!' Stu half screams, half shouts.

I twist his arm again. 'His name!'

'Don't know!' he screams, panting loudly through the pain. 'I swear! We didn't use names. Best not to. He gave me a job — I do it — I get paid... end of story.'

'Where can I find him?' I move the spray bottle closer to his eyes.

'Don't know!' he yells. 'I swear it. I'd never seen the bloke before, but... but if I ever see him again, I'll give you a call, yeah?'

'Shut it, wiseass!'

Porca vacca! None of this is helpful. I can't keep adding pressure to his hand, or else I'll really damage him. I try to switch tactics.

'Here's my problem, Stu. You've vandalised my flat, put my mother in hospital and now... well, you're not being helpful at all.' I take a deep breath and give it time for my words to sink in. 'I've had a lousy day, I'm not in the best of moods, and you made me run... and I hate running—'

'Sorry,' Stu mutters. 'Sorry, didn't mean no harm to you or your mother.' He tries to squirm free again, but I don't let him.

'—All of that leaves me with a bit of a puzzle,' I go on just as if he hadn't interrupted me. 'What do you think I should do with you?'

'Le'me go?' he tries in a weak voice, with a hint of panic.

'No, not really what I had in mind.' I lean closer and murmur to his ear, *sotto voce*, 'Tell me Stu, do you know any good places to dump a body around here?'

16

Stony Stu shudders against me, and his breathing accelerates. Heavy beads of sweat pearl on his temples. As he starts shaking, they roll down the side of his face. It makes me smile.

Objectively I think I may be enjoying the moment a little too much, but don't feel guilty enough to stop. After all, this jerk did put my mother in hospital.

'I'm s—sorry,' Stu stammers. 'S—sorry for your flat. And the paint. And your mum. You can't kill me. Please.'

'Give me one good reason not to…' I let my voice drop to a darker level. 'Give me something, Stu.'

'I—I—' he stammers, aimlessly, for a while. 'Bloke looked old, really old. And he had an accent. German, or Russian or else. Looked like he had money to throw around. Said he wanted some films. And—and that I had to warn off some PI, to put a stop to their investigation. Said they were sticking their nose in where they shouldn't. Said it was only a warning. I—I needed the cash. So I did it, but it was just a job. A job. Nothing personal, Ma'am. Nothing personal at all.'

I'm amazed at how the fear of dying can loosen someone's tongue.

'I didn't really look at him,' Stu continues, between pants. 'Looked more at his cash. Half up-front. But he had white hair, cut short, and a suit. Drove some sort of dark BMW. And glasses, he had glasses.'

I pull on his arm again, and Stu winces. 'What else? You have to give me something I can use.'

'I don't know,' he pleads. 'I don't — please, I swear, I have nothing more.'

'Did he say why he chose you? Who recommended you?'

'No. Please — I didn't ask. I don't know.' He tries to squirm again. 'Please, some guy shows up with a lot of cash — I take it, I don't ask questions.'

I believe him. *Porca vacca!* There's nothing more, I can get out of this idiot.

'That's for my mum,' I mutter, before moving my head out of the line of fire, and pushing down on the pepper-spray button.

I walk back to the main road, while Stu writhes on the ground, screaming and rubbing helplessly at his eyes. It certainly does appear that the stuff hurts… a lot!

I stuff the near-empty pepper-spray bottle away in my pocket and head back to civilisation, exhausted. My knee is hurting like nobody's business. I limp off, at a slow pace, turning left into an alley leading back towards the main road.

The alley is narrow, the buildings around it are tall, and the sun can't reach the dirty pavement. Just as I think that, if we were in a film noir the audience would at this point expect the damsel in distress to be falling into a trap, the silhouettes of two men appear in front of me. They seem to be a little older than me, and roughly my size. One's wearing a dark denim and the other dark cargo trousers and they're both wearing biker jackets. Not a good sign.

I notice instantly that the one on the right, with the cargo trousers and long greasy hair, has a metal chain looped around his forearm. I slow my steps, but keep walking, as levelly as I can, determined not to show my unease. As the distance narrows, I note that they both have the *Fivers* tattoo on their necks, and one of the two men seems somehow vaguely familiar to me. I swallow nervously, as I run through my options.

Maybe I'm imagining things, maybe they're just going to walk past me, and everything will be fine. But somehow, I doubt it.

With my knee as it is, running is out of the question. With an effort, I could walk faster, maybe turn my back on them and stagger away in the other direction. That would get me back to the open wasteground, which I could try to cross to reach the main road which lies on the far side. With a little luck, Stu will either be gone or still too blinded to be much of a problem. Or, he could be waiting, ready for round two.

I chance a quick glance over my shoulder, and see a third silhouette haloed by the feeble rays of sun that enter the alleyway from the back, effectively trapping me.

I keep walking forward, in slow, measured steps. All of my muscles are tense, my fingers tight around the pepper spray bottle still in my pocket.

The two men facing me stop a few feet ahead of me, effectively blocking the path and confirming that this is no chance encounter.

They're here for me, and I stop as well. Now that I stand closer to them, I'm certain I have already met the one on the left. His short spiky blond hair and pierced eyebrow are familiar. I can't remember his name though. Jay? Joe?

'Been a while, Lex,' comes a low-pitched voice, from behind me.

My heart skips a beat, as recognition dawns on me.

'Ben,' I mutter, breathlessly, without needing to turn round.

I hear him take a few more steps and he soon appears in my peripheral vision, with a cold smile on his face. My fingers tighten around the small plastic bottle in my pocket to the point of hurting.

Ben hasn't changed much. He still bears the same chiselled jaw, the same hazel eyes with flickers of honey in them, and the same short-cropped dark hair. He does, however, look four years older than when I last saw him. Time has marked his face, creasing the skin around his eyes, and near the dimples in his cheeks. The five-pointed star tattoo is still there, strikingly visible on the side of his neck, under the dark-brown stubble. The defiance and sense of strength in his gaze hasn't gone either.

Ben keeps his distance, as he rounds me, and soon joins the other two *Fivers* standing ahead of me.

'I almost didn't believe it when Jon here told me he saw you at Eddy's,' Ben continues, nodding at the blond man on his right.

I keep my mouth shut, my jaw clenched, and my eyes fixed on the men in front of me.

'I had to come and see you for myself.' Ben looks me up-and-down, with eyes that I could only qualify as hungry. 'So what are doing in my part of town?' he asks me.

'*Your* part of town?' I can't help but echo. Ben has never been one for modesty, but proclaiming that he runs the show is a little over the top, even for him.

He offers me a broad wolfish smile and I note that one of his front teeth is now missing.

'Like I said,' he replies, shrugging one shoulder, 'it's been a while.'

My eyes narrow, as I pay careful attention to him. His smile: relaxed; his eyes: smiling cunningly; his posture: carefree. Then I take in the whole scene in front of me, and note that Jon and what's-his-name both stand half a step behind Ben, like the good lackey they are. *Well, I'll be damned.* My ex isn't lying — he runs the show now.

'Don't worry' I say, in a voice as still as I can manage, choosing to respond to his earlier question rather than addressing this unexpected declaration. 'I'm not staying.'

Ben lets a wry chuckle escape his throat at that.

'Aw, Alexandra Neve, always the intelligent one, aren't you. You were always good at avoiding conflict, but I also remember your wilder side.' He opens his eyes suggestively wider at the end of the sentence.

'Must be your Italian side,' Ben continues. 'Italian women can be so passionate, isn't it what they say?'

I force myself not to respond, even when I hear Jon chuckle.

Ben takes a step forward, as his expression grows more serious. 'I heard rumours, Lex.' He pauses and wets his lips. 'That you've gone and joined the forces of law and order.'

I shudder inwardly, but square my shoulders, as I say, 'Not quite true.'

Not showing any signs of weakness is my only chance with Ben. He respects strength and determination, or at least he used to back then. I pray this hasn't changed. If he so much as thinks I'm lying and that I'm a police officer or any other kind of threat to him or his crew, I'll be dead meat.

'I'm a private investigator,' I continue. 'I was hired to find a stolen necklace. This has nothing to do with you or the *Fivers*.'

Ben raises an eyebrow. 'Yeah? That the truth, Lex?'

I look him square on. 'Yes.'

With regret, I force myself to let go of the spray bottle and grab one of my business cards instead. I take it out of my pocket as slowly and unthreateningly as I can. Out of the corner of my eye, I see what's-his-name move his right hand to the back of his jeans. He might be reaching for his knife.

I flick the card at Ben, who catches it between two fingers. He looks down at it with a bemused expression.

'Your mama must be ever so proud,' he says, words full of sarcasm.

His two flunkies snicker, and I swallow my retort, not wanting to add fuel to the situation. My mother never approved of Ben, and the two never got along. In retrospect, I'll admit she was right, but I saw things differently back then.

'Didn't she want you to go to university?' Ben asks. '*That* was the plan, wasn't it?'

I hear the unspoken, 'That's why you left' clearly.

'Things change,' I mutter, then force a smile on my lips. 'It was nice seeing you again, Ben, but I have places to be.'

Ben's smile falters, and his expression darkens. 'You're not going to leave us so soon, are you? It's been a long time.'

'Not long enough,' I spit, my temper getting the better of me. I blow out a breath to regain control.

'Oh, that's the Italian side I was talking about. I've missed that,' Ben drawls, a pained expression that I easily discern to be faked blossoms on his face. 'You're not still mad at me because of Brandy, are you?'

The name reawakens an old rage, and it takes a real effort of will for me to keep the insults at bay. 'As I said,' I mutter, darkly, enunciating the words clearly, 'not long enough, Ben.'

The fake wounded expression stays on. 'It was just a fling, babydoll.'

I shudder at the nickname. It used to mean so much, but now, it only feels like alcohol spilled over an open wound. 'Just a fling?' I echo in a heated tone, losing my temper. 'You don't cheat on your pr—'

The wail of a nearby police car's siren interrupts me, and I see a patrol car drive by on the road in front of us. I idly wonder if they're part of the team Stenson has dispatched to bring back Stony Stu.

Jon and what's-his-name exchange uncomfortable glances, then both men turn their attention back to their leader.

'Boss?' Jon asks.

Ben seems to be debating what to do, and I wait anxiously for him to reach his decision.

A second police car passes by, driving more slowly this time. Definitely Stenson's team then. They must have stopped at Stu's building. People saw him run away and they saw me chase after him. The officers would have no choice but to call for backup and start a search party.

'They're here for the man I was looking for. The man I left in the field some fifty feet from where we stand. I'm sure he's still there.' I courteously inform Ben, and he turns a quick nervous glance at the field we can see in the distance, at the end of the alleyway. 'They'll be here, any minute now,' I add.

Ben turns back to his men, and with one nod of his head, they walk the casual walk back to the main street. I suppose my ex could be called many names, but I remember that "fool" certainly isn't one of them. That intelligence was something that had appealed to me — in the past.

Ben turns back to face me, and notices instantly that my right hand has returned to the inside of my jacket pocket, while he wasn't looking. He smiles sadly at the gesture. I shrug my shoulders nonchalantly, and the corner of his mouth twitches up.

'Still the Alexandra I remember.' He nods. 'It was good seeing you again.'

I can see on his face that he's weighing his options, and I tighten my fingers on the spray bottle. 'Wish I could say the same.'

With one last feral smile, Ben blows me a kiss, before turning his back on me. He hurries back to the main road, rounds the opposite corner behind the other two men, and disappears from sight.

I release a long shaky breath, and realise my legs are like cottonwool. I reach up my left arm and flatten the palm of my hand on the wall for support. Talk about the past catching up with you. I remain in the alleyway for several long minutes until I get my bearing back.

I'm still reeling from the encounter, as I slowly reach the main road, limping heavily. I call Stenson on my way to Hackney Central station. Just to let him know where exactly his men can find Stony Stu, *not* because leaving the E5 district while on the phone with a Detective Sergeant with the Metropolitan Police is reassuring, of course.

'What the hell was that?' the DS asks, by way of greeting.

'Well, hello to you too.' I say. 'What do you mean?'

'One of our patrol cars just found Stony Stu, near his place. They're taking him to the hospital, because some crazy girl apparently went commando on him — almost broke his arm and doused him in pepper-spray.'

'Oh, really?' I try to sound genuinely surprise, but I'm still too shaken to put on a good show. 'How did you find him so quickly?'

'Finding people is what *we* do, Alexandra.' He lets out a frustrated sigh. 'Interrogating them is also part of *our* job.'

I get the message loud and clear and drop the act. 'Is he going to press charges against his attacker?'

'No. He didn't get a good enough look at her, apparently.'

'That's too bad.' I'm not surprised. I doubt Stu wants to explain to the police why I came after him, that would be like signing a confession to the whole breaking and entering thing. 'Did he tell you anything interesting?'

Stenson sighs, heavily. 'I'm on my way to the hospital; haven't interrogated him yet, but I get a feeling you already know the answer to that question anyway.'

'Can't admit or deny knowing anything, Sergeant.' I say, in a kinder voice.

'Alex.' The tone is full of warning.

'I know. Be careful.' I smile; some of the tension ebbing away. 'Hypothetically speaking, if I'd gone after a guy like Stu, it would only have been because I knew I could get him without a hypothetical scratch.'

Stenson chuckles on the line, despite himself. When he seems to notice, he tries to cover it with a cough.

'Don't worry; I know how to handle myself against one guy,' I continue.

'Fine, fine. Did you hypothetically learn anything useful?'

'No, but it did help confirm the suppositions I had, so it wasn't all in vain.'

'My God, Alex. You have no idea the trouble you could have been in, if things had gone wrong.' Stenson sighs again, and I hear in the background a door shut loudly. 'Look, I'll do what I can to straighten things out — clean out the mess you hypothetically haven't created.'

'I'd be forever grateful, Sergeant.'

'Yeah, yeah. You owe me a drink,' he says, before hanging up.

I reach the Tube station without further incident, and my nerves only relax as the Overground train leaves the E5 district.

It's already the early afternoon, when I get back to Egan's flat. With Stu out of the way, I can move back to my own home, and I intend to do just that, after I've told my partner what I learned today.

The flat is empty when I enter, and I pack my bag, haphazardly throwing everything I brought along into my duffle bag and zipping the thing closed. Afterwards, I slump down in the kitchen, with a bottle of Coke, a pen and my sketchbook, and settle down for the long wait.

I prop up my right leg on a chair, place an ice bag on my throbbing knee, and grit my teeth as the cold slowly seeps through the clenched muscles.

As night slowly falls over London, I sketch out the scene from Leicester Square, with Egan sitting on a bench on a fine August day. I finish the drawing about two hours later. The ice bag has gone from icy to lukewarm, the Coke bottle is empty, and my partner is still a no-show.

Leaving my sketchbook on the kitchen table, I stand up and walk back to the living room. I'm still limping but only slightly now and thankfully, the pain has diminished. It should have completely disappeared by the morning. I reach for the bag I've left on the couch and return it to its usual place under the shelf. What's one more night away from home, eh?

I turn on the main light, and return to my sketchbook to start to draw something else. I sketch the silhouette of an old man, his shoulders hunched under the weight of years. He stands in a dimly lit alley-way, next to an expensive car. He has a thick envelope in his extended hand. In front of him, Stony Stu eagerly reaches forward to grab the cash. I sigh, wishing I could draw the details of this stranger's face.

Egan walks in sometime after eleven. He moves about slowly, careful not to make a sound.

I look up, from the kitchen, as I drop my pencil. 'There's no need for you to play cat burglar, I'm not asleep.'

He freezes near the settee, looking like a child who's just been caught with his hand in the biscuit tin. On any other day, I would have found the scene amusing, but I know only too well why he feels guilty, and I'm in no mood to address this particular issue right now.

'Want to know what I found out?' I ask, coming to stand by the low wall that separates the kitchen and the living room.

Egan drops his keys, phone and glasses in the bowls carefully spaced out along the low wall. 'Sure.'

I start with a recap of the conversation I had with Angela's grandfather and the conclusions I made.

'You think Mrs Levantiner had a lover?' Egan asks.

'Sounds plausible.'

'And he would have given her the necklace?' His lips contort in a dubious twist.

'Why not. Wouldn't you offer a very special piece of jewellery to a woman you love?'

'Sure.' He shrugs. 'I just don't think she would wear it publicly; certainly not at such an event.'

'Oh, Ash — you really don't know anything about women.' I chuckle. '"What? Oh this necklace; it's gorgeous isn't it? I inherited it from my grand-mother… oh, yes it's real diamonds and rubies — worth a fortune, or so I was told,"' I declare with a higher-pitched voice, and a snobbish drawl. 'Trust me, Ash. If a woman owns such a beautiful necklace, she's going to show it off.'

He smiles at the impersonation. 'If you say so.'

He moves to the kitchen and returns with a glass of water for each of us. 'Any idea who could have given her the necklace?'

'None, but if this man's still alive, he's just taken the number one spot on our list of suspects.'

Egan nods his agreement.

'Something else's happened, today,' I tell him, sitting down on the settee.

'Has it anything to do with the fact you're limping?' he asks.

My mouth opens up in surprise, the word, 'How…?' the question comes to my lips instinctively. And then my brain manages to win the race with my vocal chords and the question remains muted. My friend is so attuned to my walking pattern; he's heard the difference as clearly as if he'd seen me.

'Sort of,' I reply.

Egan walks to his chair and sits down. I tell him about my

meeting with Stony Stu and relate his story of the man who hired him to vandalise my flat. I tell him of the running I had to do, and the little girl who bargained for the information necessary to find him. I leave out the part about the *Fivers* and running into my ex and almost getting killed in a dark alley.

He listens intently, without interrupting me once. I can see on his face that my words don't fool him. I suppose he wouldn't be good at this job if he couldn't spot a lie from a mile away, even when it's covered in half-truths. He knows I'm keeping something from him, it's plain to see. He doesn't even try to hide it, which, I take it, is an invitation for me to come clean.

Telling him what happened today is no big deal, but sharing what happened four years ago is. I remain silent, as I search for a compromise.

'It was risky of you to go alone,' Egan says at last, when the silence stretches.

Isn't it always. 'I can handle myself, Ash. You know it.'

'Why?' He scoffs. 'Because you've taken a few martial art classes and you're walking around with pepper spray?'

I frown at his words. 'How…'

'You still have some of it on your clothes, that thing makes my nose itch.'

'Sorry. I had to use it on Stu; he's not going to see very clearly for a little while.'

Egan sits a little straighter and leans forward a little. 'Lexa, I'm not foolish enough to think I could have been of help to you there.

I'd only have stood in your way, I know that, but—'

'Ash, it's—'

'Don't,' he interrupts me. 'It's the truth, and we both know it. I can't protect you, not in the field. But—' he pauses, for emphasis '— if you can't take me with you, at the very least, you can let me know where you are going.

'Just in case things go wrong, Lexa.' He swallows thickly. 'If you hadn't come back today, I wouldn't have known where to start looking for you.'

His reproachful and hurt tone cuts deep and makes me feel like a child. He's right. We both know it.

'I'm sorry, Ash. I truly am.' I don't have to make an effort to sound genuinely contrite. 'It won't happen again, I promise.

'Stu's a low-level crook, but he was dragged up in a bad neighbourhood. I was ruffled up a bit, and my knee took the brunt of it, but I'll be as good as new by tomorrow morning.'

With a nod, Egan leans against the back of his chair again, apparently satisfied with the explanation.

'An old man, you said,' he says, scratching his chin, after a short moment of silence. 'Do you think it could be Anna Levantiner's lover?'

'Well, if he was in his twenties back then — that would make him ninety-something today. Fits the description of an old man with a German accent that Stu gave me.'

'We need to find the thief. He's the only link left to this man.'

'Any idea how we could do that?' I ask. 'Should I try *hire a thief.com*, or something?'

Egan grimaces. 'I may have an idea, but you're really not going to like it.'

17

'You're right,' I say. 'I don't like it.'

Egan makes a good show of rolling his eyes, while shaking his head a little.

I still have to find an audible equivalent of crossing one's arms over one's chest and settle for one long, loud exhalation. 'It's a bad idea,' I say, sternly.

'It's not. Dimitri knows a lot of people, and he can, at the very least, steer us in the right direction.'

I sigh. Dimitri… your friendly go-to Russian guy for info of a dubious nature.

He's an old acquaintance of Egan, and a mobster? Arms dealer? War criminal? Gosh, I have no idea what he is. I've settled on defining him as a sturdy soldier-of-fortune type of person — might be dangerous, best stay away. I don't know what his business is, except that it necessitates Dimitri walking around town flanked by two armed bodyguards.

When we were investigating the Russian Mafia earlier this year, he was quite helpful in explaining to us how they operate. I chose not to be too picky, because that investigation was about Irina; because knowing who had killed my best friend was more important than anything else. This time though, I won't turn a blind eye to the man's secrets. I don't like not knowing much about characters I'm working with as, it makes for just too many unknown variables.

'Alright,' I mutter, 'who is he, really?'

Egan grimaces, not saying anything for an instant. 'A... *friend*.'

The way he says the word is so full of doubt, I don't even need to call him out on his lie. I do it anyway.

'Not good enough, Ashford.' I scold him. 'If we're going to be in any immediate danger just by being near him, I need to know about it.' I steel my tone. 'If I want to have even a fighting chance of protecting us, I have to know what to be on the lookout for.'

'You always over-dramatise things.'

'Oh do I?' I notice the volume control on my voice is going up, but I don't care. 'You two didn't really strike me as best mates the last time I saw you together. You were on your guard the whole time. So, I'll ask you again: who is he?'

Egan keeps his lips tightly pressed together, and the silence stretches out, only disturbed by a dog barking somewhere in the distance.

'Fine.' Finally he relents, drawing in a quick exasperated breath. 'He's in the import/export business.'

'Keep going,' I say, in a slow drawl.

'The not always very legal type of import/export business.' Egan smiles somewhat coyly. 'He can get you some excellent top grade caviar, for a really low price.'

'Something tells me that he also imports things a little bit stronger than fish eggs.'

Egan nods, reluctantly. 'I don't really know what he's in, alright?'

He waves a hand left and right. 'Whatever sells, I guess. I never asked, and Dimitri never told me.

'And yes, he's a criminal, and he's certainly done a lot of things that we're better off not knowing about. What matters is he knows a lot of people — he has ears in a lot of places.'

I shake my head. Damn it! I knew the guy was crooked the minute I saw him. 'So where do you fit in with all this?'

'I...' he starts, hesitantly.

'And don't feed me that crap about you saving his skin, like you did last time I asked.' I voluntarily let my tone grow darker, the vocal version of a hard stare, 'I want the whole story and I want it now.'

He purses his lips in evident displeasure. 'Lexa, I —'

I stop him with a cold voice. 'Not this time, Ash. I know there are a lot of things you don't want to share with me. That's your right, and I respect it, but *this* is different.' I take in a breath. 'When hired-guns are involved, I get to call the shots. For our own safety, both yours and mine, I need to know the whole story.'

Egan leans back in his chair, arms crossed over his chest. He fixes me with a raised eyebrow, or rather, he fixes the cushion to the left of me, but I get the point.

'What?' I ask.

'You tell me yours and I'll tell you mine,' he says, his eyebrow still silently challenging me. 'I want to know what happened this afternoon.'

I swallow. 'Nothing with any relevance to our case.'

'Oh, but I beg to differ. If you ran into some old acquaintances and this might prove a risk to *our safety*,' he makes a point of accentuating the last two words, 'I think I have a right to know.'

Touché! I close my eyes, as I inwardly curse him. Egan knows I grew up in Hackney, and he knows I haven't been back there in months. The first time I do, I start to withhold information from him — no need to be a genius to understand the logic of what's happening here. Still, I take a few moments to ponder his words.

Is there a risk? Could my recent run-in with my ex, a local gang-lord prove dangerous to us at any point in the future? I sincerely doubt it, but… as the saying goes: "better safe than sorry." I curse again, aloud this time.

'I ran into my ex this afternoon. I dumped him four years ago. I started university shortly afterwards, and never saw him again, until today.' I stand up, take a few steps towards the window, as I decide how to continue, and, more importantly, how much to divulge.

'Ben was in a gang back then. The *Fivers* they're called. Nothing major league, but a gang none the less. They're stealing stuff, trafficking drugs…'

Egan does little to hide the surprise my words cause him, and it shows plainly on his face.

I walk back to the settee, stand awkwardly next to it, with my arms folded over my chest.

'Ben got… promoted, since then. He runs the gang now.' I swallow, as I'm forced to face the truth of my tale. 'He cornered me in some dark alley. He was flanked by two other gang members and it got really tense.

'Police cars drove past us, and it sent Ben and his monkeys skittering away. I— I'm not sure what would have happened if they hadn't interrupted.'

Telling the tale aloud reawakens the fear I felt, and I sit back down with tears prickling at the corners of my eyes. I force myself to fight them off. 'When we were together, it was really intense and serious, but we didn't part on good terms, and Ben has a violent, darker side.'

Egan leans a little closer to me and turns up one palm in an open invitation. I reach out, and clasp my hand around his.

'Do you think he might be coming after you?' he asks.

'I doubt it. I didn't matter to him, as he did to me. It was just the lack of control over everything that got to him, back then.' I swallow, painful memories coming back in spades. 'I'm certain he's replaced me with some girl named Jenny or Mindy, or something, by now.

'So long as I keep off his turf, it should be fine. He has much more important things to worry about than some ex-girlfriend. At least now, if I ever have to go back to the E5 district, I know what to look out for. He won't surprise me twice.'

Egan nods, and squeezes my hand once, gently. 'Are you alright?' he asks, with obvious concern.

I squeeze his hand back. 'I'll be fine, I just… I wasn't expecting to run into him like that. It… it reopened old wounds.'

'I'm sorry.'

'So am I. Ben was a mistake,' I admit, in a rare moment of honesty. It was a foolish relationship. 'I was a lost teenager, without a father figure, who didn't know any better. He was a dangerous man, always on the margins of society. I was attracted to him like a helpless moth is attracted to a flame.'

I feel a lone tear run down the length of my face. 'I paid the price for my stupidity. I'll regret it for the rest of my life.'

I let go of Egan's hand, feeling my stomach churn. I wrap my arms around myself uselessly, knowing full well that any pains are psychosomatic, the phantom ache of a wound long healed, but unforgettable. Some scars never disappear.

Egan clears his throat, before leaning forward, his forearms resting on his thighs.

'I was in Moscow, when I met Dimitri. On holiday, to hear the Moscow Philharmonic Orchestra conducted by Mark Ermler.' He starts, sharing his tale now that I've told him mine.

I look up to him, sorry that he cannot see the grateful look on my face. He kept his word, and more importantly didn't ask me for the rest of the story.

'That man had a unique way with ballets,' he continues. 'How he conducted Tchaikovsky's... it was magical.'

Egan loves Operas, but that's not really my thing. He's tried to get me interested several times, to no avail. I know next to nothing about it, but this one name does sound familiar. 'Tchaikovsky... that's the guy who did Swan Lake, isn't it?'

'Yes,' Egan says, and it's a patient, patronising "yes", not an I'm-proud-of-you-for-knowing-that kind of yes. 'You kids — nowadays, you only know about things, if there's been a movie.'

'So, anyway,' I say, in my best *moving on* voice.

'Yes, yes. I was in Moscow, sitting at a terrace, and then this man comes and sits at my table.'

'Was that Dimitri?' I ask; curiosity piqued.

Egan frowns at me. 'Do you want me to tell you the story or not?'

'Alright, alright, I'll shut up.'

'So, a man sits in front of me,' he continues. 'He was panting heavily, like he'd just run to near exhaustion.

'"Talk to me," he said to me then. He meant for it to sound like an order, but I could hear the fear and the panic behind his tone.

'"What about?" I asked him calmly, and I think it caught him off guard somewhat.

'"Anything man, just talk to me. Like we're some old friends."

'"Okay," I said. "But only if you tell me who you're running from." I could feel he was very nervous. I guessed that people must be looking for him and they were probably drawing closer.

'"I'm just someone who likes to chat up strangers," he said to me, in an attempted humorous tone.

'I turned my head in the direction of his voice, scowled at him as best as I could, as I said, "No, you're a man afraid for his life. You're scared that whoever is after you will find you."

'That threw him off guard a little, and time was running out. He chose to tell me his story. He told how he'd been framed by his rivals, for a murder he didn't commit. He told me how he was not in *his* territory and he had no friends nearby. He told me how the cops were after him. "Do you know what they'll do to me, if they find me?" he asked me. "Do you know what prisons are like in Russia?"

'I didn't, but I could surmise,' Egan says, with a sour expression.

'So you helped him,' I understand, and I bet the excitement is audible in my voice.

He tsks me. 'Will you let me tell the story?'

'Sorry,' I mutter.

'Yes, I helped him. I told him to grab an empty glass from a nearby table if he could; I told him my name, and where I was from. We started to talk, and I urged him to relax.

'Some police officers arrived a little later. They said they were looking for a man. They only had a vague description, but it was a match for Dimitri's looks.

'"It can't be him, officers," I said. "My friend's been with me all day. I'm visiting your city, and I've hired him as a guide."

'Then I stood up and unfolded my cane. Dimitri — much to his credit — was quick to swallow his surprise. He moved diligently to my side, as an aid would.

'"I assure you," I told the bemused officers, "that I wouldn't have made it very far in your city, without his help."

'"Just doing my job, Sir," Dimitri piped in, with false modesty.

'The cops bought the story, apologised, wished me a nice stay in Moscow, and left,' Egan finishes.

I let out an amused chortle of breath. 'I can't believe it. You pulled the blind card out on them. You — and to save some guy you barely just met.'

'What can I say,' he shrugs, 'it had been a really boring holiday.'

'Unbelievable,' I quip, then a thought hits me. 'You could have been arrested. In Russia. And thrown in jail. In Russia!'

'I know, I know,' he flaps a hand about. 'I was a whole lot younger then.'

'And a whole lot more stupid,' I mutter.

'Anyway, the very next day, I got to experience Tchaikovsky from a VIP balcony seat, courtesy of Dimitri who knew someone who knew someone.' He looks contemplative for a second. 'The acoustics were just perfect.'

'I'm surprised you two kept in touch, after you returned to the UK.'

Egan shakes his head negatively. 'We didn't at first. Dimitri only moved to London a few years later. One day, I came home, stumbled over something and almost fell flat on my face; someone had left a basket outside my door.'

'Dimitri?'

'The best caviar I ever tasted in my life.' He sighs. 'And a note — in Braille, none the less — to let me know he was in town. It was his way of paying his debt, I suppose.'

'Have you seen him much since then?' I ask, curious to know the answer.

'Not really. I did thank him in person for the caviar, but I don't make a habit of hanging out with…'

He lets the sentence hang, and I finish it for him. 'Criminals?'

'Anyone,' he corrects.

I scowl at the word, but of course he doesn't see it.

'I contacted him once or twice since, to procure some rare products, at lesser prices than those of the market, but that's the extent of our relationship. The last time I met him, well... you already know all about it. End of the story.'

I let the tale sink in. I know Egan enough to discern when he's lying to me, and he wasn't when he recounted this story. It was the truth, or at least something close enough to pass as the truth. I wouldn't be surprised to find he'd carefully edited out some details, just as I had with my story. Nevertheless, on the whole, it was true. 'That's quite a story.'

He angles his head to the side, his brows drawing closer again. 'Is something bothering you, dear?'

'Are you sure he was innocent? I mean no disrespect, but I've met Dimitri, and—' I let out a long breath '—he frightened me.'

'He was,' Egan assures me. 'He was really scared, but the anger when he told me he'd been framed was genuine.'

I heave a sigh. 'Alright then, let's say I believe you. I'm not sure if that story makes me feel more or less wary of him. He may not have killed that man, but... how well do you really know him?'

Egan straightens his back a little. 'He's done me a few favours over the years. Dimitri may be working on the other side of the line, but he won't hurt us.'

'How can you be sure? And don't tell me you've heard it in his voice.'

He grimaces at my words.

I mutter a quick, 'Sorry,' at the uncalled for jibe.

'I know it,' he says, with assurance, 'because I've known him longer than you have. He may not follow the same rules that we do, but he's not a savage. He has a moral code of his own. As long as we pose no threat to him or his business, he'll be of no danger to us. You just have to be cautious of what you say or do — keep it courteous, humour him in his eccentricities and we'll be fine.'

I consider the thought an instant and weigh our options.

'Fine.' I swallow and nod. 'You win. You can call him.'

18

Egan calls Dimitri first thing Friday morning, and sets up an appointment for eleven o'clock.

The last time we crossed paths with this Russian character, it had been in a small bar in Chinatown. This time, the meeting has been set up in some fancy hotel, near Heathrow Airport.

We start by taking the Tube and then get a bus to the selected hotel, and arrive just before eleven.

'Dimitri said he'll be in the Ballroom,' Egan tells me, as we enter the huge hotel.

We cross the long lobby, pass by a large decorative fountain. I spot a large noticeboard with a map of the hotel. The "You are here" marker shows us correctly to be near the main staircase. I search for the ballroom. The hotel really is enormous, and it takes me a while to find it.

'It's up on the second floor,' I say, moving towards the stairs and Egan follows me.

'What is this?' my friend asks, on the second step. 'Stone, marble?'

I look down at my feet. 'Looks like marble, yeah. Why?'

'It just doesn't sound like your usual footsteps.' He smiles. 'Posh hotel, then?'

'There's a massive crystal chandelier hanging over the reception area,' I describe the scene for him. 'Renaissance paintings on the walls, and small candles on every single step of the staircase. So yes, I'd say *very posh*.' I spare a thought for the poor employee who must spend an hour every day lighting all those damn candles… seriously, what's the point?

'Don't let me walk into them,' Egan says, half-joking.

'I'll try my best,' I joke back. As we started to ascend the stairs, I stayed between him and the candles to keep him as far as possible from the flames.

Once on the second floor, we turn left, follow a long carpeted corridor (with even more candles), and finally come upon the Ballroom.

The sight of it simply takes my breath away. 'Well, I guess they named this one the Ballroom for a reason,' I say, stunned.

'This room has to be three times the size of my flat, the floor is made of a sort of rosy marble that sparkles here and there, and there are tall white ornate columns every ten feet or so on each side.' I explain to Egan. 'There's room for an orchestra, on the far side, and several tables at the back. The rest is empty space, presumably to welcome dancers.'

Egan nods. 'A ballroom indeed.'

I look around for Dimitri, or one of his goons, but only find waiters, setting up the tables. I look at my watch again — five to eleven — and we go right into the room.

We haven't taken five steps when a loud voice booms out from behind us.

'Alexandra, Ashford!' We stop walking and turn around. 'So good to see you, my friends.'

'Good to—' I force myself to stifle a laugh '—see you too.'

From the corner of my eye, I see Egan raise a curious eyebrow.

'You're missing out on something amazing, partner,' I mutter, almost inaudibly.

Dimitri — whom I had last seen in a duffle jacket and cargo trousers — is dressed in a smart navy-blue pinstripe suit, complete with those black-and-white shoes that were trendy in the American fifties. On his short, bulky frame the whole thing looks... wrong. Unfortunately, there's no better word for it. Just plain wrong.

'Alexandra,' he reaches forward, grabs me by the shoulders and kisses me on both cheeks. 'Always as lovely as the sun.'

I freeze uncomfortably, but let him greet me, in the traditional Russian fashion. A quick peck on the cheeks does beat the big, languid paw that landed on my thigh the last time we met.

He shakes hands with Egan, and grabs him by the shoulders to steer him to one side of the room, near the empty orchestra seats. I follow them cautiously.

'So what is it you wanted to ask me, old dog?' the Russian asks, coming to a stop near the conductor's stand.

'Alexandra?' Egan asks, with a minimal upward movement of his hand. 'Do you have one of our fine embossed business cards for Dimitri?'

I take a step forward and take his forearm, having recognised the hand gesture as a silent plea to know where I am. I reach into my jeans pocket with my free hand and take out one of our cards.

Egan gives me a discreet nod of thanks and I pat his forearm once, to let him know I understood the message.

Dimitri, who hasn't noticed any of our non-verbal communication, looks down at the card I hand to him. A rich laugh escapes him, an instant later.

'I didn't see that one coming,' the Russian says, continuing to smile broadly.

He looks again at the card, and places it in the breast pocket of his horrible suit.

'Nor did I,' Egan replies, with a cold tone.

Dimitri's starts laughing again at these words, which he interprets as a joke. It brings tears to his eyes and he dabs at them with his pinstriped pocket square.

Reminding myself why we're here, I force a smile onto my lips. 'We're looking for someone and we thought you might be able to help.'

The words seem to sober Dimitri up immediately. 'Oh, you're not involved with the Russian Mafia again, are you? I told you they're bad news.'

'No, we're looking for a thief,' I explain. 'He stole a necklace a little while ago — rubies and diamond — from one Mrs Hargrave, here in Greenford.

'We're looking for the man who actually commissioned the theft. He must be a very old man by now, originally from Germany, but established in the UK for a while now.'

'Very interesting,' the Russian says, 'and you're telling me this because…'

'I know you have ears and eyes everywhere, Dimitri,' Egan cuts in. 'We thought you might have heard something.'

'Ah, indeed,' the Russian drawls. 'Information is gold, you know that. It's essential to keep in touch with what is going on.'

'Of course.' Egan notes, with only veiled contempt.

'And assuming I have heard of anything, why should I tell you?' Dimitri asks.

'We're friends,' Egan says, and I cringe inwardly at the contempt again.

'Friends or no friends,' Dimitri continues, still with enthusiasm, 'information is—

'Gold, yes,' Egan cuts in. 'I heard you the first time.'

I notice a man enter the room, from a side door and move towards us — tall, dark hair, icy blue eyes. He's dressed in a suit, an elegant yet average suit, that wouldn't stand out in a crowd. I recognise him instantly: one of Dimitri's bodyguard.

Here come the big guns, I think and tighten my grip on Egan's arm a fraction — a silent warning to be careful.

'I saved your life,' my friend reminds Dimitri.

'And I helped you with your last case,' the Russian retorts. 'You can cash in on old favours only so many times.'

The bodyguard stops a few feet away on our left, his right hand hovering near his hip, where I know he keeps his weapon. Our gazes meet and I can read in his eyes he that he hasn't forgotten me. I clench my jaw; look at his hip pointedly, to let him know I remember him too. The hand draws imperceptibly closer to the lapel of his jacket. My free hand moves to the strap of my shoulder bag, all but ready to send the bag at him as a distraction should need arise. The corner of his mouth rises in amusement.

'Alright,' I say, turning back to Dimitri, but still watching the bodyguard out of the corner of my eye. 'What is your price for the information we want?'

Dimitri smiles at me, all teeth, and takes on the appearance of a shark. 'I don't know who stole what you're after, but I could ask some friends for their ideas on the subject.'

'How much?' I ask again. I'm sounding resigned and tired.

The smile grows bigger, and I realise it's turning almost lustful. A cold chill runs down my spine in response. Dimitri reaches a hand forward.

'This is a ballroom,' he tells me, 'we dance in it.'

What the hell? I freeze and swallow nervously. I can feel Egan tense next to me.

'Would love to, but it looks like the orchestra's on strike,' I say, with false cheer, and a nod to where the orchestra should be.

'Thomas!' Dimitri snaps his finger, and the bodyguard disappears from sight. Only a few heartbeats later, classical music echoes around the enormous empty space.

'Hidden speakers,' I curse inwardly and glare at the door the bodyguard has just disappeared through. 'How very twenty-first century.'

'This is ridiculous,' Egan mutters. 'Dimitri, we're here to do business, not take part in whatever fantasy you have — name a price, and let's be done with it.'

The Russian takes a heavy gliding step backwards, his hand still extended to me. 'I named my price Ashford—' he bows to me '—a dance, with your gorgeous partner.'

I take a step forward, but Egan halts me, restraining me with his arm.

'Lexa,' he rushes out, in a half-voice. 'You don't have to; we can get the information some other way.'

'It's alright.' I use the same hushed tone. 'If he can help us, it's a bargain.'

Honestly, it is. Of course, I know I will probably come to regret this decision, one way or another, but I don't know what we'd have done if Dimitri's price had been a thousand pounds, or ten thousand pounds, or more.

Egan's grip tightens on my arm. I cover his hand with mine and squeeze it once. His lips are pressed into a thin line as he lets go of me.

I force a rigid smile onto my lips in a rather poor imitation of those competing Strictly Ballroom couples on the telly, and take a tense step forward to accept the offered hand. Dimitri bows once more, and I come to stand in front of him.

The music is all around us, some kind of old-fashioned waltz, I think. I'm sure Egan would know the title; it's a bit like the kind of soporific opera music he likes to listen to.

I hesitantly place my free hand on Dimitri's shoulder and he places his in the small of my back. I have to make an effort to keep my fake smile in place. My dance partner takes one step backwards and I follow, rigidly.

I've never learned to dance, much less waltz. I seem to recall something about the man leading and the woman following. I concentrate on doing just that. I look down, every now and then, to make sure my feet are going in the right direction.

Predictably, Dimitri's hand doesn't take long to move south.

'This is business,' I remind him, in a cold voice, though my smile stays plastered on. 'A dance was all I agreed to.'

'Oh Alexandra, you weren't this cold the last time, we met. You were all flames: a burning temptation.' The Russian chuckles, but his hand stops. 'Ashford is rubbing off on you, isn't he?'

'Do you think you can find who the thief is?' I demand, instead of replying.

'I can ask around.' He nods to me. 'I'll call you, if I hear something.'

Dimitri glides to the left in one swift-yet-graceless move and I have to take several mini-steps to catch up with him.

My God, I can't imagine what we must look like — him in his stupid pinstripe suit and vintage shoes, and me dressed in a pair of faded old blue-jeans, a white shirt and white Converse trainers — doing what must be the worst waltz this fancy ballroom has ever seen.

Dimitri abruptly spins me round. My left foot goes right, the right goes left, and I lose balance and almost topple to the ground. The Russian takes advantage of my momentary loss of equilibrium to pull me close to his chest. What I feel, as my leg brushes against his crotch, makes my smile completely disappear.

I try to straighten up and step back, but he uses his superior strength to hold me in place. The smile on his face becomes predatory and almost feral. I am scared and swallow nervously.

'I have a knife in my pocket,' I tell him, with the coldest, most determined voice I can muster. 'I'd hate to have to dirty it with your blood.'

Dimitri's hold loosens slightly and I manage to take a firm step backwards. His hand finds its way upwards to the small of my back again, and we resume dancing.

I'm almost certain he can hear my teeth grinding even over the music, and I wonder how much longer this charade will last.

'I knew it,' Dimitri smiles at me again. 'You're still the wild animal you always were.'

'You don't know anything about me,' I spit, following his steps all the more rigidly.

We dance a little more and the piece finally ends. I move away from Dimitri the second the music dies.

'Thank you, my dear,' he says, in a sugary voice, as he follows me back, 'for making an old man feel young again.'

Egan's been waiting with a cold mask hiding all traces of emotion on his face. I thank God that he hasn't been able to watch any of my unpleasant experience. The bodyguard, Thomas, is waiting next to him, with a horrible smirk at the corner of his lips. I give him a dark glare, and take Egan's arm.

'I believe our business is concluded,' I say, turning back to Dimitri. 'You have our card; please call us when you know something.'

That said, we take our leave.

I'm just so relieved as I step through the large revolving door into the fresh air on the pavement. I stretch my arms and face up to the sun, revelling in my freedom.

'I'm terribly sorry,' Egan says once we're outside. 'You were right — it wasn't a particularly bright idea.'

'It's fine.' I try to swallow my anger and think of our case, and the big leap forward the thief's name would mean. I guess that's what people call *taking one for the team.*

'If he can turn up something for us, it won't have been for nothing.' I blow out a breath. 'And it was just a dance, anyway.'

'Uh huh,' says Egan, unconvinced.

'Alright,' I raise a hand to massage my tense neck, and force myself to relax. 'I feel like taking a shower and wish I could delete the last hour from my mind, but I'll live.'

He draws me closer to him, snakes an arm around my shoulders.

'Sorry,' he murmurs, before planting a soft kiss on my cheek.

'Tell you what,' I say, sneaking my arm around his waist, and leaning against him. 'Next time, you can be the one to dance with him, yeah?'

Egan chuckles as we walk back to the bus stop.

Sometime around four, that afternoon, Dimitri calls us. If I had known it was him, I'd have let Egan pick up the phone. Damn that unknown caller ID.

'Alexandra, my little white swan,' he says. The tone makes me feel like throwing up. 'How are you?'

'Fine, do you have a name for us?' I stand up and walk down the corridor that leads to Egan's bedroom.

'Business, business.' Dimitri, chuckles. 'You need to fit in a little bit of pleasure, sometimes. Nights are too lonely otherwise.'

I knock on Egan's door, and push it open. 'A name, Dimitri. Do you have one or not?'

Egan, who is sitting at his desk, turns towards the door at my appearance.

'Yes, I have one. It wasn't easy, but those thieves… they brag about their jobs, all the time. Of course, you need to have ears in the right places, you see.'

I sigh. 'A name, Dimitri.'

'Nimra. Arturo Nimra. Don't know who hired him though,' he says.

'Do you know where we can find him?'

'I'm afraid this information would require… further payment,' Dimitri says, languidly. 'If you're available tonight, we could discuss terms…'

My stomach heaves at the mental image his words conjure up. 'That won't be necessary, we'll take it from here. It was a pleasure doing business with you,' I say.

I hope he can hear the sarcasm in my voice. Egan certainly did, judging by his half smile.

'Pleasure was all mine,' Dimitri says, before hanging up.

I pocket the phone, and lean against the wall.

'He gave us a name?' Egan asks.

'Arturo Nimra.'

'Is he certain, it's the right guy?'

'I guess we'll know the answer to that when we find him.'

I take my phone out again, and text the name to DS Lingby — she can do the legwork.

My phone chirps with a text, late in the evening. I straighten up on the settee and fish it out of my pocket. 'It's from Lingby,' I say opening it up.

Egan lowers the book he's reading with the tips of his fingers, and redirects his attention to me.

'Nimra's a match to the guy I drew. She says she's on her way now with a team to apprehend him.'

19

Falling asleep after DS Lingby's text had not been easy. In fact it was almost impossible; to say that I was giddy with excitement might have been the understatement of the century.

If the Metropolitan Police had the thief, the case was closed. If he still had it, he'd hand over the necklace or else he would grass up whoever he'd given it to, in the hope of a lighter sentence.

I knew that, in just a few hours, Egan and I would get a call to let us know the Met had found the jewel. We would return it to Mrs Hargrave pronto, along with a bouquet of brightly coloured flowers to liven up her hospital room. She would pay us what she owes us — two weeks' worth of work, several international phone calls, some going back and forth through the city and a bucket of white paint — and the *Neve & Egan Agency* would be richer by one thousand three hundred pounds and some small change.

Egan and I would probably go to the bank right away. We'd drop the money onto our account, retaining only a tenner to buy our traditional victory treat from the little ice-cream shop two buildings down from the bank. Another case closed.

Lingby's call never came and my dreams of ice cream had flown out of the window the next morning. I should know by now things rarely — if ever — go according to plan.

When the waiting was finally too much for my nerves, at about one fifteen in the afternoon, I dial the sergeant's mobile number.

'Martha Lingby,' she replies. Her voice is strained on the phone and I wonder if she managed to snatch any sleep at all last night.

'It's Alexandra Neve,' I say, 'We… we were waiting to hear from you, still are actually. Did something go wrong?'

There's the sound of a commotion in the background. A rustling of cloth, a muffled "humph". Has Lingby bumped into someone? I strain to make out the noises. I'm sure that if Egan had been listening, he could easily have told me what was happening on the other end of the phone.

'I really can't talk right now,' Lingby says, eventually. 'Something went wrong, it's… it's complicated.'

'What went wrong? What do you mean?' I ask, urgently.

'I can't tell you over the phone.' There's a pause, and I hear the tapping of high heel shoes on concrete. 'Can we meet somewhere?'

I glance down at my wristwatch. Egan's in the shower, but we should be able to get going within fifteen minutes. 'We could come to your office, two o'clock?'

'Somewhere that is not the Arts and Antiques unit's office,' she corrects.

'Well… there's this bar we use, not far from our office. *Luigi*'s, on Camden Street?'

'Fine. One hour,' she says, hanging up quickly.

I'm lacing my red Converse trainers, when Egan enters the living room with his hair still wet.

'I just got off the phone with Lingby,' I tell him.

He pauses near his chair, waiting for the rest of the explanation.

'She didn't want to go into details over the phone, but something went wrong.'

Egan quirks up a surprised eyebrow.

'We're going to meet her at *Luigi's* in an hour.'

'I'll be ready in a minute,' he says, turning on his heel.

I watch him disappear down the corridor in a pair of black jeans and a light-grey T-Shirt. He re-enters the living room less than five minutes later, with his hair neatly arranged, and a grey turtleneck pullover on. I smirk at the sight of him. "Predictable as night an' day," as his Irish ancestors would say.

He reaches for his glasses, wallet, and phone, and comes to stand near me, palm extended and turned upward. 'Lead the way,' he says, with a smile.

We reach *Luigi's* a while later, and it's a relief to get out of the stuffy afternoon streets, and into an air-conditioned room.

'We're here on business, Luigi' I tell the Italian barista, as I pass him by, heading for the tables furthest from the door.

He nods his understanding, rearranges his red and white apron and stands a little straighter before quickly scanning the bar and taking note of all the customers present.

Egan and I sit down at our usual table, and, a minute later, Luigi comes to take our order himself.

'The usual?' he asks, and we both nod.

Luigi writes down the order on his notepad, purely for form, while he leans in closer to murmur, 'I scanned the place — two

French tourists, and some of the usual clientele — nothing suspect. You're good.'

I fight a smile, thinking that for all his good intentions, Luigi could spot an undercover cop or someone with less amiable motives, and give them a serious approving nod.

Pleased with himself, the barista turns his back to us, takes two steps away and carefully places one of the folding screens to hide our table from the rest of the room. He's clearly a man on a mission. I doubt he would take an order from her Majesty herself any less seriously.

Ever since I caught one of Luigi's employees stealing money from the till, he has held Egan and I in high esteem. He takes a great pride in knowing that real private investigators chose his modest bar as a place for their highly secretive business. His interpretation of the situation is a little over the top, and it makes me wonder if he hasn't seen one too many detective films, but he makes the best Macchiato in London so I'm not going to be the one who enlightens him.

Detective Sergeant Martha Lingby arrives a few minutes before the appointed time, and Luigi diligently directs her to us. When I catch sight of the brunette woman, my wondering about how many hours of sleep she's had comes to an end: none. She has dark circles under her eyes, her spikey hair is more dishevelled than ever and her blouse is heavily creased.

'Long night?' I ask, as she sits down.

'Yeah.' She forces her heavy lashes to open wider, and tries to stand a little straighter.

'Is this your idea of "a secure place where we can talk"? she asks, nodding at the folding screen.

'We're working on a budget,' Egan replies, with all the condescending contempt he's capable of.

'What happened?' I ask, forcefully changing the topic. 'You found the man?'

'We did.' She takes a sip of the extra-large coffee she'd ordered at the bar, before coming over to our table. 'He wasn't in our database, but I and some of the guys hit the streets with your portrait. I showed it to some people I know in the art business but none of my narks recognised him. Of course that changed once you provided us with his name.'

She narrows her eyes at me, suspicion evident in both her gaze and her tone. 'However you managed to acquire it…'

'A little bird whispered it to me,' I suggest.

'Anyway,' she flaps a tired hand about, 'that allowed us to get his address.'

'So what went wrong?' asks Egan.

Lingby turns a querying look his way.

'She's looking at you with an intrigued expression,' I tell my partner.

'It's in your voice, Detective,' he explains. 'You sound upset and frustrated — gets me thinking that something must have gone wrong.'

The sergeant smiles at him briefly, before saying, 'Our suspect, Arturo Nimra, is dead.'

My shoulders slump at the words. 'What on earth happened? Did you lot kill him?'

I see Egan sit up straighter.

'He was living in some vacant factory, near the river — former dockland, turned into over-priced lofts. The place was already on fire when we arrived.

'It took a while for the fire-fighters to secure the zone and we were only allowed to enter mid-morning. We found Nimra — or rather what was left of him — with a bullet in the chest and one in the head.'

'Are you sure it was him?' I ask.

'We're running the DNA as we speak, but the height and weight was a match. Neighbours say they haven't seen or heard anyone going in or out of his flat.'

'Surely he didn't kill himself and then set his flat on fire,' Egan says.

'No.' Martha Lingby purses her thin lips. 'This was a clean-up job.'

'Yet again the work of a pro,' I mutter, to myself. 'Someone killed him to make sure he would never talk to anyone, and then set his place on fire to destroy any remaining evidence.'

'My thoughts too,' Lingby says, after a sip.

Egan angles his head to the side. 'There's something more, isn't there?'

The sergeant narrows her eyes at him again, before letting out a deep breath. 'It's just the timing that's getting to me. The fire started pretty much at the same moment we left the station.'

'As if someone knew you were coming and was covering his back?' I ask.

'Something like that, yes.' Her lips flatten to a tight line. 'Except the only people who knew we were going to arrest Nimra are part of the Met.'

'Huh.' This case just gets better every day. 'I can see why this would upset you.'

'Any idea who the snitch might be?' Egan asks.

Lingby's gaze turns sour, and her tone defensive. 'I never said there's a rat amongst us.' Her grip on her coffee cup tightens. 'I'm just highlighting a coincidence, okay.'

I raise a palm up. 'I apologise for my undiplomatic colleague,' I say, in a calm voice. 'He didn't mean to put the blame on your division or anything. We're only interested in finding the necklace, nothing else.'

Egan shrugs, but remains silent.

Lingby's murderous gaze abides somewhat. 'I have no idea where it is. A team will go over what's left of the flat, and we'll inform you if we find something. I wouldn't hold out too much hope. One of the men from the fire department told me whoever did this washed the place in gasoline first, to make sure nothing would survive.

'Stenson's division will take over the murder investigation, so you can check with him for a follow-up.'

I can't help but notice that lack of nickname, as she mentions our sergeant friend. I guess she probably doesn't like someone taking over her case. I quite understand; I wouldn't like it either.

'Do you have more info on Nimra? Was he a professional thief?' Egan asks her.

'He was a suspect in the theft of a French painting some ten years ago, but he was never convicted, for lack of evidence. It must have taught him to be more careful, because he's remained off our radar ever since. I suppose he's probably been working exclusively on contracts, and been abroad much of the time.' She sighs. 'This man was really good.'

'And you've no idea who he could have been working for?' I ask.

She shakes her head. 'I've had a look over his bank records — large deposits in cash, frequent ATM withdrawals. Hopefully, I'll be luckier with his phone records, but I doubt it.'

'Well, thanks for letting us know.' I stand up. 'Keep us in the loop if you find anything else.'

She stands up as well, and we shake hands. 'Will do.'

I take a step closer to her, while Egan is standing up. 'Just between you and I, Martha,' I say, in a lower voice, 'do you think someone within the Met blabbed to the wrong crowd?'

She debates answering for a long time, bites her lower lip and thinks some more. Her voice is low, when she says, 'We don't know anything yet, but it wouldn't be the first time.' She seems to hesitate about adding more. 'There's a rumour circulating in the Force; there's a new player in town. No one knows who he is, but he has his spies everywhere — even in the Met. Several good officers have tried to uncover him, but they hit brick wall after brick wall.'

The description sounds familiar, and I swallow hard. 'The Sorter.'

It seems to surprise Lingby that I know his alias.

'We played a game once,' I say, swallowing heavily as bile rises up. I haven't forgotten the Sorter's little thank you note, after Egan and I shot down his weapon smuggling operation. "To a game well played" the envelope read. It was accompanied by a chess pawn and a picture of Irina Anderson.

Lingby sighs heavily. 'I'm not saying he has anything to do with this, but this man pulls a lot of strings in this city. If he's involved, I'd be very careful if I were you.'

'Duly noted,' Egan says, reaching for my arm. His fingers circle it just above the elbow, in a grip that reassures me.

Martha nods and I watch her leave the bar. I drop a few quid on the table to cover the bill, and we go out too.

The moist summer air hits us the minute we get through the door. I look up at the glaring sun, still high in the sky, wishing for some of London's legendary drizzle.

'Well,' I say, as we start walking towards the Underground. 'I didn't see that one coming.'

'Do you think it's him?'

I don't need my partner's super-hearing to notice the sudden tenseness in his voice. 'I don't know, but we'd better be careful about what we do next.'

Egan hums his agreement. 'Is your mother still at her friend's?'

'Yes, I'll call to make sure she stays there a while longer.'

'Good idea. You, huh—' he seems to stumble over his words '—you... maybe you should stay with me.'

I smile, despite the seriousness of the situation. 'I'm a big girl, Ash.'

'I know that. It would be more prudent that's all. They've already been in your flat once.'

'No need to remind me.' I haven't forgotten that intrusion, nor the deadly warning painted on my door. 'Why is it always my flat that gets it though? First the fire, now the home invasion...' What will it be next? Flood? An alien attack?

'Karma?' Egan offers.

I punch him lightly in the shoulder. 'I'll stay with you — if you're sure it doesn't bother you to have to put up with me a while longer.'

'Not in the slightest,' he says, in a lighter tone.

'It's a deal, then.' With a smile, I add, 'Your AC's better than mine anyway.'

I slow down as we near the Underground entrance and we navigate through the crowd to the stairs.

'This leaves us with the million pound question, though,' I say, coming to a stop near the first step. 'Why would the boss of a London crime syndicate be interested in a nineteen-forties necklace? It makes no sense at all.'

20

I called DS Stenson right after Egan and I got back from our chat with Lingby. The conversation was short, but he confirmed to me what his colleague had told us: his division was on the Nimra case. I elicited his promise to keep us informed of any new development before he hung up.

We remain without news from him over the weekend. So, when another wife wary of her husband's incessant absences calls up the agency on Monday morning, I do the only sensible thing there is to do when your bank account is low, bills are overdue, and you have some free time on your hands: I take the case.

Later that night, I reach into my shoulder bag for my lipstick — a scarlet red shade — and apply it liberally on my lips.

'Have you got the position memorised?' I mumble to Egan, while I do the bottom lip.

My partner's seated in the passenger side of my mother's car, angled towards the outside window.

'To the millimetre,' he replies.

'Good.' I close the lipstick, drop it in the door pocket, then look back at the rear-view mirror and check my blond wig one last time. 'I wouldn't want to be doing all this for nothing.'

Egan ignores my comment and asks, 'What's your plan?'

'Well, Mrs Hayder said her husband has a type when it comes to women—' I tug at the wig a little '—I'm doing my best to fit the description.'

'Which is?' he asks, and I don't need to look at him to know he's smiling.

'Tall, blonde, sexy and exotic.'

'Exotic?' he asks.

I frown at my own reflexion. 'I hope Italian will be exotic enough for him. I'm not sure I'm able to use any other accent convincingly.'

'I'm looking forward to that part,' Egan chuckles, tapping the little earpiece he's wearing. 'And you're really certain he'll want to have a drink with you?'

'In this dress?' I ask. 'I assure you he most definitely will. I'm going to go all Monica Belluci on him — he won't know what's hit him.'

'Monica Who?' he asks.

'She's a well-known actress. She's all curves and very popular with the male population... some of the females too.'

Egan chuckles as I open the door and step out.

'Just don't miss your cue,' I say, closing the door behind me.

I walk the length of the car and cross the street. There's a bar on the other side, snuggled in-between two large office buildings.

I wobble on my heels and have to force myself to take slow measured steps. *Porca vacca*, it's easier to walk in a straight line after hitting your head against a wall, than when wearing ten-inch heels — trust me, I've tried it.

I push the bar door open, straighten my back and walk in with a casual and assured air.

It's close to five thirty in the afternoon and the place is almost empty. There's no one sitting at the counter and I choose the third chair from the left. It allows me a nice view of the whole place.

'Evening,' the young man minding the bar says. 'What can I get you?'

'Lemonade,' I reply lazily, 'but make it look like a cocktail.'

He arches a dark brown eyebrow in puzzlement.

I look him straight in the eyes and, he nods, confused He scratches his stubbled chin an instant and then turns his back on me while he makes my drink.

There's no rule that says private investigators and drinks don't mix, but I've read somewhere it's always better to do your job sober… something about never quite knowing how the night's going to turn out.

The young man comes back a minute later with a cocktail glass filled with a clear liquid. He's taken the precaution of putting sugar around the rim and garnishing it with a lime wedge. I tip him generously.

When five thirty arrives, the first businessmen who have just finished for the day start to enter the bar. I discreetly watch every man that enters and mentally catalogue him. None of them is a match for the picture of Mr Hayder that his wife provided. Yet, she assured me — if his credit card records are anything to go by — that her husband stops by this exact bar almost every evening after work.

'What is a pretty young lady like you doing all by herself?' a man asks me, distracting me.

I had seen him enter and dismissed him immediately. Mr Hayder is almost six foot tall and rather slender, with curly brown hair. The man facing me is a good head shorter and balding on top.

'Waiting for someone,' I answer, in a tone that suggests he doesn't have a chance.

He grumbles and moves off quietly.

Out of the corner of my eye I watch him return to his pals. One of them pats him on the back. 'I told you—' I hear him say in the distance '—a girl like that's too good for you, Jim.'

I smile, thanking my short, close-fitting red leather dress, and concentrate my attention on the reflection of the door in the mirror behind the bar. I'm just in time to see yet another man enter.

I frown and look more closely. This one's tall, and a perfect match for the picture I have in my bag.

I straighten my back, flick at my hair to make sure the blond ringlets cascade nicely and take up a more languid position as I play distractedly with my lime wedge.

Kevin Hayder takes several steps into the bar and stops. I see him hesitate. He lifts up a hand, salutes some friends seated at a table on the other side and then he covertly glances at me.

After a few more seconds of standing poised in the entrance, during which I hope he will choose me over a pint with his friends, he moves to seat at the bar, two chairs to my right. Jackpot!

I swallow the lime and take a sip of my half-empty cocktail, ignoring him completely. I think I once read something about playing hard to get…

Step one; grab his attention. I place the glass back on the counter, raise a hand to massage my neck and flick my hair again.

One, two, three, four, I count in my head, *five, six, sev*—

'I don't think I've ever seen you here before,' says a deep voice, on my right.

Whoa, best pickup line of the century. I chuckle inwardly, but keep a straight face as I turn a little towards Mr Hayder and bat long mascara-coated eyelashes at him.

'I'm not from here,' I say, in a tone a little huskier than usual. I make sure to pronounce every letter to its fullest, as Italians do and even roll the 'r' a little.

Hayder's eyes widen immediately, a clear sign of his growing interest. 'Your accent?' he says. 'Where are you from…? Italy?'

'*Si*,' I say, smiling sweetly showing all my teeth, '*da Milano.*'

'I love Italy — *bellisima Italia*,' he winks at me.

I have half a mind to burst out laughing at how lame he sounds, but remind myself that I'm working.

Step two; let him play the hero. I let out a throaty chuckle that was meant to sound sexy, and finish my drink.

Hayder snaps his fingers to get the server's attention and orders me 'another one'.

I flick Hayder a smile, bat my eyelashes some more, and he takes that as an invitation to come and sit closer to me. Dear me, men can be so easy at times.

'So are you here for business or pleasure?' he asks me, and I feel like snorting at the barely veiled innuendo.

'Business. I'm only staying for the week, but—' I tuck a long strand of blond hair back behind my ear '—maybe there's a way to have both, *sí*?'

There's a little microphone tucked under the collar of my dress, and a wireless transmitter in my shoulder bag. Egan is listening to our conversation in real-time and I can imagine the smug smirk on his face at my words.

'I'm sure that's possible.' Kevin Hayder holds out his hand to me. 'I'm Mark.'

I shake his hand. 'Monica.'

'Pleasure.'

He bows a little, as he lets go of my hand, and I appear flattered.

'And, can I ask, Monica, what is it that you do?'

'Oh, boring stuff—' like spying on you for your wife, I think, keeping my smile up '—it probably would turn you off.'

'But—' I reach for his hand, and he leans a little closer to me '—what about you, Mark?'

I get an awfully long-winded answer about his job in a health insurance company. By the end of his spiel, he's almost sitting in my lap. God, this man is easy money.

Step three; reel in the fish.

I cross my legs and brush his leg, accidentally on purpose.

He inches even closer. 'So how about we leave this place and I show you something of our wonderful city?'

Show me some nice hotel room, more like, I snort inwardly. 'I would so love to.'

He drops a few notes on the bar to settle the tab and escorts me to the door.

With his arm snaked around my waist, it's certainly easier for me to walk, and I manage to stride out like a real lady. I catch sight of the man who came up to me earlier as we leave the bar. Poor Jim watches us go, a pint in his hand, a look on his face that clearly says 'what the hell does this guy have that I don't?'

My phone rings a mere instant after we're through the door. I reach into my bag for it, step away from Hayder and answer.

'*Allo*,' I say, loud enough to be heard clearly by Hayder.

'Just phoning to see if you're having fun.' Egan says.

'*Si, signore*,' I reply.

He snorts. 'If you're interested to know, I'm bored out here on my own... Monica.' The name is a vocal eye-roll.

'*Lei è terribile*,' I fake a distressed tone. '*Io arrivo subito*.'

I end the call and drop the phone back into my bag.

I turn back to Hayder, forcing a grave expression. 'I'm so sorry, something has come up at work. I have to go.'

'Oh.' Hayder's not as good as me at faking emotions. He's cross and it shows through his would-be understanding façade. 'That's too bad.'

We exchange fake phone numbers and part ways on the sidewalk.

I wobble down the street in my high heels and tight leather

dress. I round the corner; count to twenty and peer back out — Hayder's nowhere in sight.

I take off my shoes, cross the street and run back to the car, open the door and slide behind the wheel.

'Back so soon?' Egan says, with an elegant eyebrow arched up. 'It sounded like it was going so well, *bellisima* Monica.'

'Oh, just shut it,' I grumble, reaching for the large sweatshirt I left on the backseat. I remove the wig, pull on the shirt and feel like myself again.

'You took the photos?' I ask.

He hands me the camera. 'Yes, of course.'

I take it, power it back on and check the snapshots. Perfect.

'Is it okay?' Egan enquires, hesitantly.

Earlier, I'd parked the blue Fiat Punto in a spot that would give us a good view of the bar. Then I moved the passenger's seat back slightly and, as Egan sat, camera in hand, I positioned him so that he would have a perfect angle to get a good shot of Hayder and me leaving the building arm in arm.

'The pictures are good. Nice work, Ash.' I zoom in on one, which perfectly captures Hayder's heated gaze directed at my breasts. 'We have everything we need.'

'At least that's one job done.' Egan sighs, as he fastens his seat belt.

'Yeah.' I turn on the ignition and the old car putters to life. 'It may just have been a short interlude, but the money won't hurt.'

'When are you seeing Mrs Hayder?' he asks.

'I'm not. She's out of town, remember.' I move the car into the traffic and head for Egan's flat. 'I've got her email address and she has our bank details.'

'The wonders of the twenty-first century.' Egan snorts. 'You don't even need to meet your clients anymore.'

'Hey, stop complaining.' I shoot him a sideway glance. 'When some woman offers me five hundred pounds for an hour's worth of work, I don't mind it if she's only a voice on the phone.'

'I'm not—'

'Yeah, yeah, I know.' I cut him off, slowing down as we near a red light. 'Gosh, you can be so old-fashioned sometimes, you know.'

We don't stop for ice cream on the way back, even though the *Neve & Egan Agency* just wrapped up its tenth case. I don't feel like celebrating, and I don't think my partner does either. We eat warmed-up leftovers instead and are both sound asleep before Big Ben even strikes.

21

The next morning, my phone finally rings with Stenson's familiar number.

'Hello,' I say, hoping that my eagerness isn't too obvious.

'Morning, Alex.'

I decide to keep the flirting for another day, feeling far too curious not to jump straight in. 'Any news on the case?'

'Oh, I'm fine. Thanks for asking,' he chuckles. 'We got the DNA confirmation on Nimra, and had the bullets analysed; we didn't find a match in our database.'

'Find anything useful in the loft?'

'Nothing. It was burnt to a cinders.'

Damn. Professional efficiency once again. Couldn't criminals be sloppy every now and then? 'I don't suppose I could have a copy of the report?'

'That would be most irregular of me,' Stenson says, the smile clearly audible in his voice.

'Even if I say please?'

He chuckles. 'I suppose I could be persuaded.'

I huff. 'Sergeant Stenson. Are you suggesting a monetary bribe?'

'I never said anything about money — a nice dinner, in good company, on the other hand… I don't know how I could refuse.'

Huh? My mind blanks for a second or two. Is this his way of asking me out on a date?

'Sure, why not,' I mutter, hesitantly. 'Let's wait until the case is over, though.'

'It's a deal. Stop by New Scotland Yard this afternoon and I'll see what I can give you.'

'Alright, thanks. See you then.'

I'm feeling slightly dumbfounded when I hang up.

'So that's how you kids do it these days, huh?' Egan says from his nearby chair. 'Things certainly have changed since my day.'

'No-one's ever told you that listening in on other people's conversations is rude?' I turn a murderous gaze his way. It has no effect, so I throw a pencil at him.

The pencil bounces off his chest and falls to the floor with a limp thud. Egan merely raises an eyebrow.

I get up and retrieve the pencil before my blind friend inadvertently steps on it.

Egan chuckles when he hears me place the pencil back on the table.

'Oh, just shut up,' I mutter.

Later that day, Egan and I part near UCL's entrance. He has another of his meetings — the last for a while, he assures me — and I have... a date.

'Pass on my regards to Matthew, will you?' he says, with a smile playing at the corner of his mouth which warns me that innuendos are on the tip of his tongue.

'Will do,' I grumble.

'And remember to use protection.' He smiles at me. 'From the sun, of course. I hear it's going to shine brightly today.'

A soft punch in the shoulder is the only answer I give him.

Egan walks away chuckling lightly, the tip of his white cane charting the way ahead of him. I watch him go with a fond shake of the head, and a blush in my cheeks.

As I walk down to New Scotland Yard, the mantra 'it's just work' is on a loop in my head. I'm going to see Stenson to get some information out of him over some polite chat. Nothing more. The only reason I'm wearing a dress today is because of the high temperature. The only reason I'm wearing my hair loose is that it wasn't quite dry when I left the flat. *Yes,* I tell myself, firmly, *this is just work — nothing more.*

I enter the New Scotland Yard lobby with my head held high and absolutely no butterflies in my stomach. No, sir! that odd fluttering feeling, must just be something I ate.

I take the lift upwards, follow the now-familiar corridors and enter Stenson's divisional office with a nonchalant step. Pausing near the entrance, I look around but can't find the familiar mop of curly black hair anywhere. Moving forward, I stop by the man whose desk is next to Stenson's, a short man, with a thin nose and even thinner lips. I've seen him once or twice before, but I don't think I've ever heard his name.

'Hi,' I say, with a smile. 'Is DS Stenson in? I was supposed to meet him this afternoon.'

The man raises dark brown eyes up to meet me. He frowns for

an instant, probably while he searches his memory to place me, then offers me a contrite smile. He opens his mouth to answer my question, but someone else cuts in before he has the time to form the words.

An older, gruffer voice greets my ears, 'He's not here. He's been called to court at the last minute to testify in a trial. What's your business here anyway, *kid*?'

I roll my eyes at the tone. I don't need to turn around to know who this voice belongs to; I'd recognise the drawl and the insulting nickname anywhere.

'Detective Inspector Langford.' I slowly turn around. 'What a pleasure.'

'Kid.' He nods at me, and a few of the drops of sweat that have gathered on his brow, fall to the floor.

Langford hasn't changed. He's still as bald as a cue ball and a good head shorter than me. From the look he gives me, I can tell he still hates my guts. I force myself to smile.

I have to make an effort to sound polite as I ask, 'How are you doing?'

'Too hot,' he grumbles, as he traces the inside of his shirt collar with a finger.

No kidding. I have to make an effort not to giggle childishly at the sight of him. Langford is the type of man who's always sweaty. The first time I met him, it was on a cold February day, and there had been a film of sweat on his brow even then. Today, he looks like one gigantic turkey out of the oven.

'Any idea when Stenson's coming back?' I ask. 'We were supposed to discuss a case.'

The DI narrows his eyes at me. 'Not an ongoing case I hope?'

I steel my tone. 'The Nimra case.'

'Figures.' He snorts. 'I heard it was your *PI Agency*—' he says the last two words with disdain, '—who helped identify him.'

'That's right.' I nod, and can't help but add, 'We're good at what we do, and quite affordable.'

He snorts again, louder. 'That just has to be the dumbest thing I've heard all week!'

'The Art Division had all but given up on this case,' my anger is growing and my voice rises in volume, '*we* helped them identify the thief; otherwise they'd never have found him.'

'Fat lot of good that did.' Langford passes a thick hand over his brow, it comes away sticky with sweat. 'The guy's dead, and we still have nothing.'

He looks me up and down, narrowing his eyes at me behind his glasses, and mutters, 'Danger magnet.'

His attitude, as always, unnerves me. With a superhuman effort, I manage to get my voice under a semblance of control. 'Excuse me?'

'Danger magnet — it's what you are. When you take a case, people always get hurt.'

'I—'

'Sorry, sir.' A young officer interrupts, and I snap my mouth shut with an audible clack of teeth. The newcomer, a man, with curly blond hair and a face that screams fresh-out-of-school takes a few steps towards us and turns to the DI insistently. He raises a mobile to his superior. 'It's for you sir, DCS Saunders. He says it's important.'

Langford raises a fat index finger in my direction. 'I'm not done with you.' He retreats to his office with a grumble of 'What is it?'

'Saved by the bell,' I mutter, as I sit down on Stenson's chair.

As long as I can remember, I've always had a temper, but with the years, a hell of a lot of practice and Egan's calming influence, I become better at keeping it in check. Langford, for whatever reason, always manages to push just the right buttons to unnerve me.

I fold my arms on the desk and drop my head onto my forearms. In less than five minutes, that Detective Inspector has managed to give me the beginning of a headache. I close my eyes and take some deep breaths. Damn, this is not how I had envisioned my afternoon.

When I reopen my eyes, a familiar name catches my attention. Nimra. There's a dark folder on the side of the desk, with our thief's name written on its side. Raising my head again, I quickly look around me. Langford is locked in his office, still on the phone. He's facing the large fan he placed on one of his shelves, with his back to me. The man at the next desk has his eyes glued to the screen in front of him and the rest of the office is empty.

I lean back down and, as inconspicuously as possible, surreptitiously take the corner of the file between two fingers to drag it to the middle of the desk. I open it with one hand, and keep my gaze on Langford the entire time.

Stretching my back, with my head still turned slightly in

Langford's direction, I glance down at the document and discover the first few pages are Nimra's bank records. With a quick flick of my hand, I turn the page.

I glance up to check on Langford's position: he hasn't moved. I look back down and read a copy of the post-mortem file. My stomach somersaults at the pictures and I quickly turn the page over.

The next thing in the file is Nimra's phone records. I scan over the names, raise my eyes up again to check if I'm still safe, flick the page and look back down. My eyes narrow at a name: a familiar name.

'Sloppy,' I mutter under my breath, with a smile. I grab a pencil and write the number down on a post-it note, before closing the file and placing it back where I found it.

I stand up, walk to the young man nearby. 'Tell Langford I left, would you?' I ask. 'Tell him unlike some, I can't laze around all day with the air blowing in my hair. I have a business to run, criminals to catch.'

He nods, with a puzzled expression, and I leave the room. I jog down the stairs and walk out of New Scotland Yard. I have my phone ready at my ear the second I'm through the door, waiting to be connected with 118 365.

I ask the young woman who greets me for a reversed research and give her the number I've just written down. A short wait and she gives me an address in Guildford.

I try to call Egan from the cab, but get his answering machine. I leave him the address of where I'm going, obeying his rules… just in case.

I pocket the phone, and wonder if me finding the culprit on my own might be enough to give Langford a burst blood vassal. As we enter Guildford, I realise I should maybe have given my plan rather more thought. What is it some American president once said…? "By failing to prepare, you are preparing to fail." Well, that man probably didn't have my temper.

At my request, the cabbie drops me a few houses down from my destination and I go the rest of the way on foot. I walk down a small residential road, with tall hedges hiding cosy individual houses. The street is a dead-end and the house I'm looking for is the last one before a large row of chestnut trees; I slow down and move closer to the hedge. Peeking through the leaves, I see a two-storey house. Large bay windows allow me to peer inside what I realise is a nicely furnished living room. The grass around the house is well trimmed, but the façade is worn and could do with a paint job. I can see no sign of there being anyone being home at the moment.

After one last look round at the road behind me to make sure it's still empty, I move to the iron gate and scale it as swiftly as I can. I regret not having worn trousers, and once I'm on the other side I'm puffing a bit as I try to pull my dress straight.

I run to the hedge that surrounds the house and follow it around to reach the back of the house. I creep to the north wall, crouching down below a window to take a minute to catch my breath.

I take my phone out of my pocket, and turn on the camera. I rise up slowly, lift my hand until only the top of my phone peers at the window. I move my hand around gently to get a good overall view, then lower it back down again and play the video. I discover the window looks in on the kitchen, but the room is empty. There are some green apples in a bowl, and a newspaper on the side, signs that the house is currently inhabited.

I continue creeping along down the length of the wall and try another window. The new video shows me the inside of an empty bedroom. The large bed is made up, a male dressing gown hangs on a rack, shoes (all male) are shelved on the far wall. I spot a walking cane resting against a wall.

A creak behind me freezes me to the spot, and the shudder that runs through me is almost enough to make me drop my phone.

'Turn round,' a man's voice commands, in a kind of faded martial tone.

I swallow and obey, before coming face to face with an elderly man; and the barrel of his gun.

'Drop the phone,' he orders and I obey instantly. There's a dull thud as it lands on the grassy ground below.

I know I only have a few short seconds to decide what action I can take. Thoughts rush in my head as the adrenaline flares. Fact one: the man facing me looks old, really old, slow and wary. Fact two: I'm young and athletic. I could run to the front of the house and am probably able to vault halfway over the gate before grandpa has time to reach me.

Problem: grandpa has a gun. I have no idea of this man's marksmanship — even trained soldiers are sometimes wildly inaccurate. If he hesitates, if his old and tired hand wavers, just a fraction, I could make it out unhurt. Or, grandpa could be really good at shooting, and put a bullet in my forehead before I had the time to say damn.

Odds: fifty-fifty.

With a grimace, I obediently raise both hands up in a slow, unthreatening move.

'I would be much obliged,' the man says, waving the tip of his weapon to the left, indicating the direction to follow.

He follows me down the length of the house's left wall, then inside through a side door.

'Go on,' he says, as I enter a long corridor.

I've never been very big on taking orders, but some extraordinary situations do call for exceptions. Extraordinary situations include times when one finds oneself with a gun held to the back of one's head.

'That's far enough,' the man says.

I stop on the threshold of the living room I glanced at earlier. No more orders come, and I turn to look over my shoulder. I know it's a bad idea, yet I'm unable to refrain from it. I don't even have the time to be cross with myself, before a sharp pain explodes within my skull and I see stars.

I try to hold onto consciousness for as long as I can, but darkness quickly floods over me. The last thing I remember is falling to the floor.

Sometime later, I reopen my eyes with a grunt and quickly shut them again. The light is bright and blinding. I try to raise a hand to shield them from the light, but that doesn't work. For some odd reason, my right arm doesn't want to cooperate. I try the left and get the same result. With an horrible feeling that something is terribly wrong, I force one eye open, just a fraction, and peer down.

'Not good,' I mumble, as I discover some thick rope around my chest. 'R'ly not good.'

Heaving in a few deep breaths, I wait for some of the haze to dissipate and take stock of the situation. My head hurts like a New Year's binge aftermath, my stomach is in knots and I feel like throwing up.

I raise my head again and open both eyes. My vision swims for an instant and finally focuses on a Victorian salon. I look around me with a bemused expression. The chair I'm sitting on, although still plush, has to be older than me. The settee and the coffee table ahead of me are made of old, dark wood. The table has been hand-carved with intricate motifs, and the settee is covered in dark red velvet. Gosh, this place reeks of the centuries past. 'Where the hell am I?'

'Good to see you're awake,' a voice says, from somewhere behind me.

I try to wiggle and twist my head around to catch sight of the speaker, but the back of the chair is too high.

I hear the faint echo of feet padding down the carpeted floor, and a man comes into the edge of my view. An old man in black trousers, a white shirt loose over a skinny chest. Silver gray hair, cut short. Memories are slowly filtering back, but then I catch sight of the weapon in his right hand and flash back into the present.

I wriggle uselessly again, purely for effect.

The deep wrinkles etched into the old man's face crinkle into a smile at my efforts.

'Herr Strausser,' I nod to him and the smile widens.

22

Strausser sits down on the settee in front of me. That smile has developed into a contented, relaxed one. 'No one's called me by that name for a very long time.'

Although his English is very nearly perfect, there are still faint traces of a German accent that betray his origins.

'If you really wanted to disappear, you should have taken an entirely different name — not merely dropped a letter or two, Willem.'

'So this is how you found me? Did you go right through Britain's phone book in alphabetical order?' he muses, leaning forward, with the greatest interest.

'Nimra's phone record was enough.'

His smile turns sour. 'I admit that was an error on my part. A man of my age... I'm a little behind when it comes to technology, you know. Life certainly seemed easier before.'

I feel like snorting, but hold it back. 'That wasn't your biggest mistake.'

'Was it not?' he asks, with something akin to bemusement in his voice.

'Hiring that lunatic to ransack my flat, was.' I shake my head. 'He hurt my mother.'

'You may be right. I admit transforming Willem Strausser to William Strauss was maybe a bit lazy on my part. But—' he sighs '—

we hadn't planned for such a turn of events.'

We? Realisation hits me, and it hurts my head as it does. 'Anna wasn't in the car, was she?'

Strausser moves backwards and leans against the back of the settee. 'No, she wasn't.'

The pieces of the puzzle start to align and form a picture. I was right to think Anna had a lover. With Strausser, they found the perfect way to elope and start a new life together. 'Who was the woman in the car?'

'Some poor girl from the factory.' He waves a wrinkled hand about dejectedly. 'She looked a bit like Anna and we knew she wouldn't be missed, besides her ancestry was—' disgust flashes briefly over his face '—*tainted*. No one would have cared much if one of them disappeared. It happened all the time.'

'Anna faked her own death to be with you.' Just like some sick, twisted version of an old romance tale.

'Her husband was violent,' Strausser spits. 'A fanatic, devoted to the Reich, and unstoppable in his thirst for power. He had plans to overcome Von Abschütz and to take over the company. He wanted the factory to expand, to become the biggest foundry in Germany and number one in the eyes of the Führer. He had plans for every habitant of Magdeburg to work in the factory. Every single one. Including my Anna... You should have seen how he treated her. What he put her through in their home.'

'So you killed him.' I mock him. 'To save the woman you loved.'

'I did the world a true favour that night.' Strausser sneers. He closes his eyes an instant, and probably replays the events in his head. 'When he found out about me and Anna, he tried to kill her. He wasn't supposed to be home. He found us together, brought out a gun and fired at Anna.

'Luckily his aim was bad. I was able to throw myself onto him, made him drop the gun. We fought, man to man, and I killed him with my bare hands.'

A chill runs along my spine at his tone. There's a glint of menacing darkness in Strausser's eyes. I quickly look away.

'You were a soldier in the Reich,' I say. Stupid I know but I simply can't keep my mouth shut. 'You sent Jews to their deaths. What makes you any better than Claus Levantiner?'

A punch rewards my impertinent question. The blow stings, even though the old man doesn't have the strength he must once have had.

'I wasn't offered a choice. I was only a kid,' he roars. 'And we didn't know what happened in the camps.'

I find that hard to believe, but manage to bite my tongue and don't challenge him this time 'You stole the necklace from a Jewish woman, when she was deported.'

Strausser nods, but remains silent.

'Then you used the ruby heart to buy a safe passage out of Germany, for you and Anna. You started a new life together here.'

He nods again, seemingly pleased that I have the story right.

'Here's what I don't get. Why steal the necklace a second time? Why after so many years?'

Strausser sits up straighter. 'It was my Anna's necklace.'

'It wasn't!'

The old man looks at me with a fierce gaze and I fear a second blow is on its way. It doesn't come. 'It was. I gave it to her — she loved that necklace. She always regretted having to give it away. She said it was a symbol of our love.'

I can't help but let a dry laugh escape my lips. 'Yes, it is a symbol of love. It was made by a jeweller named Salzmann for his wife. Handcrafted with a dedication and patience only love can elicit.'

'A Jew, who used the German people to make money,' Strausser spits out the words.

Woah, some crap ideology dies hard. I have to bite back a retort. Somehow, I don't think antagonising the man who's just knocked you out and holds you captive in his living room is the best way to survive the day. Speaking of which, 'What am I doing here?'

'What do you mean?'

'I mean *here*—' I wiggle about on my chair to illustrate the point '—what do you want from me?'

'Oh, that,' he waves a hand about, as if it is a mere trifling matter. 'I just wanted to know how much you've learned and how you found me. We've covered the second part...'

'And then what?' I swallow. 'If I talk, what then? We shake hands and part ways?'

'I don't think so.' Strausser narrows his eyes on me, moving his weapon from left to right to illustrate the point. 'Or did you not get my warning? Surely, a woman of your intelligence understood the message.'

Give up or die. A shudder courses through me at the memory.

'How did you know we were onto you?' I demand, curious.

The old man stands up and moves towards a shelf on which rest several glasses and decanters. He pours himself a large whiskey. 'You told me so yourself,' he says, turning back to me.

I feel my eyes go wide at his words, 'What?'

'You left a message with all the Straussers in Magdeburg, didn't you?'

Porca vacca, I have. When I found the picture in the newspaper, I contacted Von Abschütz and several other people, including all the Magdeburg residents with the surname Strasser. None of them ever got back to me, so I supposed they had no connection to Willem. 'One of them tipped you off?'

He nods as he closes the decanter. 'My sister, Martha.'

I let out a frustrated breath. She was the first name on my list.

Strasser drops ice cubes in his drink and they tinkle in the silence. 'We keep in touch.'

'And Nimra?' I ask. 'Who tipped you off on him? Why kill him too? You could simply have told him to get lost.'

Strasser turns back to face me, surprise etched into the lines of his face. 'Kill him?' he asks. 'I had no idea he was dead.'

'What?'

'I assure you it's the truth.'

I decide to switch tactics. 'How did you find him in the first place? Who told you about him and Stu?'

Strausser's face darkens. 'I suppose I should call that man... an independent contractor.'

With a sigh, the old man walks back to the settee and sits back down in front of me. He rests the gun on his thigh and holds his drink with both hands.

'When I saw the necklace on the news, I knew I had to get it back. I asked around some old acquaintances, and was directed to a man who could put me in contact with the right person for the job, for a small fee.'

'The Sorter.' I snort. 'The man *sorts out all your problems*, doesn't he?'

Strausser nods, before taking a large gulp of his drink.

'Who is he?' I ask, with way too much excitement for someone in my situation.

The old man smiles at my interest before his expression sobers.

'Oh, come on,' I say, wriggling a little in my chair. 'You can tell me. I'm dead anyway, aren't I?'

After one final long gulp, Strausser places the drink on the table. His hand wraps around the gun again. A strong grip, a sure hold. If I had tried to run, he wouldn't have missed me.

'The last time we spoke,' Strausser begins, 'he did warn me about you. He told me you're smart and a worthy opponent. But, it looks like this is one game you lost.'

A game I lost... the metaphor brings back ugly memories and chills me. I choke back on any smartarse comment I may have had. Facing down the barrel of a gun can do that to a person.

There are moments in life when you take the time to ponder all of the major life-changing decisions you've ever made. You second-guess your choices, and think about the future and what you could do to make tomorrow better than yesterday. It mostly happens during really intense moments; the life-threatening kind… or so I've heard. I'm in the middle of such a moment and I wish I could be having similar contemplative thoughts. As it turns out, I'm stuck thinking I've chosen a really stupid outfit to die in. A dress, really? Me? I hate wearing skirts and dresses and very rarely do it of my own free will and there I am… minutes away from certain death, in a denim dress and low-cut denim Converse trainers. Talk about the universe having one last laugh at the expense of dear old me.

I don't think things have ever looked more grim for me. What's that old saying Mum uses sometimes, *"Finchè c'è vita c'è speranza —* Where there's life, there's hope."

Well, then, I fear there won't be *hope* for much longer. I called Egan, before coming to the house, but has he listened to my message yet? Will he do something about it?

The damsel is in distress, but where are her knights in shining armour. Are they on their way? Will they arrive too late? I sigh. Who'd have thought it sucks to be a fairytale princess.

I firmly look at the barrel of the gun, force myself not to blink as I feel cold droplets of sweat run down my spine. 'What about granting a dying woman her last request?' I ask, in an attempt to win some time.

'Well,' Strausser seems to consider my words, and I hold my

breath, eyes still narrowed on the weapon.

'That's the tradition I believe,' he says, as he lowers his weapon.

I let out a long, relieved breath.

'Yes, it is. It seems only fair,' I rush out the words. 'Common courtesy and all that.'

Strausser seems to ponder the thought. I'm glad to let him. Any second that passes without me being riddled with tiny red holes is a small victory to me.

'I regret that I can't satisfy your curiosity,' the old man says, with an apologetic shrug. Of course, why should I start to be lucky now of all times? I'm starting to think Langford was right, when he called me a danger magnet.

'Unfortunately, I don't have much to offer,' Strausser continues, 'that man was only a voice on the phone.'

Bummer, I knew I should have asked for a last meal instead of a last request. 'How did you find him?'

'I still had contacts with the people who helped us settle in the UK, after the war. One thing that can be said about German soldiers, we stick together.'

I have a sudden image of a bunch of old, wrinkled, white-haired men gathering for Nazis' annual Christmas parties. The thought actually makes me shudder.

'The message was passed on, and one day, I received a call from a man who said he could help me. He knew the right person for the job I had in mind and all I had to do, was—'

The sound of broken glass interrupts Strausser mid-sentence, and I curse inwardly at the bad timing.

The noise came from somewhere behind me — towards the entrance of the house. I wriggle in my seat, try to twist and turn, to no avail.

Strausser raises his weapon again, aims it high and a little to the right of me. He frowns and tenses.

My breath becomes even more rapid

Has someone just broken into the house? I wonder. Is there, after all, a little hope I will grow old enough to have white hair one day?

I struggle to see, but can't move my chest away from the chair. The best I can do is turn my head. This only offers me a minimal view of the wall to my right, which has a large chimney breast set in it. The angle reveals nothing of the entrance to the room.

Letting out a frustrated breath, I return my attention to Strausser. He's still looking ahead with a mix of curiosity and apprehension. Whoever has entered the house is not yet in his line of sight, and this is buying me some extra time. I wriggle again furiously, try to grip the rope with my fingers and pull on it. Nerves on fire, adrenaline searing, I try to focus my hearing to make out what is happening behind me.

Soon I hear the clumping sound of feet on the floor — but that's not all. There's another sound — a sharper sound — somewhat irregular, like a tapping noise. Strausser stands. A military stance I notice. Despite the years, his habits are still instinctive.

The odd sound echoes around us. It's a rhythm I'm familiar with and I find it hard to swallow around the lump that has suddenly grown in my throat.

The gun in Strausser's hand jerks a little more to the left. 'Stay where you are!' he shouts.

I hold my breath, my eyes fixed on the weapon and the index finger that hovers close to the trigger. The newcomer must have complied, because Strausser relaxes a fraction.

'Well, this is a nice surprise,' the old German says. 'The blind PI.'

23

My heart definitely drops at the words, as my worst fears are confirmed.

'*Porca Vacca*, Ash,' I say, and I can hear my own voice shake. 'I would love to say it's a pleasure to see you, but... what the hell?'

'Lexa,' comes the familiar baritone, and although his voice sounds collected, I can discern a faint trace of relief in the two familiar syllables. 'Are you hurt?'

'I'm fine. Just currently tied to a chair,' I inform him.

'Let her go,' my partner says, and there's something in his tone I don't like. Something hard and menacing, I've never heard from him before.

I try to move again. Damn, if only I could see his face, I would be able to understand his intentions.

'I don't think so.' Strausser straightens his hold on the weapon, and I blink at the muzzle of the gun nervously.

'You will let her go,' Egan repeats, in the same tone that sends chills down my spine.

The old man stares him down hard for a few more seconds, then breaks his stance. 'Oh,' he says, with surprise as he visibly relaxes.

'You can't see it, that's right, but I do have my gun pointed at you,' he informs Egan, with a sick smile at the corner of his mouth. He takes a few steps to the side, to face Egan more directly, and disappears from my line of sight.

'He does.' I feel the need to confirm, hoping this will dissuade my friend from doing something even more overtly stupid than being there in the first place.

'And I have a bomb in my hand,' Egan says, in a deadpan voice.

I choke down on my surprise and freeze. An instant later my brain, or at least a portion of it, reboots and I struggle against the ropes with desperate fury even though I know damn well it's completely futile. I guess a psychoanalyst would have a field day going over our current situation. I, on the other hand, don't enjoy it so much.

Egan and I have our differences, it's true. We both have our own way of approaching life and treating people. That's true too. We don't really care about all that, though, for the sole reason that *it works*. He's the ears; I'm the eyes. He has the cold, controlled attitude — I'm the carefree, fiery one. I pull the crazy stunts, he lectures me about it afterwards. That's how it goes. Not the other way around, damn it.

I've always believed that, as long as we're left alone to do what we're good at, and be who we've decided to be, things will turn out all right in the end. Now, me being strapped to a chair, unable to see what is going on, and Egan coming to the rescue, carrying a freaking bomb. That is not — by a mile — all right.

A bomb.

A bomb.

The word keeps echoing in my head, as if on a loop. I can't

believe it — hell, I can't even picture it. I try to turn again, twist in my chair, pull at the rope with all of my strength, try to make the chair move: nothing. I curse at Strausser, I curse at this stupid room I'm in with no mirrors and not even the slightest reflective surface to give me a glimpse of what is going on behind my back.

Ashford Egan, Ash, a history professor, my partner-in-crime, my best friend… with a bomb.

My voice trembles, giving away my emotions, as I plead, 'Ash, please tell me you're joking?'

'Hush, Alexandra,' he says in a tone that betrays nothing.

Alexandra, not Lexa, I note — it's always Lexa when everything's all right. The lump in my throat grows impossibly bigger. Not a joke then. Oh my God.

I hear a click, coming from Strausser's gun — he's just released the safety catch— and I can feel myself begin to panic. I make an effort to keep my breathing under control; although I know it's useless, I pull at the rope again.

'Is it really?' the old man says.

'Oh, it is. Concealed within this old tape recorder. A little gift from an old friend.' There's a bit of smugness to Egan's tone, and I find myself believing him. Has he got the bomb from Dimitri? I wouldn't put it past him to know where to find such rare items… but at such short notice?

'It doesn't look like much, or so I've been told,' Egan continues, 'but with the press of one button… boom.'

The old man sniggers. 'Then you and your young friend here will die too.'

'Isn't it what you had planned for us, anyway?' Egan asks. 'At least this way I get to take you along for the ride.' The coldness of my friend's tone chills me to the bone. I close my eyes to fight off a sudden bout of nausea.

'Our job is a dangerous one,' Egan continues. 'Violent death has always been a possible outcome. I made peace with myself a long time ago.'

A deadly silence grows steadily within the room and I find myself holding my breath. When my vision starts to swim I take a deep breath which sounds loud in my ears. I want to scream at Egan to run away. Just to leave me here, to run and save his life. It is my own stupidity that brought me here and no-one else needs to suffer from my bad decisions. In the confusion, words fail me — my mouth is drier than sand and not a single word escapes my trembling lips.

'Of course,' Egan says, still in the same go-die-and-see-if-I-care tone, 'there's another option. You put down your weapon, let me and my partner go, and we all live one more day.'

I like this option; I like it very much, I think, struggling again. I vote for it, count me in.

'And spend what little is left of my life in prison?' Strausser asks. 'I don't think so.'

'You have children, grand-children even,' Ash says. Though I couldn't give a damn about this madman's family tree, I frown in surprise. 'Wouldn't you like to see them again?'

'Great grandchildren, actually,' Strausser says.

The answer surprises me. How in the hell does Egan know Strausser has kids?

I don't have the time to give the question more thought, as I finally pull one hand free. Without wasting more time, as discreetly, but speedily as I can, I work the second one free too. The rope is off me. I glance sideways at Strausser. He's still aiming at Egan, ready to fire. His index finger covers the trigger. Any second now, he's going to shoot. Without thinking any further, I leap to my feet and throw myself at him.

The world spins around me and I hurt horribly as I land on the floor. Strausser grunts and growls. Throwing myself at a man when I was probably already concussed may not have been the best course of action. My head swirls as my vision darkens.

I hear Egan cry my name in anguish and force my eyes open. Strausser is inches away from me. Surprise is painted on his face. He's trying to find his balance, but I don't allow him any more time to do so. I punch him in the face, as hard as I can. A solid punch from the shoulder. The old man is flattened on his floor.

I push away from him, reach for the gun he lost on impact and make a grab for it. Strausser is out of breath, panting hard, as I stand up, his weapon in my hand.

I steady my grip, and take aim. Strausser looks up at me with venom. His nose is bleeding.

'Well, go ahead,' he spits. 'Shoot… if you have it in you.'

'Lexa?' Egan queries again, still with the same urgency.

'It's all right,' I reassure him. 'I have the gun, he's on the ground.'

I hear my friend sigh with relief.

Strausser steadies himself with one hand against the wall, as he pushes himself up into a sitting position. Pure hatred emanates from him, as he looks at me with fierce dark eyes.

I smile down at him. 'I think we should call the police. I'm sure they'll be interested in what you have to say.'

'You don't have the guts, do you, girl?' the German grunts out. 'You're no soldier, just a weak little girl, scared of the wolf.'

'You should never have sent Stu to my flat,' I tell him flatly.

A gun goes off, glass breaks, and Strausser is silenced forever; blood trickles down the side of his head.

I look down in frozen stupor, shocked, my mouth gaping.

Strausser's body goes limp and he slumps down onto the floor in a heap from the half-seated position he'd held instant before. I feel my stomach lurch, and fight to keep from throwing up there and then.

I want to look away, but know it's too late anyway. The image of the old man's skull with a large hole in it and grey matter pouring out of it is something I will carry with me for a long time. Or until I die.

Slowly, dumbly, I blink and reality comes crashing back in. I inhale, and hear my friend repeatedly calling out my name. The urgency in his voice raising each time.

I turn to look at Egan, see he's trying to make his way over to me. He bangs against a chair and swears loudly. The tape recorder clatters to the floor.

'Ash, it's alright. I'm fine,' I call out. My voice is trembling, but it seems to be enough to calm him. He stops by the chair, hand extended towards where I am.

'Lexa?' Egan's voice sounds as shaken as mine. 'What… did you, is he…'

'Wasn't me,' I blurt out, when he doesn't seem to be able to finish his sentence.

'I…' I'm at a loss as to what might have happened. 'I don't— I… I have no idea what happened. I didn't shoot…' I look down at the weapon, half expecting to see smoke billow out of the muzzle of the gun, '…I think.'

'Is he…'

'Dead?' I look down at the fractured skull, and the blood quickly pooling. My stomach churns again and I take a step back. 'Yes, quite.'

I move to the left and cautiously place the gun on a shelf. I look at it frowning, then at my hand. My head is still ringing, but I'm certain I didn't shoot. And there's no smoke anyway.

'It all happened so fast,' I mutter. 'One minute I was aiming at him, and the next a bullet entered his head.'

'Where did it come from?' Egan asks.

A good question indeed. I turn back to look at Strausser's body as I try to reconstruct the scene in my head. He was sitting against the wall. Yes, he was facing me, yet the bullet hit him on the side of his head.

'It wasn't me,' I declare with certainty, this time. 'Couldn't have been me, it came from the—' I let my gaze travel forward, it finds the wall, and a little to the left, a broken, '—window.'

I rush forward, side-stepping Strausser's legs, and peer outside as I reach the bay window. I'm fully expecting to see a police squad, or Her Majesty's entire army, but only find a calm, deserted bank of grass, and further ahead the tall hedge I'd seen before. 'I can't see anyone outside.'

'I heard a car driving away a few moments ago,' Egan says.

'Really?' I didn't hear a thing, but then I wasn't exactly paying attention.

I look back at him and see my partner nod solemnly, frowning ever so slightly as he does so. Right, silly me. How dare I question the man's hearing?

The reality of the situation hits me at once and I feel faint. Here I am, standing in some dead man's living room — a dead-man I've just side-stepped like it's the most natural thing in the world, and — my friend's ego is protesting I doubted his skills when we should both be in complete shock because we've just escaped death. Our skulls could have looked like Strausser's by now, and we could still be blown to smithereens any second.

My brain screeches to a halt.

'Ash — your bomb!' I cry. 'You dropped it.'

I rush back to him with quick strides (mindlessly sidestepping Strausser's body yet again) and crouch down by the chair. I reach out for the recorder but then freeze, not daring to pick it up.

'Oh, yes,' he says, coolly. 'I dropped it, didn't I? Can you pick it up?'

'Is it safe?' My hand shakes, and hovers above it. 'How do I hold it?'

'It's just a tape recorder,' he says flatly. 'You hold it like any other tape recorder.'

I blink once, twice, purse my lips and look at him sharply over my shoulder. 'Come again?'

He shrugs, and smoothens imaginary creases on one of his pullover's arms.

'You idiot!' I pick the recorder up and feel like throwing it at him. 'You giant idiot! You scared me half to death you. I thought you were serious and that you were going to blow us all up.'

He shrugs his shoulders in apology. I throw the recorder at him, and it hits him on the right arm.

'Eh!' he protests.

'A shrug, Ash. A bloody shrug… that's all you can do?'

'I just wanted to buy us some time; talk him out of shooting you.'

'By scaring me half to death?'

He shrugs, again, nonchalantly.

I exhale exaggeratedly to calm my nerves and stop myself ranting on at him. '*Porca vacca*, I can't believe I fell for that.'

I swallowed the lot: hook, line and sinker. I knew he could lie, but not that well.

He favours me with a lopsided grim, as I reach down for the recorder which had bounced off him. 'That was rather the intended point, Lexa.'

Smug bastard. I give him the recorder back. 'Where the hell would you even get an idea like that?'

He grimaces, and pockets the device. 'Spur of the moment.'

I'm gobsmacked. 'I don't know whether to hit you or hug you.'

'Well… you've sort of already done the first one, so if I get to choose I'd rath—' He looks as if he's about to say something more, but freezes and frowns.

'What?'

'The cavalry,' he says simply.

I concentrate and finally hear the distant wail of police sirens echoing faintly in the distance. They grow louder rapidly, and blinking lights soon filter through the living room. Well, it's about time they finally showed up.

'I wonder who called them.' I raise my hands up, just in case they get the wrong idea.

'I did,' Egan says. 'Called Matthew on my way here. I had a feeling you'd find a way to get yourself in trouble.'

I chuckle at the words. 'I'm surprised he didn't advise you to wait outside.'

The corner of Egan's mouth twitches up. 'He may have… but I'm afraid the reception was terribly poor, I'm not sure I understood correctly. Stay outside, go inside — with static, it all sounds the same.'

I shake my head fondly and lower my hands. 'Careful, my dear sir, I think I may be rubbing off on you.'

He offers me a sly smile. 'What a terrible thing that would be.'

'Ash,' I start, pausing to make sure that I have his attention. 'Thanks for showing up. You saved my life.'

'Can't let you be the only one who pulls off crazy stunts, faces death, and all that. I want some of the glory too.

'Besides,' he continues and his smile grows, 'I thought we agreed to stick together, for better for worse, until death do us part.'

I shake my head at the odd comment. 'You do know that last bit is from the marital vows, yes?'

A twin set of confused eyebrows rises above the rim of his glasses. 'Oh, is it?'

I can't tell if he's serious or not, but the comment, however ill-fitting it might be in the current situation, makes me laugh, and dear me, does it feel good. The fear and the tension ebb away, dissolving into rich pearls of laughter. Egan joins me shortly after.

We're both still laughing, like a pair of overgrown teenagers, when Stenson enters, gun in hand. He is flanked by two more police officers.

The young sergeant stares at us in confusion for a second or two and lowers his weapon when he realises there is no immediate threat.

'Alexandra, Ashford.' He puts his weapon away, and motions for the other two officers to do the same. 'Care to explain to me why there's a dead man on the floor?'

24

Stenson drives us back to New Scotland Yard and takes our statements separately. He isn't too keen to learn that I lifted documents from his report and went to investigate on my own.

'What can I say… old habits die hard,' I mutter, semi-apologetically

'You could have been killed, Alex.' He shakes his head reproachfully.

'I know.' I can still picture the barrel of that gun. The moment is vividly seared into my memory. 'It seemed like a good idea at the time.'

Stenson lets out an exasperated breath and pinches the bridge of his nose.

'There's no need to lecture me,' I say. 'I'm still shaken, believe me. I just meant to have a quick reconnaissance… to see if my assumption was right. Getting knocked out and tied to a chair wasn't actually part of the plan.'

'You're lucky your partner showed up, and—' he makes sure to place a clear emphasis on the next two words '—*called me.*'

'Langford told me you were in court.' I feel the need to defend myself. 'I didn't want to bother you.'

'Voicemail, Alexandra!' Stenson raises his tone. 'Ever heard of it?'

'I—'

'Didn't think about it,' he cuts me. 'Yeah, I know.'

Well, I suppose I'm still on a learning curve with that letting people know where you're going thing. I shiver in the chilly room and cross my bare arms over my chest, rubbing at them a bit. I wonder if this is a fridge or an interrogation room, or maybe it's just the adrenalin rush receding and leaving me tired and exposed.

I offer Stenson a genuinely apologetic smile. 'Sorry.'

'Damn it.' He shakes his head and stands up behind his desk. 'Don't smile at me like that.'

'Sorry,' I mutter again, but the smile stays.

It must be contagious because Stenson's grim look lifts. 'Just don't do that again. Don't stupidly endanger your life like that *ever* again, please.'

I nod. 'I'll do my best.' I don't have a death wish or anything. I sincerely didn't think it would get this bad. 'I guess I still have a thing or two to learn about the job.'

'Oh, do you really think so?' Stenson's sarcasm is mild as he's smiling in earnest now. 'Just go get that partner of yours and get the hell out of here, before I decide to lock you up for your own safety.'

I stand up, walk to the door and halt. 'Have your people found the necklace yet?'

'Yes, it was on a side table, in the study. Left in plain sight.'

I turn back to face the Sergeant with my best hopeful expression. 'Actually, Matthew, I need one more favour.'

He looks up to meet my gaze, his almond shaped eyes narrowing in confusion. 'If you're thinking about asking me for the necklace, don't bother. It's evidence — you can't have it.'

I cross my arms over my chest, force myself to sound professional as I say, 'I don't want it for myself. It's for our client. We have a job to complete.'

'Forget it, Alex. You can't have it,' he repeats, enunciating the words carefully.

I take a step closer to him. 'She's dying Matthew. It's only a matter of days.'

'No.'

'What do you even need it for? Are you going to charge Strausser's dead body with theft? The case is closed.'

Stenson shakes his head exasperatedly. 'It's procedure.'

'I'm not asking for the world, just one exception for an old lady.'

He looks at me with pleading eyes. 'I can't, Alexandra. Langford would have me suspended.'

'Fine. I'll ask him directly then.'

I turn back to face the door and push it open. Stenson's voice halts me. 'Don't bother. He can't grant you your request either.'

'Who do I have to ask, then?' I demand, halfway through the door.

I hear Stenson huff, then stand up. 'The chief superintendent, maybe…'

I force a sober expression on my face, as I say, 'Take me to your leader.'

An eyeroll later, the sergeant follows me outside.

We find Egan in another interrogation room, a bit further down the corridor.

'Are you alright?' I ask him, as I enter the room.

He stands up, his face resolutely controlled. 'Yes, I'm done here.'

I move next to him and offer him my arm. 'Langford didn't give you too much grief?'

Egan's lips contort. He's still upset. 'He was… his usual self.'

I snort and walk to the door. Stenson is waiting for us in the corridor, and we follow him to the lift.

Two floors up, he leads us through another set of offices, a rather posher than those belonging to Stenson's division, but still very much a modern mix of glass windows and stainless steel fixtures. He comes to a stop behind a door, with a plate that reads, 'Detective Chief Superintendant P. Saunders,' and knocks twice.

'Enter,' a male's deep voice beacons us in.

The senior detective and commander of the Criminal Investigation Department is a tall man. That's the first impression the dark-haired man has on me.

As Egan comes to stand next to me, unknowingly placing himself in front of the detective, I can see that Saunders has a least two inches over him. That makes him what? Six two? Six three?

The second thing I take notice right of, before the man even has time to address me, is how neat he looks. Everything from his fine tailored suit to his carefully combed hair screams of control. Saunders is the type of man who immediately inspires respect, and I'm not in the least surprised. These sort of people often hold such positions.

'Alexandra Neve and Ashford Egan,' Stenson introduces us, 'the private investigators.'

DCS Saunders holds a hand out to me and I see he has perfectly manicured fingers.

'Pleasure to meet you,' he says, with a smile that feels forced, a politician's smile bore out of long years of practice.

I force the corners of my mouth up as I greet him, remembering my mother's saying about flies and vinegar. 'Likewise.'

Egan addresses him a polite nod.

'I hear we have you to thank for finding out this thief's—' he stops as he seems to hesitate over the name to use or maybe he's forgotten it.

'Arturo Nimra,' Stenson supplies.

'Yes… for finding Mr Nimra's killer,' Saunders finishes.

I feel one of my eyebrows rise up in surprise, as I discover the policemen's theory over what happened. How narrow-minded is it of them to assume Strausser acted alone. I don't think for one minute the old man is responsible for Nimra's death.

Egan seems to share my surprise, if the sudden slight incline of his head, angled in my direction, is anything to go by.

Saunders appears oblivious to our reaction and he moves to sit back behind his large desk.

Stenson, on the other hand, noticed and addresses me a quick shake of the head. I frown at him, but decide to remain silent and let him take the lead in this conversation.

'It isn't the first time they've assisted us, sir,' the sergeant takes a step forward. 'They helped us with that ring of Russian arms dealer earlier this year.'

'I know,' Saunders says, his voice rising, 'I can still read reports.' He seems to catch himself and quickly covers the small loss of temper with another of his empty smiles. He turns his head in my direction and gazes straight at me, with unreadable dark brown eyes that make me uncomfortable. 'The City of London thanks you for your help.'

I have to force myself not to look away. His face looks amiable, but his eyes...

Saunders accompanies his words with a slow, contained nod of his head that appears more condescending than thankful. His cleanly-shaven jaw remains squared tightly shut.

In response I manage to force a meagre smile to my lips.

'We were only doing our job,' Egan replies with cold detachment.

Saunders breaks eye contact and I swallow uncomfortably.

As the DCS looks down at some papers stacked on his desk, Stenson addresses me a 'go ahead' motion, with his hand.

'We were hired by Doris Hargrave,' I begin, 'to retrieve her family's stolen necklace.' I pause for effect. 'We have yet to finish our job.'

The man's attention returns to me, at once. 'You want the necklace?'

'Strausser is dead,' Stenson intervenes, 'as is Arturo Nimra. There will be no prosecution in this case.'

'I am well aware of that, Sergeant,' Saunders says, diverting his attention to his subordinate, for a brief instant.

'Our client will sign whatever document is required; she will promise not to leave the city with the necklace and whatever other conditions you think necessary.' I take in a breath. 'Its a part of her heritage; she just wants it back.'

'Your case is closed, is it not?' Egan comes to the rescue. 'What use could you possibly have for it, now? It's just going to sit in some box collecting dust for the rest of eternity, is it not?'

Saunders eyes flashover to him, before narrowing on me again. He appears to be mulling over these thoughts. 'Langford doesn't talk very highly of you,' he begins, 'and yet he allowed you to be present on this case. I have to confess to being rather confused.'

I fight the urge to smile, and remain in control. Knowing Langford, I'm certain the grumpy bald man would even rather spend his day sweating in a sauna, than willingly letting me near any of his cases. Of course, he wouldn't be putting any of that in his reports.

Saunders turns to look at Stenson. He studies him sharply, for a long moment, before saying, 'there will be no prosecution indeed. This case is closed. You can release the necklace, under their supervision. Have them sign the forms—' he pauses for emphasis '— in three exemplars.'

The Detective Chief Superintendent returns his full attention to the papers on his desk, and it feels as if he's deleted us from his awareness altogether. We retreat from his office without the social nicety of a goodbye.

Stenson escorts us back to the lift, with his hands in his pockets. He seems as surprised as I am about his boss's decision.

'What a charming man,' I mutter through clenched teeth, still unsettled by the Chief Superintendant's general behaviour.

'Don't hold it against him; he's having a rough time… what with the state of things.' Stenson waves a hand dismissively.

'Budget cuts?' Egan asks.

The sergeant nods. 'You have no idea how hard it makes our job.'

'Yeah, DI Lingby mentioned it, when we first spoke with her.' I take a step closer to Egan, and offer him my arm. 'Well, we'd better get going.'

'Your necklace is in Holding, on sublevel one. I'll phone to let them know they can release it to. You'll have to make Mrs Hargrave sign a receipt and get that back to us.'

I give him a grateful nod. 'Thanks, Matthew.'

He gives me half a smile. 'Just doing my job.'

'Wouldn't your job be to look for the Sorter?' Egan asks. 'You know he was the one pulling the strings all along, right?'

The policeman sighs heavily. He takes a step closer to us and lowers his voice. 'I know that, but it's not the official position of this department. Until we have something more concrete than urban legends, the Sorter will remain a myth and nothing more.'

'Like disgraceful leaves to be swept under the carped, then?' Egan mocks.

I nod soberly. 'Careful Matthew, by pushing too many bloodied leaves away, your broom's going to get stained.'

'Don't lecture me about it. My hands are tied, as you well know.' He presses the call button on the lift and steps to one side to let us get past him to the doors. 'It's been good seeing you again, in spite of the circumstances.'

I feel my face soften and my lips stretch into a smile. 'Yeah, maybe one of these days we'll actually get to have a conversation, and there won't be guns involved.'

He chuckles in response.

The lift alert chimes and the doors slide open. Egan and I step in.

Stenson's voice follows us inside. 'You still owe me that drink, Alexandra.'

I turn back to face him, 'Well then, give me a call. We're in the book.'

The doors close on Stenson's bright smile and dimples.

Some thirty minutes later, Egan and I walk out of New Scotland Yard and manage to flag down the first taxi that we see. For once, I'm too tired to travel around town on public transport, and I'm so relieved to sit down on the upholstered backseat of the black cab. What a day this has been.

I keep a hand over the bulge in my shoulder bag all the way to the hospital.

Although visiting hours are over, we manage to persuade the woman at the reception to let us in, for just a few minutes, to drop off the necklace.

Mrs Hargrave is still awake when we enter her room, and still hooked up to numerous tubes and machines. She doesn't seem surprised to see us, and I wonder if maybe she's lost any real notion of time and not even realised that night is falling outside.

'Good evening, Mrs Hargrave.' I move closer to her bed, Egan lingers near the entrance door.

'Ms Neve,' she rasps, feebly.

The water in her lungs is clear to hear in her voice. It pains me to see how her condition has worsened.

'Sorry to bother you. We won't be long.' I reach inside my shoulder bag for the necklace. 'We just dropped by to return this.' I hold the jewel out to her, and her dull eyes lighten at the sight.

Whimpering, she reaches out for the necklace with a shaking hand. It only reaches halfway, before the old woman's whimper turns into a painful moan. I finish the journey for her, and place the shining heart in her palm.

'You found it,' she breathes out, closing her fingers around the jewel. She cradles it over her chest and I watch her eyes fill with tears.

'Thank you,' she rasps. 'Oh, thank you.'

'You're quite welcome, Mrs Hargrave,' I say.

The old woman opens her fingers, just an instant, and peers at the necklace— as if to make sure it's still there — before closing her fingers over it again. 'Thank you,' she says again, with a finally contented smile.

'We only did our job,' I answer.

'Yes,' she nods. The words seem to draw her back to reality and she looks up to me, with a sobered expression. 'Talk with my son about the payment of your fees. I've made the arrangements; he will settle your bill.'

'Will do,' I nod.

Egan and I take our leave shortly afterwards.

The night has fully fallen when we get back outside, but it's become refreshingly cool. Although I'm bone-tired and aching all over, I don't mind a bit of fresh air on my bare arms and legs — it somehow feels cleansing. We walk to the nearest Underground station.

I can't get Mrs Hargrave's expression out of my head. The joy and the happiness in her face reached a level I've rarely seen before.

'I wish you could have seen that,' I tell Egan. 'The light in her eyes, when she saw the necklace and her smile…' I chuckle, 'it was infectious.'

'No need. I heard it in her voice.'

'I'm smiling too, right now,' I tell him.

'Good to know,' he says, his own face lit up by a warm smile.

'All in all, this was a good day.'

I find it hard to describe how I feel right now. None of the adjectives I know seem to be accurate enough. This was little more than a regular investigator's job… but it changed someone's life. So yes, today was a good day. To see that sparkle of true happiness in Mrs Hargrave's dying eyes was worth the terror, the pain and the worry.

'We just gave that woman a part of her heritage back; a part of her old life back.' Yeah, damn right I'm happy. 'We did a good thing, tonight.'

Egan nods. 'Yes, we did.'

There's something in his tone that has me frowning, and my good mood fades slightly. It's that damn elephant in the room again. Egan has fulfilled his promise, we've solved our case, and he's now free to go. I feel the beginning of tears prickling at my eyes. Damn it, couldn't we have kept playing pretend just a little while longer? At least until we both had a good night's sleep.

'Lexa?' Egan interrupts my thinking.

'What?'

He angles his head my way. 'Everything alright?'

I frown. 'Sure. Why do you ask?'

When he angles his head downwards, I realise I've unconsciously tightened my grip on his forearm. I force myself to slacken my hold again, but don't let go of him — I doubt I could, even if I wanted to. I curse inwardly at this complicated life that forces you to make choices all the time. Why can't we have everything we want and time enough to enjoy it?

Egan slows to a stop and I do the same. He looks serious again.

Right... I realise, I haven't answered him. 'I'm just a little shaken up — facing down the barrel of a gun and all that...' It's not a lie, per se, but I choose to keep ignoring the elephant, just a little while longer.

He offers me a tight-lipped smile. 'Is there somewhere we can sit?'

I look around us. Under the faint glow of a streetlamp, I find a nearby bench, and take us there.

'Did Strausser say why he took the necklace?' Egan asks, after sitting down.

'Love.' I let out a long breath. 'Stupid, mind-numbing love… and a few psychopathic tendencies.

'They used the necklace as we thought, and he married Anna, after they eloped. She's dead now, but he still loved her. And because he wasn't right in the head, he wanted the necklace back to honour her memory.'

'Love,' Egan echoes, with a touch more contempt than I had shown.

'Yeah, love.' I sigh and swallow before adding, 'He got some help along the way though.'

Egan frowns. 'What do you mean?'

'To find Nimra. He told me he asked around, and he was put in touch with a man who *helped sort out his problem.*'

I see Egan shake his head a little. 'The Sorter,' he murmurs, surprise tingeing his words.

'Uh, huh.' I lean fully against the back of the bench and cross my arms over my chest.

'So he was involved.' Egan's hand rises up to scratch at his chin. 'Did he tell you how he contacted him?'

'That's what I was getting at when you showed up.' Something clicks in place in my mind, at the words. 'Now he won't be saying anything…'

My tone is enough for Egan to understand what I'm not saying. 'You think the Sorter's behind the hit that killed Strausser?'

'Wouldn't put it past him. Tying up loose ends, making sure no-one can trace him, fits the profile. First Nimra, then Strausser...' I swallow, 'We were just lucky that his hitman chose that moment to take his shot.'

'But how?' Egan ask. 'How did he know we were getting close. He had Nimra killed when the police identified him, but Strausser...'

I ponder the thought an instant. 'You called Matthew, before going after me, didn't you?'

Egan nods.

'And Matthew came to the rescue with a local unit. When his request for backup was processed, a call was made on the police radio, an entry made into some computer database...'

'It's all the warning that the Sorter needed,' my friend agrees.

A car drives by, and its headlights shine on us for an instant. I can see Egan swallow, his face grim and serious.

'What about us?' he asks, eventually.

It's the million pound question. 'I don't know. We have nothing on him, really.' I blow out a long breath and massage my temples for an instant. 'I guess this is the reason why we're still alive. That shooter was good, a professional — Matthew told me so himself — one single shot, over a long distance.'

I swallow. He could easily have killed Egan and me too, before Strausser's body had even hit the ground. 'The Sorter decided to let us live.'

'He doesn't think of us as threats,' Egan says, and I can hear the unspoken *not yet*.

This is the second time that we've found ourselves on the fringe of his bloody network. What is it they say about playing with fire and getting burned?

I close my eyes, my mouth suddenly drier than any desert, and, in the darkness, all I can see is the barrel of a gun aimed at me. How many more games will we play with this mystery man before he wins? How long will it be before our luck runs out?

Egan's hand settles on my shoulder, drawing me back to reality. I find it to be a comforting weight and lean into it, just a bit.

'Lexa?'

'Hmm?'

'You're shaking,' he says, quietly.

Am I? I look down at my bare arms and realise I'm freezing and… shaking. 'I was scared,' I admit. 'Really, truly scared — like I've never been before in my life.'

'I can imagine,' Egan says, darkly, drawing me closer.

I turn my head to look at him, at the revealing tone. 'You don't need your imagination to know what that felt like, do you?'

Something unpleasant stirs in my stomach as realisation dawns on me. Bound, unable to see and scared — scared for the both of us. That must be exactly how my friend felt that day, in the warehouse, and a match for how I felt today. He still has nightmares about it and now I can finally understand why. That gun, pointed at my face will haunt me for a long time to come.

I reach out for Egan and engulf him in a tight hug which he too relaxes into.

I do it, firstly because it's only polite to do so — I think I read somewhere it's the least you can do when someone saves your life – but mostly, I do it because, right now, I think I need it more than I need air to breathe.

'Thank you,' I whisper in his ear, 'for coming to save me.'

I feel him smile, against my neck, and strengthen my hold.

EPILOGUE

Mum and I move back into our flat the next day. She tells me all about her few days with Bob, and how amazing he is, and how the breakfasts and everything else were delicious. She's going to continue spending a lot of time with him… and wait and see where it all leads. Who knows? One day, she might even move back in with him.

We gradually ease back into our routines and turn the page. After a few days, I even start to forget about the blood red letters, when I glance at the entrance door. I still remember the barrel of the gun though.

On Wednesday, the next week, I get a call from Mrs Hargrave's son. The news isn't good, but not un-expected. The funeral is scheduled for the following Saturday and I pick up Egan so that we can go together in my mother's car. He's wearing a black turtleneck pullover and I have matching trousers and jacket, and a dark-grey shirt.

The ceremony is brief, and we remain in the back. I'm not sure if it was expected for us to show up or not, given how short a time we'd known Mrs Hargrave, but I liked the old woman and I want to pay my respects.

After the ceremony ends, as people are standing up to leave, something catches my eye — something red and shining. The ruby heart,' I whisper, in surprise.

'Where?' Egan asks.

'A young woman, with long auburn hair. She's sitting in the first row, and she wears it proudly, over her blouse. It must be Lyssa, Robert's daughter. She certainly has his chin.'

'It's a good thing,' Egan says. 'It's passed on in the family, then.'

The young woman, Lyssa, takes several steps towards the central aisle, and I see a man her age is following her closely. They're both wearing wedding rings. I smile, hoping that for them there is some truth to the Salzmann myth and they too will "live happily ever after".

'Yes, it is,' I say, offering Egan my arm. We wait until almost everyone has left, before we finally go out as well.

The sun is shining brightly outside and I have to stand and blink a few times to get used to the light. Thankfully, the temperatures have lowered a little, but it's still very much high summer.

'Lexa, have you got a few minutes?' Egan asks, as we approach the car.

We pause near the passenger door. Egan is poised rather awkwardly, near the door, with both hands in his pockets. He looks unsure of himself.

'I should have been with you,' he says, eventually, 'that afternoon... instead of going to that stupid meeting.' He bites at his lips for a few moments. 'If something had happened to you—'

'Look, you really must stop all that.' I reach for his arm. 'Nothing happened, because you *were* there.'

He leans back against the car, and his arm slips from my reach. 'What if I'd arrived a few minutes later? What if he'd— I can't help thinking about that.'

More of the remaining cars depart, and very soon we're alone in the gravelled cemetery drive.

'Figgins is right after all.' Egan sighs. 'Can't do both things at once.'

Well, hello elephant, I almost let the hostile thought pass my lips, *I hadn't seen you there.*

I take a step forward, and reach for Egan's arm again. 'Ash, before you say anything, I want you to know you're my friend. Whatever you decide, nothing's going to change that.'

He nods, and his smile turns sour. 'I know you mean it, but it wouldn't be the same. We both know it.'

'We'd still be friends,' I promise. 'I'll always be just a phone call away.'

I could beg, I know. I'm tempted, so, so tempted to ask him to stay. I bite my tongue, hard. It's the safest option. The worst that can happen to him at UCL is a papercut.

Egan seems to consider the thought for a second, then stands a little straighter. 'I love History, and I enjoy teaching. Sure, it's a bit boring at times — well most of the time — but it's safe. There are no guns and no-one gets tied to chairs.'

'I know, and I can't blame you for choosing safety.' God knows how Mum would love it if I made the same choice. 'It won't be the same without you though.'

He chuckles. 'You were sure that I would choose the university all along, weren't you?'

'It's the only sensible choice.'

He finds my hand and holds it in both of his. 'Why didn't you try to convince me to stay?' he asks in a soft tone. 'You could have, I know it.'

Tears prickle in the corners of my eyes as I look down at our hands. I can only tell him the truth. 'You're my friend — I care about you too much for that.'

He holds my hand a little tighter and a smile, full of emotion, blossoms on his face. 'Thank you for your consideration. It really does means a lot to me.'

'You can thank my mum, for that; she's the one who raised me with principles.' It's rather a lame joke, but it's the best I manage with the gathering tears threatening to overflow from my eyes.

His smile transforms into an expression which I can't quite decipher. 'You need someone around, Lexa. You can't do this job on your own — who would come to the rescue then?'

'Don't worry about me. I'll just have to learn to become more sensible.'

'And just when have you ever done things the sensible way?' he chides. 'In fact, when have *we* ever?'

It takes a second or two for my brain to join up the dots. Am I understanding him correctly? Is he really saying what I think he's saying?

I'm almost afraid to ask, and my voice wavers as I say, 'You're staying?'

Egan's smile broadens. 'I resigned from UCL two days ago.'

I give him one of my fiercest hugs. When I let go of him again, he's blushing, and trying to rearrange his pullover with one hand.

'Don't get me wrong, I'm thrilled about this... but are you quite sure?'

'I don't care if it's dangerous. It won't hurt me if I get home with a few scratches or bruises every now and then. I don't care if the money's not really good, or even if we have to look for damn dogs.' He tugs my hand, until I take a step closer. 'You're my best friend, Alexandra Neve — I'm not giving you up for the world.'

I grab his forearm, lean forward and kiss him on the cheek. With my best Italian accent, I say, 'Oh Ashford, you say the sweetest things. Do you talk to all the ladies like that?'

He swats at my arm in mock annoyance, but can't help laughing.

'Besides, you were right,' he continues, more seriously. 'This job matters. What we did for Mrs Hargrave wasn't extraordinary, but I believe her last few days really were made easier because of us. She died having recovered what was rightly hers, and with the knowledge that it will remain in her family for generations to come. This... this touches me.' He pauses and takes in a deep breath. 'If we can help more people, I want to be a part of it.'

This is exactly how I feel. 'I couldn't agree with you more.'

'Having said that,' he jabs a finger in my side, 'do not take this to mean you should make a habit of getting us into trouble. I intend to die peacefully in my own bed at a ripe old age.'

I snigger. 'You're already pretty old.'

The finger pokes me again. 'I'm serious.'

'Then it'll be a good thing if you stick around to keep me in check.'

'"Ice puts out the fire,"' Egan quotes from an earlier conversation.

'"And the fire melts the ice."'

'Now,' I ask. 'How about I treat us to drinks at *Luigi's*?'

Before the end of the week, Robert Hargrave has been in touch with us; Egan and I triumphantly march into the bank and put our finances back on an even keel. We take our time celebrating with ice-cream.

We walk slowly back home, and I stop in the hallway to check our agency's letterbox before climbing up the stairs to the flat. There's only one letter inside. A white envelope, with no address for either recipient or sender. It's an odd, bulky shape and has only the words, 'UNTIL NEXT TIME' handwritten in blue capitals on the front.

I take it out of the letterbox with shakey fingers and open the flap holding my breath. It contains only one thing: a wooden chess piece.

'We've got mail,' I tell Egan, and it's a wonder my voice doesn't tremble.

'Lexa?' he turns towards me, with a curious look.

'"Until next time."' My voice wavers, as I relay the message.

'That's all it says on the front.'

Egan's face grows serious, as he steps closer to me. He reaches out a hand, palm upwards.

I place the chess piece into his expectant hand. 'And this: a dark bishop.'

He closes his fingers around the chess piece, and mutters, 'The Sorter.'

'He wants us to know he has his eye on us — he knows who we are, where we are, and what we've done.'

'Until next time?' Egan repeats, the words a question.

'I don't know.' I keep looking at Egan's fisted hand and mentally review the situation. 'I guess he considers this a game.'

'A game… of chess?'

'I haven't played in a long time, but chess is all about strategy — moving your pieces on the board and thinking ahead of your opponent.'

Egan grimaces. 'It certainly sounds like something the Sorter would enjoy.'

'Yes, it does.'

His lips thin to a grim line. 'I don't like this.'

'Neither do I, but I don't think we have much of a choice but to play. Whether we like it or not, we're on two opposing sides. Our teams will probably cross paths again in the future.'

'He does have one big advantage over us, though.' Egan pauses and my muscles tense. 'He knows exactly who we are, and we don't have the slightest clue about his identity.'

I don't reply. There's nothing to say to that. All I can do is swallow, with difficulty, and try to quell my rapidly beating heart.

'So what now?' my partner asks, opening his palm up again.

I take the little chess piece between two fingers and lift it up. Contemplating it, I say, 'I guess it's time we decide what our future strategy is going to be.'

Look for the next book in the series:
DANSE MACABRE

Cristelle Comby was born and raised in the French-speaking area of Switzerland, in Greater Geneva, where she still resides.

Thanks to her insatiable thirst for American and British action films and television dramas, her English is fluent.

She attributes to her origins her ever-peaceful nature and her undying love for chocolate. She has a passion for art, which also include an interest in drawing and acting.

Find out more at www.cristelle-comby.com